"Brunke deftly weaves Shannon and [illegible] astonishing tale with a gratifying ending. [illegible] sympathetic protagonists and lively accessible prose [illegible] the emotionally intense story line completely engrossing."

—LIBRARY JOURNAL, Starred Review

"From the very first page of *Snow Out of Season*, I was pulled into the story and captivated by the author's ability to express the depth of pain a parent feels when losing a child. The author intertwines the two main characters, Shannon and Leslie, from two different time periods. *Snow Out of Season* allows one to see the difficulty of making choices and how making those choices can bring different results, results that can change the lives and futures of others forever."

—CONNIE GIBSON, author, international speaker, and award-winning English professor

"...beautifully illustrates that what first appears as an unwelcome burden may in the end prove to be her cherished legacy. The story caught me with characters so real I feel I might see them on the street, and it held me with breathtakingly clever storytelling. All good novels perfectly pirouette full circle, and Ms. Brunke brings us satisfyingly, emotionally home."

—SANDRA BYRD, author of *Mist of Midnight*

"Once in a while you have a moment with a friend that feels like a gift. *Snow Out of Season* felt like such a moment for me. Christy Brunke has written a beautifully poignant and much-needed story. From the first page until the last, you'll be drawn into the characters' lives. You'll come away pondering with a full heart."

—BRANDY VALLANCE, award-winning author of *The Covered Deep*

Snow Out of Season

SNOW Out of SEASON

Christy Brunke

Mountainview Books, LLC

Edited by Carol Kurtz Darlington

Cover photograph of woman © sbytovamn| istockphoto
Cover photograph of man and child © whiteisthecolor| istockphoto
Cover photograph of grunge snow © Artshock| Dreamstime

ISBN: 978-1-941291-26-9 (paperback)
ISBN: 978-1-941291-27-6 (ebook)

For Angie Brunke,

because your choice changed my world.

Acknowledgments

Mark—for being "Wade" and for supporting and encouraging me throughout this journey. You're the one my heart loves and the reason this story sprang up in my soul.

Michaela and Angelina—for sharing Mommy with another baby.

Dad—for helping me plot this novel and for always believing in the power of the story.

Mom—for taking me to the library, for being the first person to suggest I write novels all those years ago, and for paying for the Craftsman class which took my writing to the next level.

Debby Stafford—for helping me write the discussion questions and for conscientiously critiquing multiple versions of almost every chapter. If only everyone had such an aunt.

Nancy Holec—for inspiring the character of Gabby Diaz, believing in this book from the beginning, and being more ecstatic than I was when I discovered it would be published.

Darlene Carter, Betty Farley, Tim and Natalie Litzau, Marty Wade and especially, Angie Brunke—for babysitting the girls so I could attend writers conferences and finish this novel.

My mentors, Sandra Byrd and Kathy Tyers—for your encouragement, creativity, and faithful instruction. What a privilege it was to be taught by you!

Jerry B. Jenkins—for editing my first chapter, for pouring into new writers of which I am one of many, and for holding the Operation First Novel contest which brought this book to life.

C. J. Darlington and the team at Mountainview Books—for publishing my book in both paperback and ebook formats, designing a beautiful cover, and making my dream come true!

Carol Kurtz Darlington—for your edits that have made

Snow Out of Season so much stronger. What a pleasure it was to work with you!

Kristina Cowan, Rachel Atkison, Lori Davis, and Anthony Trendl of the Chicago Christian Writers—as iron sharpens iron, your superb suggestions have sharpened this story.

Word Weavers Lisle/Naperville, especially Mollie Bond, Justice Carmon, Sue Ekins, Roberto Garcia, Pam Holtman, Robin Melvin, and Mary Sandford—for making my book better.

Suzy Q & Mr. Suzy Q—for your coaching and courses about marketing and social media.

My agent, Jonathan Clements—for taking me on as your client and for all your advice.

Megan Elrabadi—for your insight into the ballet world.

Retired Lieutenant Mike Sarni—for making my police chapter credible.

Dr. Gina Smith—for your advice about the medical scenes.

Eunice Sarni, Sherry Yuan, Tony and Katrina Blasé, Richard Grendzinski, and my other beta readers—for your fabulous feedback and suggestions.

York Community High School archivist Barb Hoyne and former students Diana Perez, Josh Perez, Justine Nuñez, and Nicole Nuñez—for answering numerous questions about the school, past and present.

Rosemary Ashworth, Val Stewart, and Nancy Wilson of the Elmhurst Historical Museum—for helping me find the information I needed.

Marlene Bagnull, Lin Johnson, and Eva Marie Everson—for directing Write His Answer, Write-to-Publish, and the Florida Christian Writers Conference respectively, every year.

Brandilyn Collins, Jeff Gerke, and Dr. Dennis Hensley—for your fantastic fiction classes.

Angela Canton, Joanna Delejewski, Donna Hanert, Raelyn Lau, Grandmom (Pat) Litzau and Jösselly Peterson—for your powerful and persistent prayers.

Jenn Culp and Rick Cardona—for always being so supportive of my writing ministry.

Georgina Cruz, Natalie Cruz, Alicia Holec, and Judy Weber—for believing I could do it.

And, most of all, Jesus—for giving me the desires of my heart. Like a Shepherd, you have led me on one glorious adventure after another. I can't wait to see what's next!

1

Shannon: June 2014

The casket was small.

Only our three-year-old twins clinging to my legs kept me from breaking open the steel coffin and taking back my baby Lily.

Scottish bagpipes played "Amazing Grace" accompanied by whimpers.

Friends and family tossed Stargazer lilies onto Lily's grave and walked back to their lives. Back to their homes. Back to their children.

An empty crib awaited Wade and me.

I buried my nose in the white flower and inhaled the sweet-scented petals, soft as Lily's skin. A sob escaped, giving way to a barrage of salty tears.

Thunder blasted a warning just before the heavens poured.

Wade, his strong hand gripping mine, turned to go.

No. I dug my heels in. *I won't leave her.* A swan gliding across the cemetery lake paused to let her little ones climb aboard and then secured them beneath her wings.

I wrapped my arms around Katy and Daniel to shelter

them. If only I could shield them from the pain. Awaken Lily. Erase the loss from Wade's red eyes.

But my arms weren't big enough.

I sent Wade and the twins to the car and turned back to the grave.

A cemetery worker cranked a metal handle that lowered Lily into the pit. Rain drummed the coffin as he shoveled earth on top of her. Every thud screamed "Never."

I'd never hold her again, her warm cheek pressed to mine.

Never win another slobbery kiss.

Never feel her little hand wrapped around my finger.

Never hear her belly laugh tickling my heart.

Tombstones reeled around me, and lightning slashed the sky. I staggered backward and crumpled into the mud.

Wade ran back and knelt beside me, enveloping me in his arms. We wept together, our tears blending with the rain.

The cemetery worker threw the last heap of dirt over Lily, nodded at us, and hurried on his way.

I glanced back at our minivan—the only car still parked by the gravesite.

"Don't worry about the kids," Wade said, reading my thoughts. "I sent them home with my parents." He rose and pulled me up with him.

With one last glance at the ground that held our daughter, we trudged back to our car and the infant seat without an infant.

Wade swallowed hard. "I'll . . ." He cleared his throat and choked out, "I'll take that out tomorrow."

I gazed out the window, but the storm blurred my view. Wade had always said he wanted a big family. And maybe he still did. But I couldn't kiss another baby good-bye when she'd just begun to live.

2

Shannon: August 2014

Two pink lines appeared, but all I saw was gray.

I dropped the pregnancy test into the trash can where it landed with a clank. I winced. Did Wade hear? Sourness tainted my mouth as I buried the stick and its packaging under a pile of tissues.

Back in our room, I curled up on our bed and pulled my knees to my chest. A whiff of spit-up struck me. I jerked away. I must not have washed these jeans since Lily died. My eyes stung, but I pressed my face into the smell—the last I had of her—and inhaled. Memories rushed at me, tumbling one on top of another, until I wasn't sure where to look or what to feel next.

"Remember me," Lily seemed to be saying.

My gaze fell on a picture of her on our nightstand. At three months old, she wore a ruffled swimsuit, her arms and legs stretched out as if making a snow angel. Her raised eyebrows and the spark in her eyes said, "Look, Mommy! I'm so big!"

My chin quivered. How could we have another child after the way she died?

"Mommy?" Katy called from down the hall. "I can't find Rabbit."

My daughter's voice stirred me back to the present. Back to Wade's birthday. We needed to leave for his party in fifteen minutes, and I wanted to paint Katy's nails and finish my face. I swiped at my tears, threw on a smile, and hurried to the twins' room. "Can you take Piglet instead?"

"Mommy." Katy shook her head as if I'd suggested one plus one equaled three. "Snow White sings to bunnies, not pigs."

"What was I thinking?" I knelt before Katy and drank in every beautiful curve of her face. Kissing her cheek, I made a mental note to buy her a Snow White costume. With her dark hair, bright eyes, and long lashes, she'd look just like her favorite Disney princess. I took her hand and stood. "Let's go find him."

❄

After we found Rabbit behind a potted plant in the dining room, I matched a bottle of nail polish to Katy's raspberry shirt and sat cross-legged on the carpet, one eye on the Winnie-the-Pooh clock.

Five minutes until takeoff.

Then I'd have to face Wade. Wade, who always noticed when I was upset.

"Red," he called. "Where are you?"

I jerked, sweeping crimson across Katy's fingers.

"Mommy!" Katy pouted. "You messed it up."

"I'm sorry, sweetie. Let me fix it." I attempted to wipe away my mistake but only smeared it more.

"Now it's messed up even more!"

"Red?"

"In here!" *Calm down, and he won't suspect anything.*

Wade stepped into the room, his broad shoulders filling the doorway. "Are my girls ready?"

My girls. I used to love it when he called us that. But now it only reminded me of the one we'd lost. "I have to finish putting my makeup on."

"I keep telling you, you don't need fake-up. You're beautiful. Stunning." He exhaled. "But I guess my opinion doesn't count."

"Honey, it's not that." He considered me prettier barefaced, but my eyes found my flaws. I cleaned up the edges of Katy's fingers with nail polish remover and hurried to the bathroom to apply blush, mascara, and eyeliner, warm tones that complemented my copper-colored hair.

As I was fumbling with my charm bracelet, Wade strode into the room. "We gotta go."

I handed him the chain he'd given me when I was pregnant with Katy and Daniel. *To the Next Chapter* was carved onto a silver heart. "Can you help me put this on?"

"Yes, I can," he said but just stood there.

I tried to shoot him my usual smirk. "*Will* you?"

"Of course," he teased. He fastened the bracelet and kissed my wrist, his lips warm against my skin. "Why didn't you just ask?"

I straightened the chain so the twins' charm dangled at the bottom, next to the lily Wade had given me when our youngest was born. I lifted it to my lips. "She would've been seven months old today," I whispered.

Wade closed his eyes and let out his breath. With a lump in my throat, I ran my finger over the engraved heart. What would this "next chapter" bring?

Our Weimaraner puppy charged into the bathroom and knocked over the trash can to get his huge mouth around a half-eaten banana.

The pregnancy test tumbled out.

My pulse raced as I shoved it back into the can.

❄

Had he seen it? I studied Wade's face as he drove through Elmhurst. Of course not. He would've said something. It was Wade—he always said something. I reached behind me to pick up the Cheerios Daniel had dropped. Sticky crumbs were ground into the seat and carpet. Would our car ever be clean again?

"Calm down." Wade slowed to turn into his parents' driveway. "We'll take care of those later."

A car seat clicked open.

My breath caught. "Hold on, sweetie." I looked back at Daniel. "Wait until Daddy parks." Of all the tricks Daniel could've learned, why did he have to master springing from his car seat like a pint-sized Houdini?

"Relax." Wade squeezed my hand and pulled up to the brick Cape Cod-style house. "He's fine."

Daniel got out, ran down the curved sidewalk, and hit the doorbell.

"Are we going to have cake at Gram's?" Katy said when Wade opened her door.

"Uh-huh." I studied the dark clouds overhead. The sky seemed undecided whether to celebrate Wade's birthday or not.

"With a princess on top?"

"My cake doesn't need a princess." Wade hoisted Katy out of her car seat and swung her around, her chocolate ponytail flying through the muggy August air. "*You're* my princess."

I smiled, but emptiness gnawed at my stomach. If only Lily had lived long enough to appreciate what a great dad she had. If only we could've watched her grow up . . .

"Grandpa!" Daniel yelled.

I grabbed the apple pies at my feet and got out of our minivan.

"How's my little buddy?" Dad gave Daniel a bear hug and then pretended to look for Katy. "I seem to remember having a granddaughter too."

My body went cold.

Dad shot me a contrite look as if he just realized what he'd said.

Oblivious, Katy ran up the steps. "I'm here! I'm here!"

He tickled her and eyed the dessert. "Mmm." Closing his eyes, he inhaled the cinnamon scent.

Maybe it was good that I'd still brought the pies, even though the peaks of the crumb topping had turned out darker than I'd planned.

"Let's go get some chocolate chip cookies." Dad picked

up Daniel like a football, took Katy's hand, and paraded into the house where *Star Wars* music was playing.

"I'm ready for some sweets too." Wade looked me over and whistled.

"Honey!" I forced out a smile since I still wasn't ready to giggle.

He kissed me square on the lips. "I still can't figure out how I tricked a woman like you into marrying me."

"You threatened to run me over with your car."

"I wasn't trying to run you over. Just get your attention."

I kissed his stubbly cheek and ran my hands over his broad shoulders and muscular arms. "Mission accomplished. And then some."

"Duel of the Fates" came on as Wade's mom stepped into the foyer. Radiant in a canary-colored sundress, she wrapped her arms around Wade. "Happy birthday," she said, her eyes moist.

"Nice touch with the music, Mom."

"And how's my favorite daughter-in-law?"

I flashed an overly-bright smile. "Fine."

"I saved some cookie dough for you." She winked at me. "I know how much you love it."

My mind flashed to the foods-to-avoid-when-pregnant checklist—cookie dough was listed near the top because the raw eggs could be contaminated with salmonella. Pregnant women and their babies were extra susceptible to food poisoning. "Great," I said and swallowed. "Thank you so much."

In the kitchen, Wade's younger sister Margaret—just months shy of her thirtieth birthday—was rinsing plates and loading them into the dishwasher with the grace of the dancer she was, her curls cascading down her back.

How could she move with such effortless ease? I was lucky to make it through a day without breaking something.

Wade groaned. "That stupid dishwasher."

"Oh, brother." Margaret rolled her eyes. "Here we go again."

"If you're gonna go through the trouble of rinsing them, why not just wash the dishes yourself?"

Margaret snapped a towel at him.

Wade dodged it. "A swing and a miss." He hugged her. "I'm gonna make sure the kids don't put Play-Doh into the DVD player again."

"Don't forget your lemonade." Mom nodded toward his well-worn Darth Vader cup. She handed me a glass with R2-D2-shaped ice cubes and then pulled a Tupperware container out of the fridge. "Go ahead and have some now," she said, motioning toward the uncooked dough. "I won't tell anyone."

My mouth went dry. "Actually, I'm not that hungry and want to save room for lunch. Is it okay if I take it home to eat later?"

"Sure," she said and stuck it back into the fridge.

"I have so much to tell you," Margaret said, gripping my arm. "But I promised Dad I'd help him with something first." She closed the dishwasher with her foot, as if she were Ginger Rogers in a Fred Astaire film, and bounced out of the room.

❄

As Mom and I made subs—I couldn't eat them unless I microwaved the meat first, which would be a dead give-away—Wade popped his head into the kitchen.

"Anybody seen Katy and Daniel?" he said. "Dad went to put on his Chewbacca costume, and when he came back out they were gone."

A chill spread across my shoulders.

"Maybe they're upstairs?" Mom said.

"I've looked all over the house."

I couldn't breathe. "Did you check outside?"

Wade shook his head.

I flew out the front door, my chest exploding. York Street was busy this time of day. What if they'd run into the road?

No sign of them.

I sprinted to the back, meeting Wade as he flew down the deck steps.

Katy was picking marigolds out of the garden.

Daniel was digging in the dirt, his tongue curled over his lower lip as it always did when he concentrated.

I exhaled. My babies were fine. I picked up Daniel, squeezed him tight, and inhaled his sweet-smelling hair. I knelt beside Katy and clutched her warm hand. "What did Mommy tell you about going outside by yourselves?"

"I wanted to pick flowers for Gram."

"And Grandpa needs worms when he goes fishing," Daniel said as if I were keeping him from a special duty.

"That was sweet of you, kids," Wade said. "But you should've asked permission first."

"Sorry, Daddy. Can I give Gram the flowers now?"

"Sure, princess." Wade put his hand on Daniel's shoulder. "Why don't you go inside too, buddy?"

"But—"

"I'll help you find some really fat worms later."

I tried to settle my hammering heart. When would I stop acting like a veteran with post-traumatic stress disorder?

"Honey?" Wade searched my eyes. "We're doing our best, but we can't protect them every second," he said, wiping away runaway mascara. "You know that, right?"

I turned away. Weren't parents supposed to protect their children?

"What happened with Lily . . . It wasn't our fault."

A leaf fell from an elm tree in the back yard.

"There must've been something." I stared at the leaf. "Something I could've done better. Something I missed."

Wade pulled me back to him and cupped my chin. Eyes moist, he said, "You have to stop blaming yourself. For Katy and Daniel's sake." He pressed his lips against mine. "For mine."

I sank into his chest.

"We're going to get through this, Red." He wrapped his arms around me. "Together."

Sunlight pierced the clouds.

I closed my eyes and drank in his warmth. Birds chirped and the summer breeze carried their song straight into my heart. "It's beautiful outside today," I whispered, submitting to his embrace.

He swept my bangs to the side and ran his hands down my face. My skin tingled. "*You're* beautiful."

I smiled. I had so much to be thankful for. An affectionate husband. Adorable children. And in-laws I would've chosen as friends.

If I could just keep them all safe.

I slipped into my comfiest pajamas. Thank God this day was over. And no one had guessed my secret. I slipped under our silky comforter, sipped my jasmine tea, and picked up *A Christmas Carol.* I wanted to read it again since it was going to be our winter play at school.

Wade sat on the edge of the bed, his expression solemn.

I put down my book. Did he know?

"It's been a hard few months," he said, compassion in his eyes. "I know you're stressed. School's starting. The play's going to be a lot of hard work. Why don't we get away over Christmas break?"

Christmas. This would've been Lily's first. I still had the stocking Aunt Darlene had embroidered for her.

"We could have my parents watch the kids. Go somewhere for a few days. Sleep in. Relax."

I nodded. Maybe getting away would help. "How about downtown? I could make reservations at The Palmer House."

"The Palmer House it is." He locked eyes with me. "And maybe we can try again," he said, "while we're there."

I avoided his eyes, my stomach rolling. That was the last thing I wanted to do. *Had* wanted to do. On the other hand, maybe this was a good opportunity to share the news. But could I go through another pregnancy? Or worse, another first year?

He squeezed my hand. "We'll never forget Lily and we can't ever replace her. But we can't let her death derail our dream of having a big family."

I straightened the bronze tissue box on the corner of our nightstand. "I adore our kids," I said slowly, fingering the twins' charm. "I can't imagine our life without them. But I'm not ready for another baby. What if—"

"Don't think like that." He squeezed my leg. "Next time will be different."

I put a shaky hand on Lily's picture, my body growing cold.

Wade swallowed.

"And what if it's not?" I whispered.

The silence hung between us like all those sleepless nights.

"Wade, I can't live with another picture that never changes."

3

Shannon: October 2014

The oily shrimp scampi I'd eaten for lunch started coming back up. I flew to the bathroom.

"Red?" Wade knelt on the floor beside me. "You okay?"

I wiped my mouth with the flimsy, one-ply toilet paper that had unfortunately been on sale the last time I'd gone shopping. "Just nauseous," I said, my throat thick. How could I not have let him know about this pregnancy for the last six weeks?

"You're still sick? Shannon, this is ridiculous. This is what happens when you work and never rest. I'm calling your school and telling them you're not coming—"

"I'm not sick!" I bit my lip, my chest tight.

He cocked his head. "That time of the month?"

I avoided his eyes and washed my hands with the pumpkin-scented soap. "Not exactly."

"Not exactly?" He squinted. "You either got your period or you didn't." He searched my face and a smile grew on his. "Unless . . . ?"

I grinned as I shut off the water, the tension in my shoulders dissolving.

His eyes widened. "Really?"

My eyes fluttered to my belly.

He beamed and clutched my arms. "When did you find out?"

My stomach dropped. "On your birthday," I muttered and hurried to our bedroom.

"My birthday?" He strode toward me, his brow furrowed. "That was two months ago."

I closed the door behind him so the kids wouldn't hear. "I'm so sorry." I lifted my eyes to his. "I was trying to find the right time to tell you, but it never came. And I thought if I was a little further along we'd know more, and there'd be less to worry about." I took his hand. "Honey, in all honesty, I was having trouble facing the truth myself."

"But this is something to celebrate. Aren't you excited?"

I sagged onto our bed. "I am." I smiled, realizing I'd spoken the truth. "*Now* I am. But before I felt . . . disloyal." I ran a finger over the lily charm.

Wade sat beside me and put his hand over mine.

"And, most of all, scared. Scared we'd miscarry or that what happened to Lily . . ."

He stroked my hair. "Oh, Red. Why did you think you had to go through this on your own?"

I leaned into him, my chin quivering.

"Never mind. I'm here." He kissed my forehead. "And we're having a baby!"

I studied his features, and warmth radiated through me. Would our child have his prominent nose and muscular physique? Maybe my blue eyes and fair skin?

"If it's a boy, we're naming him Yoda."

"Yoda? And if it's a girl?"

"Princess Leia."

❄

"I knew it!" Gabby Diaz's voice rose through my iPhone. "I felt it in my soul. I'm going to throw you the best baby shower ever."

I straightened the orange suede pillows on our couch and

smiled. Gabby didn't waste any time. "We really don't need another baby shower, after all the stuff we got from the twins' shower and—"

"A sprinkle then," Gabby said. "I saw this paper garland on the Internet the other day that would look great over the cake table. And I think we should do cupcakes instead of a cake—it's the new trend. Plus, I've got some great ideas coming to me right now about the favors."

"I hope they're not quite as amazing as the ones at my bridal shower," I said, grinning.

Gabby snickered. "I don't think the other teachers at your school will ever forgive me for how those plants took over their gardens. But don't worry. No Rose of Sharon seeds that grow into giants and multiply."

"Maybe you better let me read the fine print, just to be sure." I put Wade's dirty socks, jogging pants, and old-man slippers on the stairs to take up later. Would he ever stop leaving things around for me to pick up?

"At least they'll never forget you and Wade. Every time they look outside, they'll remember how perfect you are for each other."

"A little more often than they'd like." I ran my hands over his navy slippers. If given the chance, I'd marry him all over again.

"We need to start registering."

I froze. Registering would make this baby real. Real enough to die. "I really don't think this is necessary. We can just use Katy and Daniel's hand-me-downs."

"Every child deserves a special celebration."

What if we ran into someone we knew at the store? I wasn't ready to go public. Not until we passed the miscarriage danger zone and received the screening results. "I'm not even past my first trimester."

"You're, what, one week away?"

"Two."

"Close enough. We need to celebrate."

I grabbed the furniture polish and paper towels from under the kitchen sink and dusted the entertainment center, lemon scenting the air. "I prep for play practice and dramatic literature class on Saturday afternoons."

"You need to throw out your schedule for once. Do you really think spending one afternoon doing something fun will make you less prepared for school? Go out on a branch sometimes."

I suppressed a giggle. I couldn't usually tell by Gabby's English that she was raised in a Spanish-speaking home. Until she tried to use idioms. "Go out on a *branch*?"

"Go out on a tree?"

"I think you mean go out on a limb."

"Yeah, I guess that's it," Gabby said, chuckling.

I pulled back the curtains and sunshine poured into the room. I still had to prep for school between errands, housework, and dinner out with Wade. "When did you wanna go?"

"I'm outside."

I laughed and looked out the window.

Sure enough, Gabby's candy-apple-red coupe was parked beside an elm tree, its leaves now saffron yellow. She honked and waved. "We can get ice cream afterwards. Or go see a movie."

I put away the cleaning supplies. I'd have to register someday. "Let me see if Wade can watch the kids."

"I promise you won't regret it."

I gazed at Lily's birth announcement still taped to the fridge. That's what we'd thought before.

But Lily would never taste the chocolate chip ice cream Gabby promised to treat her to on her first birthday. She'd never say good-bye to me on her first day of kindergarten, clutching a lunch box with a special note from Mommy. Never walk down an aisle with a tiger-lily bouquet on the arm of a daddy who adored her.

I swallowed hard, my face on fire. What I wouldn't give to kiss Lily's head one more time, her hair like feathers on my lips.

"Wouldn't Katy look beautiful in this?" I held up a green taffeta dress with a rosette-accented waist. "She could wear it to *The Nutcracker* next month."

"Forget frou-frou." Gabby pushed the cart toward the baby section. "Your next girl's going to get chic and modern stuff from me, like skinny jeans and cute little boots."

I dropped the dress into the cart. "I like frou-frou."

"I know. That's why I need to balance you out so you don't do what my mom did to me—make me wear hair ribbons and ruffled dresses everywhere I went." Gabby held up a miniature pair of denim pants. "Now this is what I'm talkin' about."

I pointed at the flowers embroidered on the back pockets. "They've still got a little frou-frou."

"A little frou-frou's okay, as long as it doesn't go overboard." She nuzzled a pair of footed pajamas made of pink fleece and covered in snowflakes. "We have to get this one."

I ran my hand over the soft fabric. "We should wait to register for clothes. We don't even know if it's a boy or a girl."

"It's a girl."

Another girl. Like Katy. Like Lily.

An infant giggled in a passing cart.

I stared at the white floor, remembering Lily's last bath. She'd laughed for the first time. Her perfectly-shaped mouth opened wide, and her whole body shook as if the source of her amusement was the funniest thing she'd ever seen. And it probably was.

Gabby's dark eyes told me she ached with me. "Let's go." She put the pajamas back. "Baskin-Robbins is calling. We can do this later. Or I can register for you, if that'd make things easier."

I shook my head. This little one deserved as much attention as I'd given Lily. This little one needed a mommy too. "I'm okay."

Gabby hesitated.

"Really." I put my hand on her arm. "And another girl would be wonderful. Maybe she'll have Lily's eyes. Or her laugh."

"Well, it *is* a girl. I feel it in my soul."

I cracked a smile as I munched on the salty popcorn I'd bought at the food court. I couldn't resist that movie-theater smell. "Your soul's been wrong a time or two."

"But you have to admit, it's amazing how many times it's been right." Gabby scanned the bar code on the PJs and the registry gun beeped.

I reached for it.

Gabby hid it behind her back. "I'll take it off if it turns out to be a boy. But it's a girl, I'm telling you. Plus, I'm inviting lots of people, so we need to register for lots of stuff."

Inviting? "You didn't tell anyone I'm pregnant yet, did you?"

"Well . . ."

Oh, no.

"I may have mentioned it to one or two people."

"In the time it took me to grab my purse and come outside?"

"I was excited," Gabby squeaked.

I groaned.

"I know. I'm sorry. But don't worry. I told them it was a secret."

I chuckled. "Like I told you it was a secret?"

Gabby hugged a duck towel to her face. "This one works for a boy or a girl."

"You're not getting off that easy."

"I won't tell anyone else. I promise. Cross my heart and hope to the sky."

"You mean, hope to die," I said, a lump in my throat.

"Are women beheaded in these homes?" Wade had asked our realtor before we bought our two-story Tudor. We had just watched *The Wives of Henry VIII*.

I smiled at the memory as I unlocked the side door and stepped into our kitchen with a plastic bag of nursing bras and yellow-hooded towels.

Gabby plopped two gallons of Bonsai Tint paint onto the porcelain floor tiles.

My eyes settled on the overflowing trash can that reeked of rotting raw chicken. Why hadn't Wade emptied it like he'd told me he would? I should've done it before I left. Gabby's house was immaculate. Her garbage would never be caught in such a state. Especially in front of company.

Wade raised his eyebrows at the paint. "You might have run this past your husband."

I set my bag on the granite countertop. "We talked about this."

His eyes narrowed. "We did?"

"I said we should turn the guest room into the nursery instead of Lily's room and you agreed."

"But we're painting it already?"

"We need to paint it so we can start setting up the room."

Wade poured himself a cup of apple cider. "I thought you said it wasn't safe for women to paint when they're pregnant."

I rubbed the back of my neck. "We'll open the windows and wear masks." But what if something happened to the baby? I'd always wonder if it was because of the paint fumes.

Wade smirked. "Masks?"

I mock-glared at him. "Or we could hire Travis. Is he still painting houses to save money for college?"

Wade opened the box of candy his mom had given him for his birthday and took out a turtle. "I'll see if he can do it over Christmas break."

Travis would be glad to help out, since Wade tutored him in math and science. I crunched on some chocolate-covered almonds. "Do you think he could do it sooner? Like next week-end? I can ask him if you give me his number."

"We still have six months. Why do we have to do this now?"

"We have to get moving." Gabby chose a piece of dark chocolate. "Time's a wastin'."

Wade focused on me, his eyes soft. "Weren't you just telling me how stressed you are about all the work you need to get done over the next couple months?"

"I'm finally starting to get my energy back, and I want to finish the room before I start my third trimester. Besides the fact that I'll be huge and probably tired and uncomfortable, I'll be directing *Once Upon a Mattress* in the spring. And the musicals are a lot more work than the plays."

Wade stuck another caramel-coated cluster of pecans into his mouth. "We don't know if it's a boy or girl yet."

"Light green works for both," Gabby said. "And we'll add pink accents once you confirm it's a girl."

Wade lifted an eyebrow. "*Confirm* it's a girl?"

"You know, at the ultrasound."

Wade winked at me. "Well, I wish I could help," he said, shifting his eyes. "But we just started Monopoly."

I put the dirty plates on the counter into the sink. "Honey, don't you think the kids are a little young to play Monopoly?"

"I gotta start teaching them now so they'll be undefeated champions like their old man." Wade struck a Superman pose. "Plus, it's Monopoly Junior."

I tried to heave the trash bag out of the can, but it was so full it stuck to the sides.

Wade rushed over. "Let me do that."

Gabby grabbed the paint cans. "I'll start packing the things we're going to move to the attic."

After she headed upstairs, I frowned at Wade. "Honey, the house is a disaster," I whispered. "You promised me you'd straighten up so I could register and get things done."

"I thought you were gonna see a movie afterwards so you could relax, not start another home improvement project."

"Nothing good's playing. Plus, that's beside the point."

Wade scanned the room. "The house looks fine. Is it supposed to look like people don't live here?"

I put a new bag in the garbage can, threw away the napkins, and started washing the dishes.

"Shannon, stop." Wade caught my arm. "Look at me."

I hung the rag around the faucet and stared at him.

"I'm sorry," he said, looking partially repentant. "I cleaned a few things, but then I got busy playing with Katy and Daniel and I forgot about the trash."

I picked at a hangnail. How could I be mad that Wade played with our kids instead of doing housework? Of course I'd like to just play with them more instead of doing chores while watching them. But then who would cook, clean, and do the laundry?

"Tell you what," Wade said in his solve-the-problem tone. "I'll get the twins, and we'll have a cleaning party."

My shoulders relaxed. He really did try to please me. I glanced at the dolls and dinosaurs strewn throughout the living room and smiled. "You guys played Jurassic Amazon again?"

"Today's episode was riveting. We discovered D-Rex is only evil because he's under a spell."

I wrapped my arms around Daddy Rex and inhaled the fresh scent of his Old Spice deodorant. "And whose spell is he under?"

"You'll have to tune in to the next episode to find out." He dipped me and kissed me.

"Daddy?" Daniel called from upstairs. "It's your turn."

I struggled to get back on my feet.

Wade dipped me farther back then pulled me upright.

I kissed him on the cheek. "Go finish your game."

Wade searched my eyes. "You sure?"

I nodded.

"I'll be up in a minute, buddy," Wade yelled.

I grabbed a couple old newspapers to wrap the knickknacks in. "Can you get the boxes out of the attic first?"

"As you wish." He blew me a kiss and headed upstairs.

My phone rang.

I wrestled it out of my purse and checked the caller ID: Dr. Beck's office. Was she returning my call about the blood test? Since Lily's death, she'd gone above and beyond to answer my questions. "Hello?"

"Mrs. Henry?" Dr. Beck said. "I received the results."

Dr. Beck's tone reminded me of the way the emergency room doctor said, "Lily didn't make it." I could almost smell the hospital disinfectant. The hair on my arms stood at attention.

"The first trimester blood test isn't diagnostic, so it can't tell us anything conclusive."

Gabby walked in and grabbed a Coke out of the fridge.

"But, unfortunately, you did test positive for Down syndrome."

The room spun. I sat, one hand gripping the black ash table. "Down syndrome?" I said, trying to keep my voice steady.

Gabby gaped at me, her eyes wide.

I flashed back to the day I'd seen my little one on the monitor. "But the ultrasound seemed pretty normal."

"Increased nuchal translucency and a non-visible nasal bone are common in fetuses with Down syndrome," Dr. Beck said. "But the techs can't always tell from the NT scan that a fetus has a chromosomal abnormality. That's why we do the blood test in conjunction with it."

My baby had appeared normal on the screen but wasn't? Had I done the ultrasound too early to set my mind at ease?

"But don't be too alarmed. One in twenty women test positive on the first trimester screening, and the majority don't have a child with Down syndrome. Testing positive just means you're at higher risk."

I exhaled. Our baby was probably fine. "How much higher?"

"Your results based on your age, your high levels of the pregnancy hormone hCG, and your low levels of pregnancy-associated plasma protein A, or PAPPA for short, is one out of thirty-three."

"One out of thirty-three?" I glanced at Gabby. "That's not too bad, right?"

She set a glass of water before me and took a seat in the other arrow-back chair.

"For most 35-year-old women," Dr. Beck said, "it's only one out of 385."

My mouth went dry.

"I recommend you have a CVS test done as soon as possible."

Exhaustion crawled over my forehead and eyes. "CVS test?"

"Chorionic villus sampling examines the tissue in your

placenta for chromosomal abnormalities. It's ninety-nine percent accurate in identifying disorders like Down syndrome," Dr. Beck said as if this were great news.

Was I supposed to be happy about that? What if the results showed my baby did have Down syndrome?

"How's Monday morning at nine?"

I opened my phone calendar and peered at the gray square with the number 20 in the middle. No appointments appeared to save me. "Fine."

"Great. I'll have Norma pencil you in," Dr. Beck said. "And Mrs. Henry?"

I sipped my water. It was as cold as I felt. "Yes?"

"Try to take it easy. Most likely, your fetus doesn't have Down syndrome or any other defect. But if it does, we can discuss your options."

Options? My eyes flew to Lily's birth announcement. Were we to lose another child?

4

Leslie: December 1978

I had imagined this moment since the first day I slipped on a pair of ballet shoes. The soft slippers I'd worn as a child bore little resemblance to the toe-crushers—as Frankie called them—I wore today. But they both transported me to a magical world where I could become the princess of my dreams or wake from my worst nightmare.

The orchestra played Tchaikovsky as I pirouetted across the moonlit stage, my shoulders back, my chin high. Snowflakes fell on my tutu and tiara, but warmth coursed through my body. Before the giant evergreen trees, I was as small and otherworldly as a fairy.

Girls in white skirts danced on either side, the tufts of tulle on their arms like drifts of snow blowing in the wind. They knelt and lifted their arms to the starry sky while a choir of angelic voices sang.

All the hours I'd spent practicing had led me here—making art with my body as I reigned over this frosty wonderland. Leslie Gardner, high school senior, was no more. I had become the Snow Queen.

Until I glanced at the audience.

Don sat in the first row.

A chill invaded my body, and my mind returned to that morning. Hands shaking, I'd read the e.p.t. pregnancy test instructions one more time: "If, after two hours, a dark brown donut-shaped ring is visible, your test is positive." I'd glanced at the tube every thirty seconds, but the minutes limped by.

I noticed the yellow flower that must've fallen off another dancer's costume too late. My foot lurched forward and turned my *chassé* into a split, my legs slamming into the stage. My teeth jammed into my shin and pierced my lip. A metallic taste filled my mouth.

Every face gawked.

The room spun under the hot spotlight. A trickle of sweat and stage makeup rolled down my cheek. My costume squeezed my ribs. I couldn't breathe, couldn't think, couldn't see. Nothing but that dark circle in the e.p.t. tube that threatened to swallow all my dreams.

Yet the show must go on. Wasn't that what everyone said?

In my head, Ms. Petipa's voice reminded me of the routine I'd practiced for months. *Grand jeté, arabesque.*

I stood, but pain pierced my calf. I took a deep breath and performed the next step somewhat stilted and then the next more gracefully. I needed to ignore Don, tune out the crowd, let go of everything but the dance.

When the "Waltz of the Snowflakes" ended I stood at the front of center stage, my arms up, my left leg pointed behind me.

The audience roared.

Were they clapping out of pity?

❄

While the musicians played the last notes of the finale, I scurried to the dressing room. I sank into a gray chair, the floor boards creaking, and pulled off my pointe shoes with trembling hands.

Blood tinged the sweaty paper towel between my tape-wrapped toes and the rigid box at the end. A blister taunted my big toe.

I dropped my head into my hands. How could I have gone all the way with Don, in the back of his Nova, no less? My dream of becoming a professional ballerina had seemed within reach. Now I'd have to take care of a baby and bag groceries to make ends meet. What would my parents say? My classmates? My teachers?

I grabbed the rubbing alcohol and wiped my toe. Forget about months from now when I would start showing. What would Ms. Petipa say today about my fall? Did she regret casting me as the Snow Queen? Would she reject me as a possible lead for the spring production? Starring in *Giselle* would've looked nice on my resume, maybe even gotten my foot in the door of a ballet company.

A few dancers squeezed my shoulder or offered a hug as they hurried into the room.

Others who wanted my part looked at me.

If only I could find a secret passageway between the backstage and my bedroom. But there wasn't one. Not in the real world. I stood and grabbed my clothes. After I got dressed, I'd sneak out before anyone else saw me.

Terri pranced in and peeled off her burnt-orange Arabian veil, reminding me of the many times we'd played dress-up in my attic during elementary school. "Don't worry about it. It happens to all of us. Plus, it could've been worse."

Not *much* worse. I summoned up my sincerest smile. "*You* were dynamite."

She wriggled her eyebrows. "Guess who's here?"

I let down my hair and rubbed my head where the bobby pins had stabbed me. My bun had added waves to my straight tresses, not unlike the waves now rippling across my heart. "Jack Manningham," I said, referring to Don's role in our school play.

Terri put her hands on her hips. "Why didn't you tell me he was coming? You're supposed to keep your best friend informed, ya know."

"I didn't know. Not until the end of the snowflake scene."

"So that's what happened."

A couple girls snickered and turned their backs to us.

Where was that secret passageway when I needed it? Perhaps it could lead to a world where it was always spring but never Mother's Day. At least until a girl was ready to be a mommy. I hid behind a dusty, full-length mirror and slipped out of my tutu. The sequins seemed to mock me.

"The snow *pas de deux* was perfect," Terri shouted over her blow dryer.

Perfect? Not exactly. I pulled on my lavender top and stepped out from behind the mirror.

Terri tugged off her sheer pantaloons, her dark hair now feathered like Farrah Fawcett's. "See what he brought?"

I shook my head.

"After the finale, I saw him pull a dozen roses out from under his seat."

My heart jumped. Maybe he did love me. Maybe he'd be excited when I shared the news. I bit my lip. Excited? Who was I kidding?

Terri squinted at me as she squeezed into her leather jeans. "You're not having second thoughts about him, are you?"

My mouth fell open. "Oh no, I just—"

"Off in La La Land again?"

I smoothed my skirt. "Something like that." How *would* Don react? I pressed my lips together. However he'd react, I needed to tell him and soon.

Terri popped a stick of Freshen Up gum into her mouth and flashed the smile that made all the boys drool. "Want one?" She held out the green, mint-flavored pack.

I took a stick and slipped into my backless mules, adding inches to my height. I spritzed Anais Anais on my wrists and breathed in the scent of freshly-cut flowers.

"Come on, slow poke. Let's get out there before another girl snatches him."

❄

I stepped into the buzz of the auditorium and spotted Don.

His dimples, wavy hair, and dreamy eyes screamed hunk.

My throat thick, I moistened my lips, thankful for my minty mouth.

He laughed at something Peggy Richter, our class president, said.

I blinked. Had Peggy come with Don?

Maybe I should slip out before he notices. I turned to go out the other way and bumped into Frankie.

He wrapped a long arm around my shoulder and squeezed. "Good job, kid," he said as if he were my older brother instead of my friend. He handed me a tin of Band-Aids. "I only got one pack." He jerked his head toward the stage. "Apparently it wasn't enough."

I swatted at him.

"For real, though," he said, noticing the blood on my lip. "Are you okay?"

Just as I was about to answer, my family approached through the throng of people.

Mom looked stylish as ever with her striped blouse and matching circle-button earrings. "It's okay, honey," she said and hugged me. "You were really wonderful, so talented and graceful. The way you move your arms . . . I could never dance like that."

Maybe Mom was finally seeing I was meant to dance. Maybe she'd finally stop pushing me toward a "sensible" career like nursing or teaching.

My five-year-old niece Heather held up a baby's-breath bouquet and stared at me with wide eyes.

My older sister Patricia laughed. "When Heather saw you dance, she asked if you were a princess."

I knelt to embrace her and take the flowers. They smelled like sour milk. Guess I better get used to it. "*You're* a princess." I leaned back to admire Heather's tulle skirt and tiara.

Patricia took Heather's hand as I stood. "We gotta get you to bed, missy."

"But Mommy, I wanna stay with Aunt Leslie."

Frankie chuckled and tickled her. "Don't we all?"

Don sauntered over in his gray-and-orange plaid blazer and handed me the bouquet of long-stemmed roses. "You amaze me." He took my cold hand. "I couldn't take my eyes off you."

Not even when I tripped? I inhaled the sweet scent of the purple petals, the paper sleeve crackling in my hand. "They're beautiful."

Frankie cleared his throat. "Les, I gotta go."

I hugged him good-bye. "Thanks for coming."

"We should be going too," Mom said as Frankie hurried off.

"Actually, Mrs. Gardner . . ." Don put his hand on the small of my back. "I was hoping I could take Leslie out to dinner."

Mom glanced at her watch. "All right, but don't stay out too late. You've both got school tomorrow."

On our way to Don's car, he told me he'd made reservations in the Macao room at Kon-Tiki Ports—he'd gotten some early Christmas money from his grandmother. "I've got something to tell you," he said with a smile that couldn't be tamed.

He had something to tell *me*?

❄

We followed an Asian waiter past red booths and bronze statues, through hanging beads that rustled as we walked by, to an elegant table with mother-of-pearl accents.

I scanned the Polynesian menu and decided on chicken and a virgin version of the Gold Cup, one of their signature drinks.

Don ordered sliced sirloin in curry and a South Seas Cooler, which the menu described as a fruit-filled beverage with honey and a hint of ginger.

When our balding waiter, dressed in a Chinese tunic suit, returned with our drinks, Don pushed an envelope across the table.

Something told me I wouldn't be happy about the contents. With an ache in my gut, I opened it.

"Congratulations!" the letter read. "I am pleased to offer you admission to the University of Southern California for the fall 1979 term."

Fall 1979. Right after our baby was due.

"Hollywood, here I come." Don lifted his cooler in the air and took a big gulp. "Just you wait, Les. I'm gonna be the next John Travolta."

I tried to smile.

"Wanna come with me? You could be the next Olivia Newton-John."

I rubbed my neck, my chest heavy.

"Don't look so serious. I'm just kidding. I know you've got other plans."

Had other plans.

He reached across the ebony table and took my hand. "You were born to dance. Anyone can see that."

He studied my face, his eyes melting my defenses.

"Just when did you decide to become a ballerina?"

My mind visited February 1965. "I saw Margot Fonteyn and Rudolf Nureyev star in *Romeo & Juliet* at the Royal Opera House in London."

"London? Must be nice to have a judge for a dad."

I sipped my sweet lime-and-almond-flavored drink. "It has its perks."

"Who's Margot—"

"Fonteyn?" I beamed. "One of the greatest ballerinas of all time. And Nureyev's been her dance partner and friend for years. The first time they performed together he said, 'When she left the stage in her great white tutu, I would have followed her to the end of the world.'"

"The end of the world, huh? That's love."

I searched Don's face. Would he do the same for me, even if it meant staying in Chicago?

He took another drink. "How old were you?"

"Four."

Don raised his eyebrows. "Four? I don't think I was even a real person then."

I laughed. "I was almost five. It was two months before my birthday."

"Well, that changes everything." He chuckled. "What are you going to do after graduation? Still planning to go to NIU?"

I wrapped my fingers around my chilled goblet, and the ice seeped into my veins. How could I break it to him? "I was going to apply to their School of Theater and Dance."

"Was?" He winked. "Coming to L.A. with me now?"

My mouth went dry.

"Chicken manuu?" Our waiter placed a plate of vegetables, pan-fried noodles, and chicken breast strips before me. "And the pounded steak," he said to Don.

Don smiled at the waiter and dug into his curry. "I'd never ask you to give up ballet, Les, just like I know you'd never ask me to give up the silver screen. Dancing means as much to you as acting's always meant to me."

The egg noodles I was chewing turned into boa constrictors.

"Did you change your mind about going to college first?" Don stabbed a potato. "Gonna audition for a company right after graduation?"

"I could try out for companies this summer," I said, my fork unsteady in my hand. "But with more training, I could probably get into a better one."

"From what I saw tonight, any company would be lucky to have you."

"My parents are big on me finishing my education first. Dancers' careers are short so it'll be good to have a bachelor's to fall back on." At least that's what Mom and Dad said. But were they insisting I get a degree because they thought I couldn't make it as a professional ballerina?

Don chewed a pineapple fritter. "How short?"

"Most ballerinas retire around age thirty. Some earlier if they have a lot of injuries. Or a baby." *You can do this, Les. Just tell him.*

"A baby?" Don's eyes widened.

I swallowed, the hope in my heart deflating like a popped balloon.

"I mean, don't get me wrong." He lifted his hand like he was stopping traffic. "I want kids. When I'm older. But we're only young once, right?"

I nodded, my eyes on the sesame-seed-covered chicken I was trying to force down.

A lady wearing a Mandarin gown played a Chinese violin, the mournful notes resonating.

"There's just so much to see, so much to do," Don said, gesturing with his fork. "Like I can't wait to hang out with you in New York."

New York. How could I have forgotten?

"We can see a Broadway play and take the elevator to the top of the Empire State Building like in that movie we watched."

"I haven't auditioned for summer intensives yet, and the School of American Ballet is the most distinguished dance academy in the country. So many people are competing for a place—"

"You'll get in." Don pushed his plate aside and pulled a ring box out of his blazer. "I was going to wait until dessert, but now seems like as good a time as any."

My jaw dropped. Was he about to propose? No. He couldn't be. We were still in high school. But if he was that serious about me, maybe we could make this pregnancy work. Sure, we'd have to change our plans a little, but wasn't it worth it?

He handed it to me. "Open it," he said, his eyes shining.

I opened the velvet box and stared at his class ring.

Don covered my hand with his. "Will you wear it when you're at NIU? Two thousand miles can't separate us."

My finger traced the scarlet gem in the center. Garnet for January. I turned the ring to the side.

Two masks with a banner over them that read, "Speech and Drama." His greatest loves.

Don fidgeted. "So? He pulled out a gold chain, slipped his ring onto it, and fastened it around my neck. "No one could ever love you as much as I do."

I fiddled with the chain and looked up at him. "Of course, I'll wear it." *But it won't be the only sign I'm taken.*

5

Leslie: December 1978

Captain & Tennille belted "Love Will Keep Us Together" from my alarm clock radio.

I pushed snooze again, pulled my velvet bedspread over my head, and clutched Don's ring. He loved me. Of course he did. If I could just sleep a little longer. Maybe then I wouldn't feel so sea-tossed. Maybe then I'd have the energy to get through this day.

I groaned. No matter how exhausted I felt, I had to get up. And I needed to tell Don about the baby. I swung my legs over the bed and wiggled my toes in the carpet. My eyes fell on the wilting roses on my nightstand, the ones Don had given me last weekend. Hopefully, their fading beauty wasn't a symbol of our love. I shook my head. Why did I always read into things?

After I picked out my clothes, I paused to touch my first pair of pointe shoes that hung around a post at the bottom of my bed. I kissed the slippers for good luck and dragged myself to the bathroom, forcing myself into the shower.

"Frankie's here," Mom yelled as I was drying off. "Don't make him late again."

"I'm coming." I threw my clothes on, ran a comb through my tangles, and hurried downstairs.

"Your hair's soaking wet," Mom said. "You can't go out like that. It's thirty degrees."

"Twenty, with the wind chill," Dad piped in from the living room.

Frankie honked.

"I gotta go," I said and pulled on my tweed coat.

"At least put this on." Mom grabbed a crocheted hat from the hall closet, the rust-colored one I hated. "Don't forget to tell Don you can only go out once a week. You're wearing yourself out dating him on top of your homework and ballet practice. If you want to get the lead again . . ."

Now she was taking my dancing seriously? "I'll tell him."

Mom handed me my book bag and two muffins wrapped in paper towels. I hurried to Frankie's orange Coupe de Ville, the Windy City's icy tentacles whipping around my neck.

"What it iz? What it iz?" he said as I handed him a muffin, his dark afro wilder than usual. He was one of the few white guys who still sported one, and though I couldn't say I liked it, somehow with his one-of-a-kind personality he was able to pull it off.

"Don's play *Gaslight* opened last night." I tore off my fuzzy cap, clicked my seat belt into place, and sat back in the leather bench seat. "I had practice so I couldn't go. But Terri and I are going tomorrow. Wanna come?"

Frankie shrugged, pulled out of our driveway, and took a long drag of his cigarette.

I put a piece of muffin into my mouth, the blackberries and brown sugar sickly sweet. "Don's starring as the suave murderer, Mr. Manningham. He tries to make his wife go insane and flirts with the servants."

"Figures."

Frosty air crept under my skin. "What figures?"

"That Don would play a skirt-chasing poser."

My jaw dropped. "You hardly know him."

"Like you know him so well? He just transferred to our school."

"He's been here since August. Plus, we've been going out for months."

Frankie's jaw twitched. "I noticed."

My hands shook as I fiddled with the black strap on my bag. "Why don't you like him?"

Frankie blew out smoke, the stench of tobacco filling the car. "Little things."

Like what? I cleared my throat. "So I take it you're not coming?"

He patted the dashboard with his grease-smeared hands. "I gotta work on this baby."

I smiled. Frankie had been ecstatic the day he saved enough to buy the 1974 Cadillac. He spent every Saturday modifying it.

He jerked his head toward the gift in the back seat. "Early Christmas present."

I lifted my eyebrows. "For me?"

"No. Rudolph the Red Nosed Reindeer."

I unwrapped the package and ran my hands over a pale pink box painted with gold and violet butterflies. I opened it and a ballerina twirled to the theme song from *Swan Lake*, the ballet I'd always dreamed of dancing in. Tears sprang to my eyes. "It's perfect."

Frankie grinned. "Figured you'd like it, Twinkle Toes." His eyes flashed to mine then back to Saint Charles Road. "My parents keep asking about you. They want to know when you're coming over again."

I pulled out my pocket calendar and flipped to December. "Maybe next Sunday?"

"Don't forget. And remember, I was your friend long before that turkey showed up."

❄

"Hand in the rough drafts of your short stories," Mrs. Evans yelled over the fourth-period dismissal bell.

I laid my incomplete fantasy on top of my growing pile of assignments, still trying to decide what should happen to

Queen Velia and her pet monkey in the end. Maybe her rival could return the lost pet, prompting reconciliation between the sisters that ultimately saves their kingdom. My mind in the Land of Yamanu, I bumped into Don in the hallway and dropped my binder, papers spraying onto the moss-green tiles.

He laughed and helped me gather my things. "How's my graceful dancer?" He put his arm around my waist and strolled toward the cafeteria.

I studied his face. "I need to talk to you about something."

"Shoot."

"Not now. After school."

Phil Kostas and Sarah Schiller, the longest-standing couple at York, strolled out of the cafeteria, Phil's arm around Sarah's shoulders.

Warmth eased the tension from my muscles. High-school relationships *could* stand the test of time. They'd been dating, what, three years already?

"Hey," Phil said, smiling at us.

Sarah caught Don's eye and nodded.

My breath quickened. What was that about? I rolled my eyes at myself. She was just saying hi.

Charles and Rhonda, seniors in my child development class, walked in front of us. Rhonda's bobbed hair swung side to side.

"You know those really pretty, snobby girls?" she said to Charles in a hushed tone.

I strained to hear.

Charles buttoned his plaid blazer. "You mean, like Leslie Gardner?"

"Exactly."

My mouth fell open. *Snobby?* I was just shy. And maybe a little wrapped up in the world of my own imagination. I'd have to make an effort to be friendlier so people didn't feel snubbed. Of course, they had said I was really pretty too. Did they actually see me that way?

Don coughed. "Dorks."

Peggy slammed her locker shut, straightened her gray cowl-neck sweater, and started walking with us. "Great job at

The Nutcracker last Sunday," she said, her blue eyes fixed on me. "Terri said you're auditioning for the lead in the spring production."

My stomach contracted into a tight ball. "I've always wanted to play Giselle, but I'll be happy with any part." My chest tightened at the lie. Of course, I *should* be happy with any role, considering my condition.

"I heard Ms. Petipa usually hires guest artists to do the leads."

I scratched the back of my neck. Maybe Peggy thought I was arrogant for reaching for a role professionals typically performed.

"From what I saw at *The Nutcracker* though, I'm sure you could handle it."

"Of course she could." Don winked at me.

A smile grew in my heart and bloomed on my face.

We followed Peggy into the lunch room and stood at the end of the line, the greasy smell of the food turning my stomach.

"What's the show about?" Peggy said.

I considered how I could sum it up quickly. "*Giselle* takes place in Germany in the Middle Ages. A peasant girl falls in love with a duke who's disguised as a commoner. He comes to her town to woo her before marrying the daughter of a prince."

"What a jerk." Peggy handed us scratched-up plastic trays. "What happens next?"

"When Giselle discovers who the duke really is, she grabs his sword and runs around madly until she collapses and dies from a heart attack." I put a carton of skim milk on my tray, the cool condensation moistening my fingers.

"It ends with her dying?" Peggy passed out napkins and plastic forks. "Sounds depressing."

"That's just the first act," I said. "In the second, it's nighttime, and the duke is mourning Giselle's death in a meadow near her grave, but he's frightened away by the Wilis—"

Don raised his eyebrows. "The Weelees?"

I laughed. The name did sound funny. "They're the spirits of women who men betrayed. They dance men to death to get revenge."

Don nodded. "Righteous."

I decided on Salisbury steak with peas and mashed potatoes and snuck a hot bite of gravy-drenched meat before continuing. "The Wilis welcome Giselle then disappear. Soon afterward, the duke comes looking for her grave. She appears, he begs for forgiveness and she forgives him, her love for him strong as ever."

"She still loves him?" Peggy shook her head as she paid for her pizza and tater tots. "Sounds crazy."

I squeezed Don's hand. Would I be crazy to forgive him if he ever betrayed me?

❄

Ten minutes after school, I walked past the auditorium, my leather boots clicking on the marble floor. This part of the building, with its high ceilings and exterior doors, always felt drafty. I rubbed the goose bumps on my arms.

Someone started playing "Fur Elise" on the theater piano.

The beauty of the music called to my arms and legs. If only I could slip on my ballet shoes and paint a picture with my body. As if the other students didn't think I was strange enough.

Don was sitting on the stairway just where we agreed to meet, the amber scent of his cologne drawing me to him. "Hey, beautiful." He pushed up the long sleeves of his yellow T-shirt, a number two emblazoned on the front.

I set my backpack down and stumbled. I grabbed the cold metal railing.

"You okay?" Don helped me sit and put a supportive hand behind my back.

"Just a little lightheaded." I breathed deeply while a ripple of nausea passed over me.

Basketball players in hunter-green jerseys bounded through the lobby, whooping and slapping each other on the back.

Don squeezed my knee, sending shivers through my body. "You need a break. You've been working too hard."

If only working hard were the reason I felt tired. I ran a hand through my hair, and my fingers caught on a knot.

"Wanna go see *The Warriors* tonight?" he said, his eyes brightening.

I chewed my lip. I hated disappointing him. Hated disappointing anyone. "My mom thinks I'm overdoing it and thinks, with school and ballet and everything, we should just see each other once a week. She wants me to focus on my future."

"I thought she saw ballet as just a hobby."

"She's coming around." If only it had been sooner.

Don squinted. "Are you saying we can't go out anymore?"

"No, I just need some extra time to prepare for *Giselle* and the summer intensives audition. After it's over, we can spend more time together." I swallowed. "Maybe a lot more time."

"But that's three months away."

"We can still go out on Sundays, when I don't have practice." But I'd promised Frankie at least one Sunday. "Or Saturday nights after rehearsal."

Don stared at the white floor. "I need to tell you something too," he whispered. He lifted his gaze to mine.

I froze at his somber expression. The notes of "Fur Elise" grew agitated, the D minor chords echoing in my heart.

"Sarah told me she likes me."

Bile rose in my throat. "Sarah Schiller?" I stammered, picturing her and Phil walking together just a few hours before.

He nodded.

Spots blotched my vision. "When?"

"Today in Spanish class."

Who shares their feelings in Spanish class? "Why would she say that?"

He fidgeted on the stair, peering across the foyer at the exit. "She's been flirting with me for weeks, and in fun I guess I was playing along. I didn't think it meant anything," he said quickly. "But I guess she likes me and . . ." He locked eyes with me. "I realized I like her too."

How could he do this to me? Especially now. "Did you say anything to her? Tell her you liked her?"

He stared at me, his lips a thin line.

My heart stopped. It was one thing for him to have passing feelings for another girl. It was quite another for him to express those feelings. Especially when we had a baby on the way. I stood and grabbed my bag.

Don caught my hand. "I told her I wanted to stay with you," he said, his eyes wet. "And she wants to stay with Phil."

I exhaled. That was good. But he shouldn't have been flirting with Sarah in the first place.

"This doesn't have to change our relationship."

I perched on the end of the step and peered at my stomach. If Sarah didn't change our relationship, someone else certainly would. And if I couldn't count on Don to be faithful for a few months, how could I count on him to help me raise a child?

The song ended.

My fingers fumbling with the clasp, I took off the necklace Don had given me and handed him his ring.

He pushed it away. "I don't want to break up."

"But—"

"Just think about it over Christmas break."

I stuffed the ring and necklace in my backpack and leaned back, the metal-capped step jabbing my spine. Since he'd told me about it, maybe I could trust him. Plus, we had a child to consider. And shouldn't that child know its father?

6

Shannon: October 2014

Down syndrome. The words were like a life sentence on our baby's future. This son or daughter might never go to college. Never marry. Never have children.

I rolled over for what must've been the hundredth time that night and pulled the silky comforter over my chilly shoulders. I considered feeling through the darkness to find my socks but instead pressed my frigid feet against Wade. His devotion was the one thing I could count on these days. That and more sleepless nights.

Sometimes I still thought I heard Lily crying and staggered out of bed to nurse her, only to return with empty arms and an emptier heart. I bit my lip to fight the tears, but they fell anyway, dampening my brown pillowcase like the rain had drenched the ground at Lily's burial service.

I curled toward Wade and caressed my rounding belly. Not only was our little one's career and family at stake, but kids with Down syndrome often had heart and lung problems. Or so I'd read online as soon as I'd gotten off the phone with Dr. Beck.

Our newborn might need a heart operation. What if something went wrong during surgery?

I laid my head on Wade's smooth chest, his heartbeat steady under my ear. As he'd reminded me, our baby only had a one in thirty-three chance of having Down syndrome. Odds were, our little one was fine. And worrying about a possible disability wouldn't help.

Wade was right, of course. Besides, I had the twins' birthday to prepare for and a high school play to direct.

I sat up and sipped my mug of chamomile tea. When I swallowed the last drop of honey, I sprayed my pillow with lavender and vanilla and turned up the river sounds on my phone. I snuggled close to my human heater and ordered myself to sleep.

But hours later I continued to toss and turn, the uncertainty eating at my stomach. Was this child destined for defeat? Would this baby die even younger than Lily?

"Spirit," Andrew said from stage left, a script in his hand. "Tell me if Tiny Tim will live."

I fidgeted in my front-row theater seat and it squeaked. When I was a four-eyed and freckle-faced preteen, my family decorated the tree together every year then watched *A Christmas Carol.* In honor of them, I hoped this would be the best play I'd ever directed.

Ravi gazed stage right where the students playing the Cratchit family gathered around a fake fireplace. "I see a vacant seat in the poor chimney corner," he said, his burly back to me.

"Don't turn your back to the audience," I called out.

"Sorry, Mrs. Henry." He spun in a mock ballerina twirl until he faced me.

Grinning, I shook my head. "Stand diagonally between Andrew and the audience." I strode on stage and demonstrated. "One foot pointed toward him and one toward them, so you can see him and they can see you." Dust tickled my nose, and I sneezed.

"God bless us every one," Ravi said in falsetto.

"Hey, that's my line." Sam, a freshman with blond Justin Bieber hair, stood and raised his arms.

His brother Ben, a six-foot-four senior, flicked him in the ear.

"Ow!" Sam winced. "That hurt."

"Boys." I attempted a stern look. "That's enough."

"I was just joking anyway, Mrs. Henry." Sam scowled at Ben. "You don't think I'd seriously be mad at him for saying my line, do you? It's just a stupid play."

I pressed my lips together. Stupid play? That's not what he'd said during auditions. "Would you rather I get someone else to play Tiny Tim? Several students would be happy to take your place."

Sam's jaw dropped. "No, Mrs. Henry. I'm sorry." He shot daggers at his brother.

I returned to my seat and sighed. Getting this play off the ground would take a bigger miracle than the three ghosts who visited Ebenezer Scrooge on Christmas Eve. But wasn't that what Christmastime was all about? "Let's take it from the top." I bit into my juicy pear and nodded at Andrew.

Not only was he my best actor, but he looked like a young Ebenezer with his pale skin, high forehead, and angular nose. "Spirit, tell me," Andrew said, pleading with his eyes, "if Tiny Tim will live."

"I see a vacant seat in the poor chimney corner," Ravi said as if he were a spook in a haunted house. "And a crutch without an owner, carefully preserved. If these shadows remain unaltered by the future—"

"Ravi," I said, suppressing a smile. "I appreciate your exuberance, but can we tone it down a bit?" At least he had too much expression instead of not enough. I'd had the opposite problem with the junior high kids I'd taught before.

His face sobered. "Sure thing, Mrs. Henry." He cleared his throat and looked at Andrew. "If these shadows remain unaltered by the future, the child will die."

"No." Andrew stepped back and shook his head. "Oh no, kind spirit. Say he will be spared."

I rubbed my thumb against my belly. "Say he will be spared," I prayed silently. My eyes watered, but I gritted my teeth. I couldn't cry here. Not in the middle of play practice.

❄

Rain pelted me as I hurried across the black parking lot. I shivered and hunched under my trench coat, but I couldn't hide from the questions that assaulted me.

Had Tiny Tim been born crippled? And if so, did Mrs. Cratchit blame herself? Maybe if she hadn't stumbled when she was pregnant. Or lifted that heavy crate. Or worked so late.

I climbed into our Odyssey, clicked my seat belt into place, and unbuttoned my dress pants. I'd have to start wearing maternity clothes soon. That or continue to struggle breathing as my trousers strained against my swelling stomach.

I made a right onto Saint Charles Road. In five minutes, I'd be at Elmhurst Memorial Hospital for my CVS test. Would it hurt? And, more importantly, what would it reveal about our child? At least Wade would be there with me.

I turned right onto York Street when another round of questions assailed me. Did kids at school or in the neighborhood make fun of Tiny Tim? What would happen to him once his parents died? Could he earn a living? Or would he have to live in a poorhouse? Or burden their other children, who were struggling to make ends meet themselves?

I put a hand on my stomach. This child might not only be physically disabled like Tiny Tim, but mentally disabled as well. If so, what kind of life could it lead?

"And now for 'Autumn,' a piano solo by Ryan Stewart," the radio deejay said.

The melody was as enchanting as the falling leaves outside.

A chill rushed over me. I loved October in its ever-changing glory. The romance in the crisp air as the leaves turned colors and fluttered to the ground. Hay rides and fruit picking with Wade and the twins. The sweet Golden Delicious apples I loved to munch on and the tart Granny Smith apples I baked pies with.

I caressed my belly and imagined our youngest sitting on hay bales, wandering through pumpkin patches, and jumping in piles of leaves, the sound of laughter in the air.

My phone rang.

I answered it, trying not to rear-end the SUV in front of me.

"Hey sweetie," Wade said. "Bad news. I had an accident—"

"An accident?" My grip on the wheel tightened. "What happened? Are you okay?"

"I'm fine. I just side-swiped someone when I was pulling into a gas station. But I won't be able to make it to the hospital in time. Tell me about it when you get home?"

❄

Dr. Beck pulled on white gloves, the stench of latex infecting the room, and filled a syringe.

I rubbed the goose bumps on my arms. Was I doing the right thing? I'd heard that chorionic villus sampling could cause a miscarriage. Of course, Dr. Beck had assured me the risk was low—only one miscarriage for every 100 to 200 tests performed. But still, was I endangering my child's life just to find out if he or she had a disability? What if the baby was perfectly healthy but died as a result of the test? I'd never forgive myself.

Dr. Beck ran a transducer over my exposed belly and static filled the room, a blur of ice-blue blobs appearing on the ultrasound monitor. She poked my stomach then injected the fluid from the syringe a little at a time. With another needle, she pricked my skin.

I flinched. Could that have been the fatal blow?

But the worst hadn't come, for she soon pulled out the longest needle I'd ever seen.

My breath caught and my pulse started racing.

She inserted the foot-long needle into the other one still piercing my belly, which I now saw was a port. She drew up fluid into the syringe then squirted the watery-red contents into a petri dish.

I felt sick. Would these sample cells doom our little one's future?

Two days later I dumped water, Spanish rice mix, and a can of diced tomatoes into a pot on the stove and turned on the heat. Hopefully, I could get dinner ready and the house tidied before Wade's student arrived.

When I was a child teaching my stuffed animals and later acting in school plays, Wade had been building robots and competing in science fairs. Little wonder, he now taught physics at Willowbrook High School. Travis was one of several students he tutored on the side.

I grabbed the rice box and empty can and headed for the trash bin but tripped over a plastic school bus.

The can clattered over the floor, spraying tomato juice onto the freshly-washed tiles.

I rubbed my forehead, feeling a headache coming on. Why was I always dropping things?

"Clumsy Mommy," Wade said.

My blood pressure rose. "Daniel's toy was on the floor. And pregnant women are clumsier."

Wade lifted his eyebrows. "I would think that wouldn't be until the end of the pregnancy when you're bigger."

I grabbed a knife from the silverware drawer. "The extra weight is not the only reason."

"So you weren't clumsy before you got pregnant?"

I shot a look at him and grabbed avocados from the fridge.

He stooped to clean my mess. "What's this on the mat?"

"Comet I spilled. I shook most of the powder into the garbage can but didn't have time to wipe the mat off yet. If you want to get it clean, you can take a rag—"

"Wait." He held up his hand like he was stopping traffic. "You lost me at 'If you want to get it clean.'"

I grinned and swatted him with the dish towel.

My phone rang.

I glanced at the caller ID: my mom. I didn't really have

time to talk right now, what with dinner to finish and the house to tidy, but I didn't want her to feel ignored. She'd already left two voicemails in the last two days that I hadn't returned. "Hey, Mom."

"Hi, honey. How did the test go?"

"It went okay," I said, an ache in the back of my throat. "We're expecting the preliminary results today or tomorrow."

"Let me know as soon as you find out."

"I will." I pulled red bell peppers out of the fridge. "But remember, no one except you, Wade, and Gabby knows I'm pregnant," I said, lowering my voice and turning away from the living room where the kids were playing. "Not even the twins. And I don't want my in-laws finding out on Facebook."

"Don't worry. I won't tell your brother."

Despite my fears I had to laugh, thinking of the time Mom told my brother I was in labor. He'd posted it on his timeline before I'd even had a chance to tell Gabby or Wade's mom. They'd found out when they read their news feeds that morning.

"Mommy," Katy said when I hung up fifteen minutes later. "Is my boyfriend coming over tonight?"

"Your boyfriend?" Wade picked her up and spun her over the porcelain tiles. "You're not allowed to have one of those."

What if he dropped her and her head split open? Unlikely, I admitted, but possible. "Can we do that in a carpeted area next time, just in case?" I finished cutting up the avocado, popped the last piece into my mouth, and wiped the slimy residue off my hand with a napkin.

Wade squinted. "Who's this Case guy?"

"Case guy?" I frowned.

"Justin Case? Is he someone you're seeing on the side?"

I laughed just as the doorbell rang.

"I'll get it," Daniel yelled from the living room.

I glanced at the clock above the sink. A little early for Travis. "Don't open the door unless you know who it is." I hustled to the front entrance, Buster barking at my heels. I put my hand on Daniel's shoulder and peered out the window.

Travis stood on the concrete landing. He wore his baseball

cap backwards, held a skateboard under his arm, and had a backpack slung over one shoulder.

I smiled and opened the door.

Buster jumped all over him as if he were his long-lost brother.

"Good to see you, Travis," I said, trying to get our Weimaraner under control.

"You too, Mrs. Henry." He pet Buster then crouched before Daniel and mussed his chestnut hair. "How's the little man doing?"

"I'm gonna be four next week."

Travis lifted his eyebrows. "Wow. That's big. You're gonna be taller than me before you know it."

I made a mental note to pick up presents for the twins' birthday, especially walkie-talkies for Daniel and the Snow White costume for Katy. "Got physics homework for Wade to help you with?"

"That and trig." Travis stood. "And I heard you have a room for me to paint? Thought I'd check that out too while I'm here."

I swallowed. Wade had asked Travis to paint the nursery even after I tested positive on the first trimester screening. "That would be great. How much would you charge?"

Travis scowled. "I can't take money from you. After everything you've done for me?"

He sniffed the air and his eyes lit up. "What smells good?"

"Fajitas and Spanish rice," I said, leading him into the living room. "But we want to help you save money for college."

"I wouldn't even be going to college if it wasn't for you guys. I'd probably be a pothead and a high school dropout."

Daniel tugged on my pants. "Mommy, what's a pothead?"

Travis gawked at me, his coffee-colored eyes contrite.

I grinned. "That's okay. We'll just have you explain it to him."

"Uh . . ." Travis twisted the silver stud under his lip.

I laughed. "I'm kidding. Come on." I gestured for him to follow me. "The room's upstairs."

My phone rang.

I pulled it out of my back pocket and glanced at the number—Dr. Beck's office. My stomach rolled. I answered the call, my voice more stable than I felt.

"Mrs. Henry?" Norma said. "Dr. Beck received the results from your CVS test. Can you and your husband come in tomorrow morning?"

7

Shannon: October 2014

A chill marching up my spine, I followed the nurse to a patient room at the end of the hall and took a seat.

Wade sat beside me and put his arm around my shoulders.

I stared at the charts and pictures on the ice-blue walls. If the results were good, someone would've let us know over the phone. Wouldn't they? So the doctor calling us in could only mean bad news. Unless this was the standard way to deliver CVS test results.

Dr. Beck swept into the room, her face somber, and sat on the black, rolling stool. Her dark, close-set eyes fixed on me and then Wade. "I'm so sorry, Mr. and Mrs. Henry, but the diagnosis isn't good."

A wave rolled over me.

"Unfortunately, your child does have Down syndrome."

I brought a shaky hand to my forehead and closed my eyes.

Wade rubbed my back. "But these are only the preliminary results, right? Couldn't they be wrong?"

Her brow furrowed. "Rarely. The FISH test is around 98% accurate." She pushed her glasses over her chestnut hair. "That being said, we can wait a week or two until the final results come in to discuss your options. If you'd prefer."

"What kind of options are we talking about?"

"Termination of the pregnancy, for one."

Termination? I peered at my empty hands.

"If you continue with the pregnancy, you should start reading up on Down syndrome and prepare for the possibility of a long NICU stay after your child is born. Babies with Down syndrome are often born with a heart problem or other birth defects that may require immediate surgery."

Wade squeezed my hand.

Dr. Beck's eyes softened. "Go home and prepare yourself for this. Then give me a call when you're ready to make a decision." She stood, clipboard in hand. "But don't wait too long. If you decide on abortion, the earlier we do it the safer and easier it will be."

❄

Everywhere we went, people would stare. Point. Comment. And not because my adorable daughter wore a flower headband as big as her head like they'd done when I'd taken Lily out, but because my child was disabled. Retarded. Abnormal.

I gritted my teeth, a sour taste in my mouth, as I pulled a tomato-red sweater over my head. How dare they ogle my little one? How dare they call my kid those names?

My chest tightened. Should I really be mad at them—whoever they were—or at myself for thinking like this? I should be as proud of this child as I was of Daniel who could do math in his head and Katy whose vocabulary far exceeded her friends.

I glared at the half dozen water bottles littering Wade's nightstand. I trudged through his discarded clothes, grabbed the nearly empty containers, and threw them in the trash. One fell out.

I picked up the rebellious cylinder, plastic crunching in my hand, and dropped it into the can. No matter how many times I asked Wade to finish them and toss them, they continued to pile up. And his pants, socks, and T-shirts on the floor were growing into Mount Everest.

His black physics tee with "May the [Mass Times Acceleration] Be With You" on the front smelled like he'd played basketball in it, so I threw it in the hamper. I folded the "10 Things You Need to Know About Chuck Norris" shirt and put it back in his drawer.

Exhaling, I sank onto our bed and glanced at our wedding picture on Wade's nightstand.

We were walking down the aisle after we'd said our vows, a bouquet in my hand and a boutonnière on his lapel. He must've just said something funny because I was laughing and he was grinning at me, my free hand clasped in both of his.

My gaze fell from the photo to my belly and the problem before us.

Wade loved attention and might enjoy making a scene as he went out with our slightly-different son or daughter. But I'd always shied away from the spotlight. Unless I was acting.

Now I'd always be on stage, in a role I could never escape.

I ran my hands through my hair. How could I be so selfish? So heartless? This was my child. A child who might not even live long enough for people to stare.

❄

"Ben and Sam Cooper," Principal Peggy White's high-pitched voice echoed through the hallway. "My office now."

I capped the blueberry-scented dry erase marker I'd been writing with and placed it in the whiteboard tray. Were Tiny Tim and Mr. Cratchit about to be suspended again? Would I have to find replacements?

The boys shuffled out of the classroom across the hall and followed Peggy's clicking heels.

"You think they put another snake in her office?" Ravi said from his front-row desk.

I gasped. "That was them?"

Peggy was a force to be reckoned with. Until a garter snake slithered up her leg.

Ravi's jaw dropped. "Um, no," he said, looking side to side. "I mean, yes, I mean, who knows who it was?"

The fifth-period dismissal bell rang.

"Saved by the bell," Ravi muttered, laughing.

"Don't forget, your papers on the themes in *A Christmas Carol* are due Monday."

My students shoved their books and binders into their bags and pushed back their chairs, metal squeaking across the white square tiles. They headed off to their next class, talking and laughing about what prank Ben and Sam must've pulled this time.

I slipped my notes into my briefcase. I'd hate to be on Peggy's bad side. And if I didn't tell her about this pregnancy soon, I probably would be. I couldn't hide my rounding stomach much longer. After all, I'd be three months along on Tuesday. But I needed time to decide what to do first.

"Do you need the Cooper brothers for play practice this week?" Peggy stood in the doorframe, her short, blonde hair roller-curled and hair-sprayed.

I tapped my pen against the oak desk. I liked Ben and Sam and would like to spare them if I could, but I didn't want to stand in the way of Peggy running the school as she saw fit. "It would be helpful. Why?"

"A six-foot-four gorilla showed up in the girls' locker room," Peggy said, her blue eyes flashing.

I clamped my lips together to keep from grinning.

"And a bear jumped out of a stall in the girls' bathroom."

"I see," I said, nodding. "If you want to suspend them for a few days, we can just practice the scenes they're not in." I latched my briefcase closed. "I've been meaning to ask you, would you mind if we make the Sunday, December 14 play performance a matinee? It's my sister-in-law's birthday, and we were hoping to have the party at our house that night."

"Sure. Just send me an email to remind me." Peggy sat on a corner of the desk and peered at me. "You haven't been yourself recently." She peered at my belly and lifted her penciled eyebrows. "Is another Henry on the way?"

My mouth fell open. What could I say? I refused to lie, and beating around the bush with Judge Judy, as the students called her, never worked.

"Tell you what." Peggy stood. "You're free for the next two periods, right? Let's talk over lunch. My treat. I'll meet you outside in ten minutes, after I knock some sense into those Cooper boys." She winked and strode out of the room.

❄

I bit into my Cajun chicken wrap, my favorite entrée at Jack's Silverado Grill, but only chewed the sharp cheese and spicy meat mechanically. How much would I have to eat to convince Peggy I wasn't pregnant? And could I hold it down?

"So, let's have it." Peggy wrapped her manicured nails around her cup. "Should I start looking for a substitute for your maternity leave?"

That didn't take long. "Well," I said, wiping my mouth.

"I knew it!" Peggy giggled like she was fifteen instead of fifty-something.

Her sweet laugh was one of the things I adored about her, but today I couldn't share her enthusiasm.

She frowned. "What is it? Are you worried that what happened to Lily will happen again?"

My chest ached as my mind returned to June 22. I'd woken at 6:46 a.m., surprised Lily had slept through the night. Still tired from months of broken sleep but eager to peek at my daughter and wish her a happy four-month birthday, I snuck into the nursery. I bent over the chipped, white crib and brushed Lily's forehead.

Cold skin met my hand, and a chill jolted through my body.

"SIDS is rare, you know," Peggy said, pulling me out of the memory. "It's unlikely it'll happen again. And you can't let fear stop you from living the rest of your life."

"The baby has Down syndrome," I blurted out. I couldn't think about SIDS today. Not with everything else I had to worry about.

Peggy's hand flew to her chest. "Oh my dear, I am so sorry."

Would Peggy think something was wrong with me and Wade for having a child who was less than perfect?

She squeezed my hand. "I know it's hard to get that news."

Hard didn't begin to describe it.

"Will you need to quit working for several years, since your child has special needs?" Peggy lifted another forkful of crab cake. "I'd hate to lose such an organized, talented, and popular drama teacher. But family comes first."

I bit my lip. I hadn't considered the effect this child could have on my career. I loved my students and enjoyed using my creativity to produce plays and musicals. "I'm not sure if I'm going to continue with the pregnancy."

Pursing her lips, Peggy's face tightened as if she'd swallowed a bag of lemons.

My body went rigid. Why had I shared such a personal decision with the most opinionated woman I knew? I should've kept my mouth shut.

"Can I tell you a story?" Peggy let out her breath and sat back in the wooden booth. "Just between you and me?"

I crossed my legs and nodded, my skin tingling. Peggy shared more news about people than the *Chicago Tribune*, but she'd never asked that a story be kept confidential before.

Peggy pushed her plate to the side, rested her arms on the table, and wove her fuchsia-painted fingers together. "When I was a senior in high school—you probably weren't even born then—I knew a very sweet and talented girl. She had a lot of dreams and plans for her future, but then something unexpected happened."

I threw a salty French fry into my mouth. "What?"

"She got pregnant."

"Can I get you ladies anything else?" Our waiter grabbed Peggy's empty plate.

"Dessert?" Peggy lifted her eyebrows at me.

I shook my head, eager to hear the rest of the story.

"Just the check." Peggy glanced at her watch and her eyes widened. "We've got to go," she said, pulling cash out of her wallet. "You're late for class."

❄

After school, I scrubbed our white stove as if washing away the spaghetti sauce spatters from the night before could somehow blot out the extra chromosome in my baby's DNA.

Wade came downstairs whistling "Heigh-Ho" from *Snow White and the Seven Dwarves.* "Red, the house looks great. You don't need to keep cleaning."

Maybe I wouldn't have to spend so much time cleaning if he learned to pick up after himself. I dropped the black grates and burner caps from the stovetop into the sink and attacked some stubborn bread crumbs. "Can you stick the chicken tenders in the oven for me?" I said, gesturing toward the bag on the counter.

He studied the back of the bag. "What's a lined baking sheet?"

"Tinfoil. Lined with tinfoil."

"And what is a baking sheet?"

I grinned and pulled one out of the cabinet. "What are the birthday boy and beauty doing?"

"Daniel's playing with his cars."

"And Katy?"

"She just put on the Snow White costume you got her."

I smiled and turned on the faucet. Warm water poured over my hands and the sponge, rinsing off the pasta sauce and the honeysuckle-scented soap.

Wade plopped down on a stool and grabbed a nectarine from the fruit bowl. "She wants you to paint her nails."

"I'll go up soon," I said, wiping the oven door.

"Come into the living room and sit with me a few minutes before everyone gets here."

I grabbed the pumpkin hand towel, but he gently seized my wrist. "I was just going to dry my hands," I said.

He squinted. "A likely story," he said but released me.

Something in his eyes reminded me of our life before Lily, of our life before today.

I dried my hands and raced him to the couch.

He jumped in the middle and sprawled out, no room left for me.

I stuck my hands on my hips and mock-glared at him.

"What? Did you wanna sit?" He sat up and moved over. "Come here," he said, his voice soothing.

I curled up next to him and rested my head on his shoulder.

He rubbed my arm. "Talk to me. Tell me what you're thinking."

I swallowed hard. "I know the preliminary results are rarely wrong, but there is still a chance, right?" I searched his face. "That our child will be normal? That our life will be normal?"

"Normal?" Wade cocked an eyebrow. "When have we ever been normal?"

I tried to smile.

"You're not in this alone, you know," he said and squeezed my hand. "I'm going to take tomorrow off, and we can spend the day on the couch."

"Don't you have midterms?"

"A substitute can give those."

There was a soft rap on our front door.

I jumped up.

Wade tugged me back onto the sofa. "I'll get it." He stood. "You relax."

As I watched my protector walk away, I pulled an ivory chenille blanket over my legs. Staying home tomorrow did sound awfully good. If only I could abandon the housework and sleep for days. Maybe when I woke I'd feel like a new person.

A few minutes later, Wade strode into the room carrying two gift bags and a plate of monkey bread. He handed me the bags. "For the twins. From Rebecca," he said, referring to our next-door neighbor

I peeked inside the bag at the candy-corn socks. "She always remembers their birthday."

Wade pulled the plastic wrap off the pastry and held the plate out to me.

Caramel and cinnamon stuck to my fingers as I tore off a piece and bit in. "Mmm." I didn't realize how hungry I was. The baby must have a sweet tooth. I reached for another piece and froze. "I should've invited her to the party tonight."

Wade propped his feet up on the coffee table. "I told her you didn't want her to come."

My jaw dropped.

"Just kidding," he said, laughing. "But seriously, though." He stared at me, his lips pursed. "She hates you now."

I smacked his arm. "Honey! What did you say? Did you explain it's just family? And their godmother, Gabby?"

"Stop worrying. I invited Rebecca, but she can't come. She's going out with her bully, I mean, boyfriend. They just got engaged."

My stomach sank. "Oh, no."

"I told her she doesn't deserve to be treated like that," Wade said, his jaw tight.

"I thought she was going to break up with him."

"Maybe she will," Wade said, his tone grim. "At her funeral."

❄

"Can I borrow your comb?" I asked Wade as I freshened up for the twins' party. I held up my chewed-up one. "Buster ate mine for breakfast."

"You know I don't use combs."

"I think I would've noticed if you never did your hair."

He whipped off his baseball cap to reveal brown tufts shooting out at odd angles. "Does it look like I do my hair?" he said, wiggling his eyebrows.

A smile threatened to reach my lips just before the door-bell rang.

"I'll get it," Wade said, putting his hat back on.

Once everyone arrived we gathered in the living room to sing "Happy Birthday" and cut the cake—Spiderman rescuing Snow White—a unique creation by Aunt Margaret. We dug into the layers of chocolate fudge, licking the butter-cream frosting off our lips as the twins opened their presents.

Katy squealed when she opened the stuffed orangutan from Gabby, the ballerina books from Aunt Margaret, and the art supplies from Gram and Grandpa.

Daniel loved the action figures Gabby got him and the

Spiderman pajamas we'd bought, but his favorite gift was the car Gram and Grandpa insisted on buying him. We had to bribe him with candy to get him to stop driving around in it long enough to say good-bye to everyone.

After everyone else left, I told Gabby about the preliminary CVS test results.

"Through thick and thin, I'm here," she said and hugged me, the heat from her body soothing my nerves. "But you might have to be the thin part, 'cause I'm a little thick already."

8

Leslie: January 1979

With one last swig of grape juice, I hurried outside. Icy air blasted me in the face. I bolted to Frankie's flame-colored Cadillac, the smell of smoke in the air.

"What it iz, what it iz?" he said with his easy grin.

Had he seen Don flirting with Sarah? Was that one of the "little things" Frankie had mentioned? And, if not, could I hide it from him? I avoided his gaze and clicked my seat belt into place.

He jerked his head in the direction of the blaze. "The house at the end of my block's on fire."

I gasped. "Oh, no. I hope everyone's okay."

He backed down the driveway. At a break in traffic, he whipped the coupe onto York Street.

I gripped the hand rest.

He shifted gears and slammed on the gas, tires squealing.

My stomach flipped.

"Today," the radio announcer said, "the Windy City's negative nine degrees, or negative twenty-five with the wind chill. We're not quite going to beat the negative eleven record set in 1942 though."

I shivered and tightened the sky-blue woven scarf Terri had given me for Christmas. "Any problems starting the car this morning?" I dared a glance at Frankie.

He turned left onto St. Charles Road. "This baby's V8, 472 Big Block turbo 400 transmission purred like a kitten as soon as I started her."

I laughed.

"How's Casanova?"

I stared out the window at a fire engine speeding by with sirens blazing and fingered the chain around my neck. Don hadn't called me over the break. Was he just trying to give me time?

Frankie's jaw tightened. "He better be treating you right or I swear, I will beat the—"

"I asked him for some time to get ready for *Giselle*."

"Which of course he'll give you if I have anything to say about it."

I tried a smile. "Like you do?"

Frankie glared at me as he unbuttoned his black-and-mustard coat. "We've been friends since we were in diapers. I deserve more of your time than that doofus." He exhaled and loosened his grip on the wheel. "Look, what's really going on? What's the deal with the time off?"

I shrugged.

"You know you're gonna tell me."

"He likes someone else," I blurted. "And she likes him."

He raised his eyebrows. "Who's the lucky lady? That blonde from his movies class?"

My mouth fell open. How many girls had Don been flirting with?

"Break up with him, Les. He's no good for you. You deserve a guy who only has eyes for you. And there are plenty of us out there."

I touched my throat. Plenty of *us*?

The second-period bell echoed off the cinder block walls.

I scarfed down a mouthful of stale saltines, gulped water from the fountain, and hurried to child development class. Hopefully no one would notice how many notes I was taking. I pushed open the door just as Miss Dixon tried to close it.

She stumbled backward, and a plastic baby dropped onto the wood plank floor.

My hand flew to my mouth. "I am so sorry," I cried, sweat creeping under my arms. Was this a sign of my future parenting skills? I picked up the doll and handed it to the twenty-something teacher who doubled as the girls' volleyball coach.

Her boy-cut hair was disheveled, and a piece of lint fell onto the pointy collar of her paisley shirt.

"Sorry," I mumbled again and shuffled to the back corner. So much for lying low.

"Nice one." Terri grinned as I took my seat next to her.

"This semester," Miss Dixon said to the class, "we're going to learn how to care for children. Hopefully, you won't need this information for quite a while." She winked at me.

My stomach turned. I stared at my desk. Did she know?

"Except when babysitting, of course." Miss Dixon spread her hands.

I fidgeted in my rigid plastic seat.

Charles eyeballed me through his horn-rimmed glasses, his B.O. extra pungent today.

My cheeks burned. Could he see the scarlet *A* emblazoned on my chest?

Peggy raised her hand. "Are we going to talk about miscarriage this semester? My aunt just miscarried."

"I'm sorry to hear that." Miss Dixon cleared her throat. "But that's a good question."

A *really* good question. Maybe I could miscarry and avoid all the problems this pregnancy was going to cause.

I grimaced. Peggy's aunt—and their whole family—must've been excited about her baby.

"Unfortunately, fifteen to twenty percent of pregnancies end with a miscarriage." Miss Dixon pressed her lips together. "Usually in the first trimester."

I clasped my hands under my chin. "God," I prayed

silently. "Please forgive me for what I did with Don. I promise I won't go that far again until I'm married. But could you . . . would you . . . *please* let me miscarry?"

After class, I hurried over to Peggy. "I'm sorry to hear about your aunt."

"Yeah, and she'd been trying to get pregnant for a long time," Peggy said, fingering the cross hanging from her neck.

If only we could trade places.

❄

The dismissal bell jolted me awake. What was wrong with me? I never used to fall asleep in school, but now it happened almost every day. I rolled my eyes. Never mind. I was about to see Don.

I put a mint into my mouth, my hands shaking. We would talk and eat lunch together like always, Sarah a forgotten memory. Maybe he'd even give me a Christmas present topped with a gold bow.

"Please leave the final drafts of your short stories on my desk on your way out," Mrs. Evans said.

I pulled my story out of my binder. I hated turning in something less than my best, but I hadn't had the energy to stay up any later last night. I shoved the rest of my supplies into my backpack and snuck a peek at Mrs. Evans.

She was erasing the board, her short curls like a cap on her head.

If I hurried maybe I could get out without her seeing me.

I hightailed it to the front of the classroom and set my paper on top of the rest.

Mrs. Evans plunked down her wooden eraser with a puff of dust. "Miss Gardner, may I speak with you in private?"

I froze.

She pulled me aside and smiled, but her brow was furrowed. "Have my classes gotten boring?"

"No," I stammered. "I love your class."

She put a hand over mine. "You are one of the most creative students I've ever had. And you've always handed in your assignments on time and with excellence." She brushed chalk off her pleated skirt. "But recently your work hasn't been as strong. And now you're falling asleep in class."

My ears flamed. I clutched my arms to my chest.

She tipped her head. "What's going on?"

I eyed the exit and shifted my feet. *Just a baby growing in my belly. No big deal.*

"Why didn't you eat with us today?" I took a seat on the hard, speckled step behind the auditorium next to Don. I had to tell him I was pregnant. No more stalling.

He gazed at the floor.

Butterflies beat against my stomach, frantic to get out.

"I kissed Sarah," he said.

A fist punched my gut. He'd *kissed* her?

Someone played "Moonlight Sonata" on the piano in the auditorium. The melancholy notes rang off the white marble walls.

I bit my lip. My feet yearned for my ballet slippers.

Don lifted his eyes to mine and exhaled. "I'm sorry. I never meant for this to happen." He rubbed his hands down his wide legged jeans. "I saw Sarah at a party, we started talking, and one thing led to another."

Did they do more than kiss? "You said you wanted to stay with me." My voice trembled. "And she wanted to stay with Phil."

"I wanted to stay with you, but you broke up with me," he said, his voice hard. "What was I supposed to do?"

My mouth fell open. "I was thinking about breaking up with you, but you convinced me not to," I cried.

Don shook his head. "That's not how I remember it."

A volcano erupted in my body.

He moved closer and squeezed my knee. His woodsy cologne brought back our nights at the forest preserve.

"I'm sorry I hurt you," he said, his tone soft. "That's the last thing I wanted to do."

I dropped my head into my hands and tried to breathe, but I caught sight of my belly through my splayed fingers. I twisted a loose black thread on my pants. "Does Phil know?"

"Sarah told him."

If Phil could forgive Sarah, maybe I could forgive Don. Eventually. Perhaps it really was a misunderstanding. "Where do we go from here?" I whispered.

He rubbed the back of his neck. "Sarah and I are dating."

The room spun. I grabbed the cool, wrought-iron railing.

"I wish things had turned out differently," Don said.

He *wished* things had turned out differently? Like it wasn't under his control? "We can still be friends." Don beamed at me. "Sarah knows how much I care about you."

"But . . . now that you know I didn't break up—"

"Sarah and I are already seeing each other," Don blurted, his smile gone. "She left Phil for me. I can't leave her now."

The peach cobbler I'd eaten at lunch started coming back up. I grabbed my bag and bolted outside.

❄

Thank God. No one was home.

I ran upstairs to my room, locked the door behind me, and rolled onto my bed in a fetal position. As soon as my face touched my pillow, lava-like tears streaked my cheeks.

"No one could ever love you as much as I do," Don had said last month.

I unhooked the necklace he'd given me to show off his ring and flung them both on my nightstand. Would he give it to Sarah now? My eyes fell on a copy of *Gone with the Wind*. I'd dried the roses Don had given me between my favorite pages. Should I dump them into the wastebasket? Or wait? What if he came back?

The Nutcracker performance was the first night he'd seen me dance. I'd never forget it. Or the first night he'd kissed me two months before that, after we'd split a strawberry sundae at Peterson's. But that sweet memory soured when I imagined him sucking face with Sarah.

Sarah. What was she thinking, flirting with *my* boyfriend? And what was Don thinking, flirting back?

Fighting memories and mental pirouettes, I drifted into a world where knights stayed true to their ladies.

A loud honk startled me. How long had I been asleep? I glanced at my watch: 4:56.

I moaned and hugged my damp pillow. I needed time to write in my journal, not a grueling technique class. I dragged myself out of bed and peered in the mirror over my dresser. My face was blotchy and my gray eyes bloodshot.

The car beeped again.

I wiped away smeared mascara, grabbed my ballet bag, and ran to Terri's black Chevette.

"What took you so long?" she said when I opened the door.

"Sorry. Just woke up from a nap." I plopped onto the chilly vinyl seat and picked up a *Ladies Home Journal* Terri must've borrowed from her mom.

Mary Tyler Moore graced the cover along with teasers about the articles inside. One headline screamed, "HOW CHILDBIRTH HAS CHANGED: A Compelling Report Every Woman Should Read."

Terri turned onto York Street. "I flunked my English lit test." She rolled her eyes. "Oh well, it's not like I'm gonna be a writer or anything."

"I can help you next time if you want." How was I going to tell her what I should've told her three weeks ago? Of course, at the time I'd thought it best to tell Don first, him being the father and all.

"How'd your talk with Don go?"

I took a shaky breath. This was it. "He . . . kissed Sarah."

Terri's jaw dropped. She gawked at me a moment before turning back to the road. "What a jerk," she said, pronouncing every consonant.

"I have been kind of preoccupied. Maybe he felt neglect—"

"You've been spending plenty of time with him. And it's not like this happened out of nowhere. He's been flirting with her for who knows how long."

I leaned against the plastic door and gazed at all the beautiful homes with happily married couples inside. I always assumed I'd be one of them someday.

"You're going to break up with him, right?"

I swallowed the ocean threatening to drown me. "He thought I already did," I whispered. "He's dating Sarah now."

"Of course he is. Why am I surprised?" Her eyes flashed. "Did you slap him?"

I shook my head.

"Punch him?"

"I left. I was afraid I was going to puke on him."

"Would have served him right." Terri unbuttoned her leather jacket. "You're too nice. I would've thrown my pointe shoes at him."

I grinned. "Didn't have them with me."

"Then I would've shoved pencils up his nose."

I giggled.

Terri let out her breath. "If he thought you broke up with him, why'd he bother telling you he wasn't going to eat with us today?"

I shrugged. "Maybe he thought I assumed we'd still be eating together as friends?"

"Or he's just yanking your chain. You've gotta stop being so naïve. Not everyone's as wonderful as you think they are."

My hands trembling, I flipped through the magazine. After pages of cigarette, hair color, and laundry detergent ads, my eyes locked on "e.p.t." in big, bold letters.

In the center of the page, four women beamed as if to say, "I've just gotten the best news ever." And there, in the bottom corner, stood the mustard-colored box with the dark circle.

Terri glanced at me and then at the pregnancy test ad. Her onyx eyes widened. "Aunt Flo's late?"

I flinched. "Worse."

Her jaw dropped. "You can't mean . . ."

I chipped the polish off a nail.

"Are you sure?" Terri cried, her voice rising. She swerved to avoid hitting a VW Bug in the oncoming lane. "What a nightmare."

I closed my eyes and tears drenched my lashes.

"Didn't you use anything?"

I choked back a sob. "We usually did. But the first couple times, I never thought it would go that far and . . . I guess he didn't either."

"Or he just wanted to jump your bones and didn't care what happened." Terri braked for a stop sign. "This is not good. Not good at all. You can't be pregnant now. This is the worst possible time."

I closed the *Ladies Home Journal* only to be confronted with a baby bottle on the back cover with a tube of Crest toothpaste inside. The white letters declared, "The sooner the better." I threw the magazine into the back seat and hugged my bag to my chest.

"What are you gonna do?"

What *could* I do?

"Do you have morning sickness?" Terri peered at me. "I've got pretzels in the glove box."

I ruffled through maps, condoms, and sunglasses until I found the bag of knotted hearts.

Terri turned right onto Butterfield Road. "I know of a good abortion clinic nearby."

I stiffened. Abortion?

"I'll make an appointment for you." She glanced at me. "When do you get back from New York?"

"Thursday. But I can't do that."

"What other choice do you have?"

I stared at the dashboard, the hard, salty dough crunching in my mouth like bones.

9

Shannon: November 2014

Night came early now that November had blown in.

Through the glass doors of the auditorium lobby, I watched an indigo ocean of clouds turn purple and float away as the sun slipped below the horizon.

My phone vibrated in my pocket, and I pulled it out.

"Mrs. Henry?" Dr. Beck said. "I received the final results."

I held my breath.

"I'm sorry to tell you your baby definitely has Down syndrome."

I lowered my head and exhaled. So that was it. Our last hope had disappeared with the setting sun. I shifted my feet. At least we knew for sure. Now we could prepare.

"Have you and your husband decided what you want to do?"

I frowned. "Not yet."

"I know it's hard, but try to make up your mind soon. You're fourteen weeks already. If you choose to terminate the pregnancy, sooner is always better."

I thanked her for calling, hung up, and glanced at my watch. With three minutes until the end of bathroom break, I still had time to pray—something I'd been putting off for weeks. "God," I whispered as I spun my charm bracelet around my wrist. "I don't know what to do. Will You show me?"

"Mrs. Henry?" My assistant director poked her head out of the theater. "You might want to come back in."

I hurried past her in time to see Ben and Sam sword fighting with Tiny Tim's crutches. "Boys, can we try to keep the set from being destroyed this time?"

Ben leaned on a crutch. "I was just helping Sam figure out how to use these things."

"Thank you for your assistance, Mr. Cooper, but I'm sure Sam can figure it out on his own." I resumed my place in the itchy seat and picked up my script and grape-scented pencil. "Let's try the middle of Act Two. Page fifty-one." I glanced up. "Ravi and Suresh, put on your costumes, please. You'll feel more like your characters."

The Indian cousins headed backstage.

A few minutes later Bhangra music started playing, and an exotic beat filled the theater.

Ravi appeared wearing a red, curly beard. A large torch in his hand, he danced across the stage to the high-energy drums, his green, fur-lined robe trailing behind him. He bent forward and a holly wreath fell off his head.

The students roared.

I smiled despite myself. "Ravi, thank you for the entertainment, but can we save Bollywood for after practice?"

"Sorry, Mrs. Henry." Ravi cut the music on his phone and put his crown back on.

"Let's start with 'Beware this boy.'" I put my script and pencil in my lap and grabbed my plastic container of pineapple pieces from the floor. I forked a chunk into my mouth, and the tart juice sweetened my tongue. I glanced at my stomach. If we had this child, would he be able to act or memorize lines like my students? Or would he forever be relegated to the sidelines, merely observing life as it passed him by?

"Beware this boy," Ravi said in the voice of Father Christmas, "for on his brow I see that written which is Doom, unless the writing be erased."

The boys continued to read their lines, but I barely listened until Suresh's towering form appeared cloaked in black. Ominous music trailed behind him.

Andrew fell to his knees. "I am in the presence of the Ghost of Christmas Yet to Come," he said in a high-pitched voice.

Suresh inclined his head.

"You are about to show me shadows of the things that have not happened but will happen in the time before us. Is that so, Spirit?"

Suresh lifted his arm, only his spindly hand revealed.

"Ghost of the Future," Andrew stuttered. "I fear you more than any spectre I have seen. But as I know your purpose is to do me good, and as I hope to live to be another man from what I was, I am prepared to bear you company, and do it with a thankful heart. Will you not speak to me?"

Suresh pointed onward.

"Lead on," Andrew said, accompanied by wind sounds. "The night is waning."

❄

I stared at the corn, macaroni, and chicken patties I'd made for the twins to eat while Wade and I went to Maggiano's. "I don't know whether to put the food away or leave it out for Gabby. I'm not sure if she's eaten dinner yet."

"Well, you know," Wade said glancing at my phone, "there's a rectangular device that would allow you to find the answer to that and many other questions."

I swatted him with a wet dish towel.

Buster took advantage of my temporary distraction to jump on the counter and finish off the chicken.

"I guess there's your answer," Wade said as Buster beat a quick retreat out of the kitchen.

The doorbell rang.

"I'll get it." I hurried to the front door. What would Wade and Gabby say when I told them about the test results?

I opened the door and Gabby held up her phone, the screen fractured like an elaborate spider web.

"Oh no," I said, covering my mouth.

"Yeah." She looked sideways. "Broke it again. Dropped it on the sidewalk one too many times."

I exhaled. "I'm sorry."

She took off her boots. "Oh, well. When the world gives you pumpkins, don't let them beat you down."

I chuckled. "You mean, when life gives you lemons, make lemonade?"

"Is that how it goes?" She shook her head. "So," she said, her eyes lighting. "I was surfing the Web and got a fabulous idea. You guys should get a zebra rug. With the orange and ivory in your living room, it'll look amazing."

I chewed my nail. "Are you joking?"

"No, seriously, I got inspired. I have a new favorite store—Home Goods. Yorktown Center has one, and we must go." She hung her windbreaker on a hook behind the door. "If Heaven has it, it'll be great. I know Heaven isn't about me, but I sure would appreciate decorating everyone's mansion. Anyway, I saw this picture in a Home Goods blog." She handed me a printout of a sitting room.

I peered at the picture. I liked the paint color, the hardwood floor and the sofa sectional and pillows, but the zebra rug seemed a little garish. "Hmm . . ."

"Trust me." She gripped my arm. "If you get this rug, you will not regret it. You'll get compliments on it for an eternity. I feel it in my soul."

"Well . . ."

"Oh, pretty please!"

I rubbed the back of my neck and glanced at the paper again. "Let me think about it. Can I get you some lemon iced tea before we leave?"

"Oh, yes." Gabby plopped onto the couch and grabbed a suede pillow.

I scurried to the kitchen and pulled two plastic tumblers from the cabinet.

Wade downed the last of his apple juice. "Time to go?"

"Just about. But I want to tell you and Gabby something first," I said, my stomach clenching. "The kids upstairs?"

Wade nodded. "Everything okay?" His brow furrowed.

"Might as well tell you both at the same time."

Wade put a supportive hand on my back and followed me into the living room.

"Happy anniversary!" Gabby shouted. "Seven years. Can you believe it?"

I studied Wade's face. Seven years with this brilliant, funny, good-looking man who adored me and our kids and lavished us with love. It was a lot to be thankful for. I tried to smile despite the news I was about to share. Handing Gabby a cold cup, I sat with Wade on the couch and took a deep breath. "Dr. Beck called with the final results of the CVS test." I swallowed hard. "Our baby has Down syndrome."

"Wow." Wade wrapped an arm around me. "Our lives are really going to change."

I leaned into him. The fresh scent of his deodorant reminded me of the beachside resort where we'd spent our fifth anniversary. Before Lily. Before this diagnosis.

"I really don't know what to say," Gabby said, her eyes wet. "I know this must be really difficult to process. Sometimes when I have to process something really difficult emotionally, I make cookies. I mean, I don't make them from scratch, of course."

I grinned. "Of course not." Gabby hated cooking.

"I just buy those break-away kind. I put them in the oven and the smell of cookies helps me process my emotions." She grimaced. "I'm sorry—that's really insensitive, isn't it? What I meant to say is that I'm here for you in any way, even if that means making you cookies." She shook her head. "That didn't make sense—I'm just going to stop talking now. I love you and I am . . . Okay, I'm done. I love you." She squeezed me once more, reaffirming in her own way that she hurt with me.

❄

After we got home from dinner where we discussed the

diagnosis at length, I opened a bottle of aromatic oil and arranged the reeds inside the diffuser on our dresser.

Berries, spices, and vanilla sugar scented our bedroom.

I straightened a few things and then slipped into a coral negligee. I ran my finger over the black lace on the hem. How much longer would I get to wear nightgowns before having to switch to flannel pajamas? Probably not much, between the pregnancy and winter coming. I put a hand on my belly, and my throat constricted. Not tonight, I told myself. Tonight was for celebrating our marriage, not worrying about the Down syndrome diagnosis.

Wade came up behind me, wrapped his arms around my waist, and kissed my neck, his warm lips lingering on my skin.

"Happy anniversary," I whispered. I opened a frosty bottle of sparkling apple cider and poured two flutes. "Thank you for putting your clothes away." I gestured toward the bare floor by his side of the bed. "And throwing away your empty water bottles."

"Uh . . ."

Sipping sweet bubbles, I handed him a glass.

"While I wish I could take credit, it wasn't me."

"It wasn't you?" I frowned. "Are you sure? Maybe you forgot?"

He chuckled. "Pretty sure."

I rubbed my forehead. "Well, it wasn't me this time. And I doubt the twins would've done it. You think Gabby came up here and cleaned while we were out?"

Wade lifted his palms and shrugged.

"Who else could it have been?" I said.

"The fairies?"

"The fairies!" I laughed. "I thought they only lost stuff."

"Maybe they're reforming."

I stared at the place on his nightstand where our pearl-studded frame usually stood. "Did they also move our wedding picture?"

Wade squinted. "I could've sworn I saw it there this morning."

I searched underneath the bed.

No photograph.

Hours later, I drifted off to sleep, still wondering where it could have gone.

❄

I woke. My body was trembling, but I felt Wade lying beside me. I exhaled and my muscles relaxed.

He's here.

He's safe.

The river sounds coming from my phone brought back my nightmare's images of Wade hurtling toward a waterfall. I switched the sleep machine app to the sound of an air purifier instead.

The ceiling fan whipped up goose bumps on my arms, my satin nightie paper-thin.

Grabbing my phone for light, I slipped out of bed and tiptoed to our walk-in closet, the bamboo floor cool beneath my feet. I pulled out my favorite blanket for cold, Chicago nights—a brown, microplush throw scented with lavender.

I crept back to bed—empty.

The hair rose on the back of my neck. Where was he? Had I imagined him there a moment ago?

The floor creaked behind me, and someone grabbed my shoulders.

I screamed.

Wade laughed and wrapped his arms around me. "Red, what are you doing?"

I turned to face him. "You died."

He lifted an eyebrow. "So I'm a ghost now? Is that why you screamed?"

"I screamed because you grabbed me."

"Grabbed you? Is that what you call it when a husband massages his wife's shoulders?"

I propped my pillow against the headboard, climbed into bed, and drank the apple cinnamon tea leftover from the night before. "I had a nightmare."

Wade plunked onto his side of our queen-sized mattress and locked eyes with me.

"I was screaming for you in this abandoned house when I saw the striped shoes Daniel used to wear." I pulled the teal comforter over me and spread the throw over it. "And then I stepped on Katy's doll and broke her face. You know, the one Peggy bought her with the blue eyes and curly hair?"

"The one that looks like her?"

I nodded. "Then this spider crawled up a wall, the same color Travis painted the nursery. But everything was turning to dust, and I knew you were in danger, but I didn't know where I could find you, but then I ran outside and I saw you," I said, searching his eyes. "I cried for help, but no one came, and I tried to rescue you myself, but . . ." I swallowed. "I was too late."

Wade lay on his back and patted his heart. "Come home, Red."

I snuggled into his toasty chest and slung a smooth leg over his hairy one. "My love," I whispered. "And my heater," I added with a smile.

"I love you." He kissed my forehead.

"Honey, please don't die."

"As long as I have anything to say about it, you're stuck with me."

I pushed myself up with one hand. "Don't ever go near a river with a waterfall. Drive carefully and always wear your seatbelt. And take your vitamins—you always forget to take them."

Wade opened his phone's calendar app.

I cocked my head. "What are you doing?"

"Canceling my Niagara Falls swim plans."

"I'm being serious."

"Me too. Those tickets aren't refundable so I'm taking a hit there, but at least I won't die."

"Babe, that dream really scared me. It seemed so real."

He put his phone away and pulled me back to him. "It wasn't real, Red. I'm right here, and I don't even know where the nearest waterfall is. Pretty sure there aren't any in Chicago."

"That's not the only way I could lose you."

"We could play this game all night, sweetie," he said, brushing my bangs to the side. "The world could end tomorrow.

Aliens might abduct me on Wednesday. I could vanish into another dimension on Thursday." He pulled me closer. "But I'm here now and I love you today. Let's enjoy that and get some zzzs."

I closed my eyes and tried to rest, but sleep eluded me.

10

Leslie: January 1979

"Did you talk to Don about giving you some space?" Mom said as we crossed into Indiana, her black hair cut into a chic wedge for our trip to New York City.

I fidgeted in the back of Dad's new Chevy Impala. Space I had gotten. "Yeah," I muttered, my chest hollow. I peered out the window at the suburban houses whizzing by. How could I tell them Don had left me for another girl? And, even worse, that I was pregnant? Maybe if I kept quiet and avoided their questions long enough, everything would work out on its own. Don would come back, begging for forgiveness, and I would miscarry.

Mom helped Dad out of his checkered suit coat.

"Light a cigar for me, will you, Vivian?"

She lit a White Owl miniature and handed it to him.

He took a long drag, and gray smoke curled into the back seat.

A wave of nausea rolled over me. I lowered my window and breathed in the icy air.

"Leslie, what are you doing?" Mom looked back at me. "It's freezing outside."

I gagged.

Her eyes softened. "Car sick?"

Sure. That was it. I nodded.

"John, pull over." Mom pointed at the shoulder.

"She'll be fine. Just let her keep the window down a few minutes."

I leaned back against the vinyl seat and breathed deeply to settle my stomach. As if my morning sickness wasn't bad enough on steady ground, now I was stuck in a stuffy car for thirteen hours, not counting stops for gas and food. And if Mom and Dad found out I was pregnant, this would be an even longer ride. At least I didn't have to do anything today. I had as much energy as the dead squirrel we'd run over a few miles back. How could I dance tomorrow?

"Did you remember everything you need for your audition?" Mom said, her feet propped on the dashboard where Barry Manilow crooned, "Can't Smile Without You."

Shivering, I raised the window and lay down on the steel-blue bench seat. "I think so." I pictured myself dressing for the competition and groaned. "I forgot the paper towels and medical tape for my toes."

"Leslie." Mom frowned. "I told you to double-check. We're not going to have much time in the morning."

I bit my lip. "I know. I'm sorry." The hard-boiled eggs I'd eaten for breakfast rose in my throat. I covered my mouth and swallowed.

Mom handed me a peppermint Certs. "Suck on this. It might help you feel better."

I unwrapped the green-flecked mint, the wrapper crackling. I closed my eyes and tried to fall asleep, but all I could see was Don beaming at me, saying, "No one could ever love you as much as I do."

If only it were true.

"Did Don understand why you can't go out as often?" Mom looked back at me. "I didn't mean you had to stop dating him. I just thought you were wearing yourself out."

I pushed myself up and sighed. Apparently, avoiding their questions wasn't going to work. Better to face them—at least the ones about Don and me—straight on. "He's going to the University of Southern California."

"Good for him." Mom dipped her head. "What's he going to study?"

"Acting."

"Acting?" Mom snorted. "That's almost as practical as dancing. So I guess you'll both be starving artists?"

My belly knotted. Starving might be in my future, but being an artist probably wasn't. "We broke up."

There. I'd said it.

Mom raised her perfectly-shaped eyebrows. "Because he's going to school out West?"

I stared at the couple in the red Monte Carlo next to us, laughing and holding hands.

Dad glanced at me in the rearview mirror. "I never thought he was right for you."

My mouth fell open. Dad, who knew me so well and judged cases every day, didn't think Don was right for me? If he was right, maybe it was good Don and I had split up. If only I wasn't pregnant.

"If you really want to be a ballerina." Mom's eyes bored into me. "You should marry someone with a stable career who can support you."

She turned back to the road, and I put a hand on my stomach. That was easier said than done. And what about true love? Was I now allowed no girlish dreams?

❄

As we emerged from the Lincoln Tunnel, black skyscrapers rose before us, twinkling with thousands of lights.

"Welcome to Manhattan," a sign declared.

New York. The City of Dreams.

Somehow I'd thought I would feel differently when I finally got here. Of course, until last month I never expected to be bringing someone along for the ride. I lowered my window to get a better look.

An attractive couple with a boy and a girl sat on a metal

bench sipping hot drinks. The dad had a twinkle in his eye when he looked at the mom. They might have been part of a Norman Rockwell painting, they looked so perfect together.

I couldn't deny I wanted that someday. But now? In any case, I'd probably ruined any chance I had with a quality guy when I'd slept with Don. I stared down at the blue-gray carpet. Why did I go that far with him in the first place? Hadn't I been taught better?

Mom, who'd probably never compromised herself with a guy, pulled down her sun visor, flipped open the mirror, and applied her lipstick with quick, practiced strokes. "There's the Lincoln Center," she said as we drove past the imposing building where I was supposed to audition the next morning.

So many talented dancers were competing to get into the summer intensives program at the School of American Ballet—dancers who weren't struggling with morning sickness. Of course, the odds hadn't scared me off before. But even if I was chosen, I'd be seven months pregnant when classes started on June 25. Of course, there was still a chance I could miscarry.

I munched on the crackers Mom had given me to settle my stomach, but they tasted like cardboard and expanded in my mouth, making it nearly impossible to finish them. Maybe Terri was right and I should schedule an abortion. How could I have a baby now, when my career as a ballerina was on the line?

A snowflake landed on my nose.

I brushed it off and it melted on my hand.

"Hand me my sports coat," Dad said at a red light. "Someone keeps rolling down her window like it's seventy degrees out instead of seventeen. And we're almost there."

Mom helped him put on his blazer and then reached for her own coat. "Leslie, do you remember my friend Janet's daughter? You went to grade school with her."

"Mm-hmm."

Mom slid her gloves on. "She just eloped with some guy she was secretly dating. I guess she felt she couldn't tell Janet about him. I'm glad you and Patricia have always been able to share things with us."

Goosebumps rose on my arms as if my body had just registered the fact that it was winter outside. I rolled up my window.

The light turned and Dad stepped on the gas.

I studied the high-rise buildings passing by. What if I just ended it? Then I'd never have to tell my parents I was pregnant. Never have to watch Don and Sarah fall more and more in love. Never have to watch my dreams drown in that dark circle of the e.p.t. tube.

❄

After a sleepless night on a stiff hotel mattress, Dad snoring in the bed next to mine, I waited my turn to audition at the School of American Ballet.

Founded by George Balanchine and Lincoln Kirstein in 1934 and affiliated with the New York City Ballet, SAB was one of the preeminent schools in the country. Even Rudolf Nureyev and Mikhail Baryshnikov had attended classes here in the 1960s. What would it be like to study under teachers of this caliber? What opportunities might come my way if I was noticed by the right people? Maybe one day I'd even dance for the New York City Ballet.

With trembling hands, I tacked a number six to my black leotard and stretched and pirouetted along with the twenty-one other girls in my age group: sixteen-to-eighteen-year-olds. None of them were covered in welts like I was. Bed bugs must've feasted on me during the night. I scratched at a particularly itchy collection on my forearm, but that only made them scream with hot rage.

Mom had given the hotel manager a piece of her mind on our way to breakfast. "My daughter has a very important competition this morning, and then we were planning to tour the city. But now look at us—I'd be surprised if people don't run the other way when they see us, thinking we have chicken pox or something worse." She'd demanded they refund our money and give us a bug-free room to spend the night in tonight. And, of course, they'd agreed. But what if they didn't have any bug-free rooms?

I rolled my head back and forth as I watched slender fourteen-to-fifteen-year-old girls dancing on pointe in the large classroom. Certainly, none of them were growing babies in their bellies. But my main competition was the group of girls waiting beside me.

I eyed the hallway leading to the front entrance. Was it too late to back out?

Yes. I hadn't come this far to quit before the door of my destiny.

The younger girls finished and hurried out of the room, a mixture of triumph and tragedy on their faces.

"Next." A man with bushy eyebrows and gray sideburns stuck his head out of the room.

Our group filed in, prepared or not to prove we were talented enough to be part of this elite school for the summer.

"Good luck," I whispered to the girl in front of me.

She jerked her head back and glared at me as if I'd slapped her, her green eyes flashing.

So much for friendly competition.

"We'll start with the barre," Mr. Eyebrows said. "Move on to center work and then finish with pointe."

Pasting on a smile, I danced the best I could, doing my best to ignore my fatigue, the itchy bug bites, and the blisters rubbing against my pointe shoes. Would I dance well enough to get in? Did it even matter?

❄

"How'd it go?" Mom asked as we ate lunch in Little Italy.

I forked a piece of chicken parmesan into my mouth, the mozzarella cheese gooey on my tongue. If I said it went well but didn't get in, I'd seem overly confident. If I said it didn't go well, they might try to talk me out of a career in ballet. "It went okay," I finally decided on. "There were a few moves I wish I'd done better."

Dad rolled more spaghetti onto his fork. "When will you hear back?"

"Around a month."

"Well, nothing you can do about it now," he said. "I'm sure you did your best."

After we finished, Dad paid the bill and we trudged outside.

A pay phone called to me from the corner.

If I told Don I was pregnant, maybe he'd come back to me. Maybe he'd even stay in Chicago. He had said he wanted kids someday. But even if not, he still had a right to know.

Mom hailed a cab.

"Can I make a call?" I blurted before I could second-guess myself.

"Leslie, it's freezing out here," Mom said.

A blast of wind struck me in the face as if to reinforce her point.

Mom opened the car door. "Why don't you wait until we get back to the hotel?"

"Aren't we going sightseeing and then to see the Rockettes? We won't be home until late tonight."

"Are you getting in or not?" the taxi driver said.

"Sorry." Dad shut the door and waved him on.

"Who are you calling, anyway?" Mom said with a longing glance at the departing cab. "We'll be back home tomorrow."

I played with the zipper on my coat. "Just a friend. I need to tell them something."

Mom sighed. "Okay, but make it quick."

I dialed Don's number and stole a look at my parents. I couldn't tell Don I was pregnant with them standing there. I spotted an Italian bakery. "Why don't you wait in there where it's warmer?" I nudged my head toward a red-and-green neon sign that boasted that the Veniero Pasticceria had been around since 1894. "I'll come get you when I'm done."

My parents hurried into the bakery as the phone rang, its noisy *brrrring* stretching from New York to Chicago.

"Ashby residence," an older woman said.

Don's grandmother? My muscles tightened. "Is Don home?"

"I'm sorry, honey, but he went out with his girlfriend to see *Love at First Bite*."

His girlfriend. That used to be me.

"Can I take a message?"

I'm pregnant and it's his. "No, thank you."

The sound of Don's laughter spilled through the phone.

"Oh, wait. They just got back. Hold on a second."

She set down the receiver before I could stop her.

"Hello," Don said after a moment, still laughing.

I made a fist. Why did he get to move on with his life without a second thought while my entire future was destroyed? I hung up, feeling more alone than ever.

❄

I couldn't sleep that night. Every little thing that brushed my skin felt like a bed bug about to chomp. Shuddering, I slipped out of bed. I needed to get out of that cramped hotel room. Maybe some fresh air and a view from the top of the city would cheer me up a bit. Drag me out of this sinkhole that was threatening to swallow me.

At 10:46 p.m., with Dad snoring and Mom curled up beside him, I snuck out. After I got directions, I took a bus to Fifth Avenue and 34th Street and trudged into the lobby of the Empire State Building. I pressed the button on the wall and stood before a black-and-silver art deco elevator that reminded me of a casket.

The coffin opened.

I hesitated a moment and stepped in.

A thirty-something couple got on after me with a boy in a Superman costume.

"Eighty-six, please," the man said.

I hit the floor number.

"Can we get pizza later?" The tow-haired little guy looked up at his dad.

His mom shook her head. "You're already up *way* past your bedtime."

"But Superman doesn't get tired."

The woman yawned. "Mommies do."

Ding. The doors opened, and the family hurried out.

I shuffled behind them onto the observation deck and gazed out at the skyline. This was supposed to be where my dreams came true, starting with summer intensives and ending with Don and me celebrating our love at the top of this very building.

But I'd lost it all. Don. Dancing. College. All I'd worked for.

After awhile, the deck emptied and I was alone in the cold. If only I could escape. Free myself from this impossible situation.

I climbed on top of the weathered concrete wall, using the fence above to pull myself up. The frigid wind whipped my hair around my face. I looked down. So far down. My whole body trembled.

If I jumped, I'd never have to tell my parents I was pregnant. Never have to see my dreams deflated one by one. Never have to hear the mocking whispers of my classmates.

I put one foot on the first diagonal rung of the fence followed by the other.

Superboy came back to collect a figurine he'd dropped.

He looked about the same age as my niece, Heather. What kind of example would I be setting for her if I killed myself? How would Patricia explain how I'd died? I fingered my crocheted hat, the one Mom insisted I bring to New York. If I jumped, I'd leave my family gut-wrenching sorrow and a million haunting questions.

I couldn't do that to them. I couldn't do that to anyone.

I leaped onto the deck and rushed inside to warmth and safety. On second thought, I ran back and planted a kiss on Superman's cheek.

He smelled like bananas and peanut butter.

"Don't ever let anyone tell you you're not a hero," I said, my voice choked with emotion. Ducking past his wide-eyed parents, I hurried to the elevators, my eyes welling up.

I was going to live. I glanced at my belly.

We were going to live.

11

Shannon: November 2014

Honey, you cannot wear those pants today," I said. "There's a huge paint blotch on the butt."

Wade plopped down on Daniel's Winnie-the-Pooh bed. "What's the big deal? We're just going to Mom's."

"For Thanksgiving." I sipped my tap water, which had a fishy taste today, and helped Katy into a turtleneck. "Even if they weren't stained, sweats aren't appropriate."

"Why not? They're comfortable."

I pulled a ruffled jumper over Katy's head, the one with the turkey on front I'd ordered from an online boutique especially for today.

"Mommy, can I wear my Spiderman pajamas?" Daniel's eyes lit up.

I groaned and glared at Wade, my vision for family pictures spiraling to the ground like the dead leaves littering our front yard.

"No, buddy, you need to wear this awesome football shirt Mommy bought you," Wade said, holding it up. He turned back to me and shrugged. "Holidays aren't that big of a deal to me."

"Today is the day we thank God as a family for our blessings. I would have one more thing to be thankful for if my husband didn't look like a homeless man at Thanksgiving dinner."

"Why does it matter if I look like a hobo? Who cares what people think?"

"What about what *I* think? I'd like to get some pictures we can use for our Christmas cards."

Wade put his hands up. "I'm not saying I'm right. I'm just being honest. I don't get this garbage."

I put a matching headband in Katy's hair, and she twirled.

Wade chuckled. "Doin' a turkey dance?"

"Do I look pretty, Daddy?"

"You're my princess, and you look gorgeous." He kissed her forehead. "Just like your mama who's gonna pick out something for me to wear."

I grinned and hurried back to our bedroom, enjoying the scent of pumpkins and cinnamon coming from the candle on our dresser. I laid out clothes for Wade and then stepped into khakis, pulled a knot-front top over my head, and studied myself in the mirror. My belly was getting rounder every day. How much longer could I keep this pregnancy a secret? People must suspect already.

Wade ambled in and grimaced at the wrinkled shirt. "Is there anything that doesn't require more work?"

"You don't have any other button-down shirts in a Thanksgiving color."

"So today I'm not only supposed to eat pumpkin, but look like one too?"

A smile played on my lips as I pulled dark jeans out of his highboy.

He pulled off his T-shirt and pants and dropped them onto the floor. "All right. I guess I'll just iron it."

I picked up the clothes. "Are these dirty?"

"Not sure." Wade pulled on his Levi's.

I smelled his discarded clothes and threw them in the hamper conveniently located two feet from him.

"I was going to get those."

I sighed. Next month or next year? I opened the jewelry box drawer where I always kept my charm bracelet.

Empty.

I bit my nail, the polish bitter on my tongue. Where could my bracelet be? I hunted through the other drawers. Had I left it on my nightstand? I hurried over to the bed.

Not there either.

"Mommy, can I watch a show?" Katy said, ambling into our room.

"Sure, sweetie, but do you know where Mommy's bracelet is?"

She shook her head.

"Hmm," I said, rubbing my lips. "Can you help me find it?"

"Where did you last have it?" she said as if she were fourteen instead of four.

I grinned. How many times had she heard me ask that? "Put the toys in your room away, sweetie, and then you can watch the Thanksgiving Day parade." I hurried downstairs into the living room to turn it on but froze mid-step.

Someone had replaced our box TV with a flat screen.

I shook my head. I must be seeing things. I walked closer, but sure enough, our big television that was usually covered with kids' fingerprints had been swapped for a smaller, cleaner, flat-panel. I flew upstairs to our bedroom. "Did you buy us a new television set?" I asked Wade.

He squinted at me as he pulled on his socks. "No."

"What happened to our old one?"

"It's not working?"

"It's gone."

His eyes widened. "Gone? As in, stolen?"

"Only if the robbers were nice enough to leave a replacement." I rubbed my chin. "Could your parents have bought a new one for us and snuck it into the house this morning?" Not that they usually did things like that—sneaking into our house without permission.

Wade ran downstairs.

I continued hunting for my bracelet under and around the bedroom furniture.

No luck.

I put my hands on my hips. Had it fallen off when I was out? I could've sworn I put it in the drawer last night, right after I'd slipped into my pajamas.

Sounds from the Macy's Thanksgiving Day Parade floated upstairs.

Wade came back chuckling. "Very funny, honey, but it's Thanksgiving not April Fool's Day."

"What do you mean?"

He lifted an eyebrow. "Unless that was a Christmas hint?"

I frowned. "A Christmas hint?"

"It's the same TV we've had since we got married."

My mouth fell open. "Did you actually *look* in the living room? Closely?" He had a habit of not finding things I sent him to get.

Scowling, he spread his hands. "Of course. I think I'd notice if it was different."

"But it *is* different."

Wade stared at me as if I'd just arrived from Pluto.

I made a beeline for the living room.

Empty.

Quiet.

Where were the kids, and what had happened to the parade? I stared at the black screen on the unfamiliar Samsung. I ran a hand along its cool surface, and a chill crept up my spine.

My wrist still bare and my head still spinning, I found the kids playing hide-and-seek and ushered them downstairs and into their jackets. My fingers shook as I tried to push the buttons through the slits in Katy's pea coat.

"I can do it myself." Katy finished the job. "I'm a big girl."

"Yes, you are." I kissed her soft cheek and breathed in the freshly washed smell of her hair. "Got the keys?" I asked Wade.

He nodded.

"We've gotta go." I pulled on my trench coat and grabbed my purse. "We're gonna be late."

"Calm down." He pulled me into an embrace. "You know my mom's always running behind."

"Can we bring Buster?" Daniel crouched beside our Weimaraner and rubbed his ears.

"I don't know." I bit my lip. "All that food might prove a little too tempting."

"But, Mommy, we can't leave him all by himself on Thanksgiving."

Buster barked his agreement.

"We can keep him outside," Wade said. "Ready to go?"

"Actually, I better run to the bathroom first." I grinned at Wade. Now *I* was the one holding everyone up.

After I used the toilet, I rinsed my mouth with Listerine, the cool mint tingling my tongue. I glanced in the mirror and did a double take.

My hair was wavier than it had been in years—since before the kids.

I spit out the mouthwash and stared at my mane again.

Back to straight.

My knees went weak. What was happening to me? Was I losing my mind?

❄

"Pass the bird, please." Wade nudged my knee under his parents' dining room table.

I handed him the roasted turkey and took a deep breath. I needed to put aside the Down syndrome diagnosis and all the strange things that had been happening and enjoy this special day with our family. Maybe that's all I needed to get my sanity back. That and a little sleep.

"Are you sure Gabby won't mind us starting without her?" Mom said from across the table.

Wade speared a slice of poultry. "She does this all the time—makes plans with us and then cancels."

"Honey." I frowned as I cut up Katy's food. "Gabby always lets us know if she can't make it. It's not like her to just not show up."

"Maybe she lost her phone again," Margaret said.

"You're probably right." I spooned mashed potatoes into my mouth and closed my eyes to savor the lumpy goodness. Homemade tasted so much better than instant. "Think we'll get as much snow this winter as last? I felt like I was living on the frozen tundra for four months." I shivered just thinking about it.

Dad reached for the corn on the cob. "That was nothing compared to the blizzard of '79."

"Oh, no." Margaret rolled her eyes. "Not this story again."

"January was brutal," Dad continued, unfazed. "We already had ten inches on the ground leftover from New Year's when we got slammed with another nineteen. Firemen put poles with red flags on the fire hydrants so they could find them under all the snow."

"Wow," I said. "That's crazy."

Dad bit into his corn. "We had to shovel our roofs so they wouldn't cave in. You could walk right off the houses onto the snow drifts," he said, chuckling.

"Some of our neighbors' garage roofs did cave in." Mom cut up her creamed asparagus tips, her knife clanking against the plate. "And remember that shopping center in Mt. Prospect, honey?"

"That roof was a goner. But you didn't have to worry about your roof, did you, babe?" Dad winked at Mom, and she smiled back as if they were still a couple of love-struck teenagers.

"Your father braved that storm to shovel the roof of my parents' house. This house, actually. And we weren't even dating at the time."

I offered a weak smile. Mom and Dad had inherited their home from her parents when they'd died in a car accident. At least Mom was grown up, even married, at the time. But what if something happened to me and Wade while our kids were little? Who would take care of them? I shook off the thought.

Today I should be thankful for all I had, not worried about all I might lose.

"Just thinking about all that snow . . ." Mom passed the cranberry sauce to Margaret. "Isn't it a miracle that no two snowflakes are alike?"

Wade bobbed his head back and forth as if considering what she said. "There's some debate about that."

"But Gram read us the story last week," Daniel said, his tongue curling over his lower lip.

Mom ruffled his hair. "That's right. Snowflake Bentley photographed over five thousand snowflakes and each of them was unique, just like each of us."

Margaret raised her eyebrows. "They're so small. How could he tell?"

Mom put another helping of green bean casserole onto her plate. "He attached a microscope to his camera so he could magnify each one up to 3,600 times its size."

Katy pushed back her chair and stood.

Wade cocked his head. "Where you going, sweetie?"

"To get the book," she said and hurried out of the room.

"It's in our bedroom," Mom called out behind her. She buttered a roll then turned to Wade. "How are your physics classes going?"

"Pretty good. We went to the gym last week, and I had the kids throw some balls around and measure how much force they threw them with. They seemed to enjoy it."

"Shannon told me you've been having quite an impact on your students this year, as always."

"He's an amazing teacher," I said, beaming at him. "Not only does he make science fun for the teens, but he's counseled some of his students through some pretty hard stuff. I don't know where they would be if he wasn't in their lives."

"One of my students—a guy named Travis—won the art award."

"Thanks to your mentoring him." I took a bite of stuffing.

"Not in art. You've seen my stick figures."

"But your tutoring and influence helped him stay in school and pursue his passion."

Katy paraded in and handed the children's book to Mom. "Gram, your room looks like a bomb went off."

My jaw dropped. "That's not a very nice thing to say, sweetheart."

"But, Mommy, that's what you say after Daddy watches us."

I laughed.

Wade narrowed his eyes at me. "I see how it is," he said and grinned.

Mom winked at Katy. "My mom used to tell me the same thing." She pushed her empty plate to the side, opened the book by Jacqueline Briggs Martin, and started reading. "I found that snowflakes were masterpieces of design. No one design was ever repeated. When a snowflake melted, just that much beauty was gone, without leaving any record behind."

No one design was ever repeated. I swallowed my last spoonful of sugared cranberries and started collecting everyone's plates.

Wade handed me his. "It's true that snowflakes can't be *exactly* the same all the way down to the molecular level. But in 1988, a scientist found two snowflakes that *appeared* identical, at least from what she could see under a microscope."

Mom smiled at Katy and Daniel. "Maybe some snowflakes come in twins."

❄

"Buster!" Dad hollered from the kitchen.

I hurried in to see our Weimaraner devouring the pumpkin pies. "Oh no," I said, rubbing my forehead. "I am so sorry."

Dad waved my concern away. "Don't worry about it."

The doorbell rang.

"I'll get it," Wade yelled.

I corralled Buster into the chilly back yard. I knew we shouldn't have brought him. How could I apologize to Mom for all the time she'd spent making those pies? Maybe I could run to the store and pick up some more—not that they could compare to hers or make up for it.

As I tied Buster to the elm tree, its last leaf fluttered to the ground. Winter would arrive soon, and with it, memories of my last trimester carrying Lily and her birth a week after Valentine's Day. With a sigh, I trudged back inside.

"Look who finally decided to show up," Wade said.

Gabby stood in the living room, dressed in her usual Thanksgiving Day garb—a hoodie and stretchy pants.

"What happened?" I said. "We've been worried about you."

"Well . . . I left my phone at home so I went back to get it, but then I had to use the bathroom and I dropped it in the toilet."

I grimaced. "Not the new phone you just got last month."

"Yeah," she said with a lopsided grin. "So now I've got it in a Ziploc bag full of dry rice. Hopefully, I won't need to replace it."

"Again," Wade coughed.

"Anyway . . ." Gabby brightened and pulled out a home decorating magazine. "This would look *perfect* in your living room." She pointed to a floor vase with willow branches inside. "Right next to your entertainment center."

Wade peeked over my shoulder. "No way. That's where I draw the line. We're not putting a jar of sticks in our house."

I grinned and led Gabby into the dining room. "Sorry you missed dinner. We just put the food away, but I can make you a plate."

"Are you kidding?" She surveyed the dessert table. "I made it just in time for the best part." She helped herself to a slice of French silk pie. "Glad someone had the wonderful idea of not serving pumpkin pie. I don't understand why anyone likes it."

"Yeah, pumpkin pie's dog-awful." Wade said, glancing at me.

I giggled.

Just then, Mom walked in and my mouth went dry.

"I'm so sorry about the pies," I said. "We should've left Buster home. Or at least kept him out of the kitchen."

Mom smiled and wrapped an arm around me. "We have plenty of other sweets."

"Like this one." Wade grabbed a piece of the chocolate mousse pie Gabby was gobbling up. He took a seat and dug in.

12

Shannon: December 2014

"Palmer House, Jessica speaking," a woman with a husky voice said. "How may I help you?"

I pulled a pancake box out of the kitchen cupboard. "I'd like to reserve a Hip & Historic King—the Just Chillin' package—for Monday, December 22."

"Sure," she said over the sound of keyboard clicks. "Your name?"

"Henry." I chose the two ripest bananas out of the fruit bowl. "Wade and Shannon."

I gave her my credit card information, and she gave me our confirmation number. "You're all set."

"Great. Thank you." I hung up. If I could just make it through the hectic pace of the next few weeks, I'd have a couple days to relax and spend time alone with Wade before Christmas.

I closed my eyes and imagined sleeping in, kicking back in bed, and watching movies.

Wade ambled into the kitchen. "Dang, girl, you're looking fine."

I chuckled and shook my head. "I booked a room for our

getaway," I said, pouring the pancake mix into a large bowl. "Breakfast and hot chocolate included."

He pulled me close and kissed me. "Sounds delicious."

"The Adler Planetarium is only a mile from the hotel."

Wade lifted his eyebrows. "Be still my heart."

"The Magnificent Mile is even closer. I thought we could drop off our luggage—"

"Luggage? I thought we were only staying one night."

"We still need luggage."

"A backpack, maybe."

I pulled the griddle out of the cabinet, and an army of pots and pans clattered out with it. "Anyway," I said, stacking the rebellious cookware back in its place. "After we drop off our *bag*, we could eat lunch at a restaurant on Michigan Avenue—the holiday lights should be stunning—spend some time at the planetarium, check in at the hotel and rest for awhile, and then maybe head out again for dinner and a show at the Lyric." I smiled. "Which is only six blocks away."

"Sounds awfully busy for a vacation."

I turned on the stove and poured vegetable oil onto the griddle. "Or we could stay at the hotel after check-in at 3:00. Order room service for dinner. Watch some pay-per-view."

Wade wiggled his eyebrows. "Now *that's* what I'm talkin' about."

I glanced at the clock. "I gotta get these pancakes going or you'll be late." I chewed on a pecan then stirred the rest in with the mashed bananas.

Wade plopped down on a stool. "Why are we going for just one night? Why not get away for a few days?"

"Sunday the twenty-first is the last play performance in the afternoon, and then we've got your sister's birthday party in the evening. Wednesday's Christmas Eve."

Wade groaned. "So that Monday's the twenty-second?"

I narrowed my eyes at him. "Yeah . . . why?"

"I told Travis I'd help him with college applications, and Dad and I are going to a Blackhawks game."

"Honey!" My shoulders slumped. "I mentioned the date to you several times before I booked it."

"I know, I'm sorry. I completely forgot."

I threw water onto the griddle and it sizzled.

"I'll reschedule with Travis," Wade said, caressing my shoulder. "And see if my dad can go with someone else."

I exhaled. "No, don't do that. I'm sure your dad's really looking forward to it. I'll see if we can move the Palmer House to the following Monday." I poured batter onto the griddle. "Can you double-check that you don't have anything going on the twenty-ninth or thirtieth?"

He pulled out his phone, opened an app, and studied it a moment. "We're good."

When the edges of the pancakes started to bubble, I turned them over, set the stove timer for one minute, and dialed the hotel. The smell of sweet batter made my stomach rumble.

"The Palmer House, Jessica speaking."

"Hi, Jessica. Shannon Henry again. I just booked a room for the twenty-second, but I need to change it to the twenty-ninth."

"Can I have your confirmation number?"

I relayed the odd assortment of letters and numbers I'd written down.

"I'm sorry, ma'am, but I don't have anything under that number. What was your name again?"

"Shannon Henry. Or maybe you have it under Wade Henry."

The stove timer beeped.

I pulled a platter out and transferred the pancakes onto it.

"Nothing under either of those names."

My mouth fell open. "But I just talked to you."

"I'm sorry, ma'am. You must've spoken to one of my associates."

I frowned and ran a hand through my hair. Her throaty voice sounded the same. "Is there more than one Jessica working there?"

"No, ma'am. I'm the only one."

I rubbed my stiff neck. How could she not remember? I shook my head. Never mind. No use arguing since I wanted to change the date anyway. "So you're sure we won't be charged for the twenty-second?"

"Quite sure," she said, a hint of ridicule in her tone.

My face flamed. "Can you put us down for the twenty-ninth? And can you make sure you enter it into the computer this time?"

❄

I gobbled up my last bite of banana-nut pancakes smothered in butter. "Don't forget your lunch," I said to Wade.

"Will do." He grinned. More often than he remembered his lunch, he forgot it. He put his plate in the sink and then grabbed his coat and briefcase.

"More syrup?" I asked the twins.

They shook their heads, their mouths full.

I put the syrup back in the pantry and then wrapped up the leftover pancakes and put them in the fridge. "Here's your lunch," I said to Wade, setting the bag on the counter.

He peeked inside. "Beef soup again?"

I suppressed a smile. "I'm cleaning out the fridge."

He wrapped his arms around me and the twins, and his face grew serious. "Can I tell you something I want you to remember always, just in case?"

I squinted at him. "Just in case what?"

"I don't make it back from work."

I smiled at him, but my hands trembled. "Honey, don't scare the kids." We'd had enough tragedy in this family.

"This isn't a joke." He raised his eyebrows. "You never know."

I swallowed. I *had* been having all those nightmares.

"I love you, and I enjoy you." He searched our eyes but lingered on mine.

"I love you, darling." I put my hand on his stubbly cheek.

He grabbed his briefcase and turned to go. "Have a good day," he called over his shoulder.

I started on the dishes. Scanning the kitchen to see if there were any that hadn't made it to the sink, I spotted Wade's lunch.

Forgotten.

Again.

Darn it. I hadn't reminded him that crucial third time as he walked out the door.

I grabbed the bag and ran outside. Dead leaves blew over my feet. Hadn't Wade told me he'd raked and bagged those already?

I looked down the driveway.

His Fusion was gone.

Our next door neighbor Rebecca's fiancé Eric clambered out of his red convertible and clenched his fists. "I drove all the way out here to spend time with you," he shouted. "And you're not even giving me the time of day."

"But Eric," Rebecca said in her soft-spoken way. "I told you last week me and the girls were going out for Donna's birthday."

Eric jabbed his finger in her face. "Fine." His eyes flashed. "Go with them. Obviously, they're more important to you."

"That's not true," she stammered. "I just wasn't expecting you."

"Yeah, you're right!" He punched the car. "It's all my fault. You know what? I hope you have a great time." He jumped into his sports car, slammed the door behind him and peeled out, tires squealing.

I shuddered, glad I wasn't married to him. "Are you okay?" I went over and put my arm around Rebecca.

She cringed as if I'd touched a sore spot. "I will be." She sighed. "Headed to work?"

"Not yet. Just bringing Wade his lunch." I lifted my hand, but it was empty. My chest tightened. How had I forgotten his lunch too?

❄

The windshield wipers swished back and forth, trying—and failing—to keep up with the rain.

If only the traffic on North Avenue was moving as quickly. Sighing, I braked again and glanced at the clock on the dashboard.

Preschool started ten minutes ago and my dramatic literature class was starting in fifteen. I couldn't be late today—their final was this week, and we had so much left to cover.

In the back seat, Daniel belted out "Away in a Manger" with his favorite Christmas CD. "Be near me, Lord Jesus, I ask Thee to stay, close by me forever and love me, I pray."

"Bless all the dear children in Thy tender care," I sang along. "And take us to Heaven to live with Thee there." My breath bottled up in my chest. When I passed from this life into the next, would I see Lily again? I put a hand on my belly. Was this baby another dear child in the Lord's tender care? Or had God been distracted by greater things when our little one received her twenty-first chromosome? I pulled into the parking lot and grabbed my umbrella, a bitter tang on my tongue.

"Mommy," Katy said as I got her out of her car seat. "Why you got red cracks in your eyes?"

"Red cracks?" I hoisted her onto my hip. "You mean my eye shadow?"

"No." She pinched her thumb and index finger together and pointed at my eyes. "In your eyes. You got red cracks in your eyes."

I laughed and blinked away the tears I thought I'd hidden. "They must be bloodshot, sweetie. Mommy didn't get much sleep last night." *I dreamed I lost you and Daniel.* I clutched Daniel's hand and hurried into the concrete building. "Good morning, Mrs. Henry," the Brazilian receptionist said with her Salma-Hayek smile.

"Good morning, Camila." I closed my umbrella, rain soaking my hand and the sleeve of my tweed coat, then steered the children down the hallway with the mural of zoo animals.

Katy smiled at the monkeys swinging from the vines. "Can we go to the zoo this weekend?"

I offered her a lopsided smile. "I'm sorry, honey, Mommy's busy the next couple weeks getting ready for the play, but we can go after it's over. I'll check Brookfield's schedule to see when they're having the ice carving, laser shows, and Christmas light festival."

Katy stuck out her bottom lip. "But Emma's going this weekend."

Daniel ran into their classroom, hung his coat and bag on a hook, and sat on the midnight-blue carpet with gold stars, the odor of Lysol in the air.

"Hey, Daniel," a boy in overalls said. "I got a new truck."

"Whoa." Daniel picked up the plastic dump truck and rolled it along the carpet.

I helped Katy out of her coat and straightened the ribbon on her shirt. "If Emma's parents invite you to go with them, you can go. Otherwise, you'll need to wait until after the play." I stood and gave Katy a firm look. "And don't invite yourself."

Miss Jing, her hair up in a ponytail, was helping a blond boy put together a puzzle at a short table.

"Miss Jing!" Katy ran over to her. "I can tie my shoes by myself," she said, counting on her fingers. "Get dressed by myself, brush my teeth by myself, go to sleep by myself, eat dinner by myself."

Jing smiled. "Wow. That's amazing."

Mrs. Morales swept over in a red dress, her curvy hips swaying. A smile lit up her round face, and her chocolate eyes twinkled.

I whistled. Or tried to. Wade always made fun of me for that. "Juan's favorite color. Hot date tonight?"

Maritza chuckled in a way that always lightened my heart. "It's our sixteenth anniversary. Juan told me to dress up but didn't tell me where he's taking me."

Screaming came from the other end of the hall. "I don't wanna go," a red-headed boy whined.

A wiry woman marched him down the hall. "Did I ask you if you wanted to go?"

I winked at Maritza as I turned to go. "Have fun tonight!"

❄

After dinner, the spicy taste of Old Bay still on my tongue, I grabbed laundry baskets and sorted stinky clothes from our bedroom hamper. Where were Wade's? He usually had more dirty clothes than me, but today there wasn't even one holey sock. They must be next to the bed or one of the other places he considered "the lowest shelf in the house."

I checked. Nothing. Not even one pair of underwear.

Maybe the "fairies" moved his clothes liked they'd moved our wedding picture—which I still hadn't found, come to think of it.

I hurried downstairs where Wade was dancing with the kids.

"Join us, Mommy," Daniel called over the heavy bass beats.

We hopped around the room to the "Harlem Shake," Buster jumping on us and barking.

When the song ended, we fell onto the couch giggling.

Wade started tickling me, his fingers digging into my sides.

"Stop!" I shrieked.

He put his arm around me and the twins. "Family hug," he cried and squeezed us close.

Katy looked up at him. "Daddy, I want to marry you one day."

Wade exchanged a grin with me and then turned back to Katy. "I'll tell you what I'll do. I'm always going to be your daddy, and one day I'll help you find a good man to marry."

"But I want you to be my husband and mommy to be my . . . daughter."

I laughed. "Your daughter? I thought *you* were *my* daughter." I glanced at the clock on our DVD player. "Time for your baths."

"Just one more song, okay, Mommy?" Daniel said as if he were a lawyer negotiating a plea.

"Not tonight, buddy." Wade lifted him onto his back. "It's late already."

"Honey," I said. "Where are all your dirty clothes? You didn't have any in the hamper, and I couldn't find any by the bed or in the bathroom."

He shrugged. "I've been putting them where I always do."

I squinted at him. "You sure?"

He nodded slowly. "Pretty sure," he said as if it were a stupid question.

"I guess I'll check again." I lumbered upstairs to the twins' room to check their hamper—maybe he'd stuck them in that one—but when I turned the knob it fell off. "I thought you said you fixed this doorknob yesterday," I called over my shoulder.

"I did." Wade came up behind me, the kids in tow.

I held up the cold metal knob. "How'd it get loose again so quick?"

❄

After we got the kids to bed Rebecca came over to "sleep-sit," and Wade and I walked to a coffee shop as a soft snow began to fall. We ordered two steamed milks, almond for me and vanilla for him. Nursing our hot, fragrant cups, we meandered back hand-in-hand, or rather glove-in-glove, since the temperature had dropped to below freezing.

"Babe," I said between sips of my sugary drink. "Can I ask you something?"

He stopped and searched my eyes. "Of course. What is it?"

I took a deep breath. "Do you think I'm . . . losing my mind?"

"Why would you think that?"

"The TV, the clothes, the hotel reservation. What's happening to me?"

He sighed. "I don't know, Red. You've been under a lot of stress—Lily, the play, the baby having Down syndrome—it's a lot to take in. That's why I keep telling you that you need to rest." He pulled me close as a car whizzed by. "Sleep. Hang out with your friends. Forget about the housework and all your to-do lists. Working from seven in the morning until nine at night isn't exactly a healthy schedule." He gripped my arms and glared at me. "Especially for my *pregnant* wife."

"But things need to get done. I can't pretend I don't have classes to prepare for, laundry to clean, dinners to cook."

"I can start helping with the laundry, and we can eat peanut butter and jelly for dinner every night, for all I care. I'd rather have a happy, healthy wife than a house that looks like a Martha Stewart magazine."

I smiled and planted a kiss on his cheek. How had I gotten so lucky?

We snuggled close and headed home, our feet leaving impressions in the white quilt below us. When we came upon a nativity scene in a neighbor's yard, we paused to admire it. A shepherd and three wise men journeyed toward a stable where Baby Jesus slept. Mary and Joseph kept watch on either side of him. "It's beginning to look a lot like Christmas," we sang and started walking again.

Once we got home, Wade hurried in to use the bathroom while I collected the newspapers and sales flyers piling up on our doorstep. I drank in the lights one more time, and warmth radiated through my body. Then my eyes swept over the sidewalk, and my stomach turned to stone.

Only one set of footprints led to our door.

13

Leslie: January 1979

I trudged toward the school gym, the weight of my backpack making me slouch. How much longer would I get to be just me before becoming "that pregnant girl—you know, the one who was going to be a ballerina?"

"How was New York?" Terri came up beside me, as skinny as ever in cigarette-leg jeans.

"Pretty good." I forced a smile. "Except for these." I raised my green sweater and showed her the army of welts. "They came complimentary with our hotel stay."

"Ew." Terri cringed. "Bed bugs?"

I nodded. "I've been trying not to itch them. Just makes them worse."

"How'd your audition go?"

I shrugged. "I'll find out next month."

Don came down the hall, his arm around Sarah. She smiled at him, the light playing over her shiny waves.

I hid behind some varsity basketball players.

Don leaned over and kissed her as if no one else were in the room. Like he used to kiss me. My eyes watered, and the hard-boiled eggs I'd eaten for breakfast started coming up.

I dashed to the washroom.

Terri ran after me.

I vomited into the toilet, and the smell of rotten eggs filled the stall. The thought of my face so close to a bowl where scores of students had relieved themselves caused another bout of retching. Tears trickled down my cheeks.

"You okay?" Terri said.

I wiped my mouth with the rough toilet paper and then unrolled more to blot my face.

"Les?"

I took a shaky breath. "I'm fine."

"Doesn't sound like it."

I came out of the stall, and Terri handed me a mint. "I have more if you need them."

I unwrapped it and stuck it into my mouth.

"I am so sorry," Terri said. "If I'd known what a jerk Don was, I would never have encouraged you to go out with him."

"It's not your fault, Terri."

"He seemed so crazy about you."

Seemed was right. I leaned over the sink and splashed cold water onto my face, careful to avoid my eyes. I already had dark circles from lack of sleep. If my mascara smeared too, I'd really look like a raccoon.

"And then to be pregnant on top of it." Terri locked eyes with me. "But don't worry. I'll call the clinic today and make an appointment for next week. Then you can move on with your life and forget all about this."

I winced, my stomach as tense as a tightrope. "I don't know. I mean . . . it just doesn't seem right."

Her jaw dropped. "Les, you cannot have a baby right now. You're seventeen years old."

"I'll be eighteen tomorrow," I said with a strained smile.

She glared at me. "*Giselle*'s just two months away. How are you gonna dance if you're sick all the time?"

I stared at the ceiling, blinking back tears, and then brushed them away. "I'd be killing my own baby."

"No," she cried. "Are you kidding me? It's not even a

person yet." She fixed her onyx eyes on me. "Don't ruin your life for a blob of tissue."

A toilet flushed, and my throat constricted.

Peggy Richter peered out of the stall farthest from the door, not a hair or a piece of jewelry out of place. "I'm sorry," she said, looking down. "I wasn't trying to eavesdrop. I just . . ."

I let out a big breath. "It's okay. But can we keep this just between us?"

"My lips are sealed."

The bell rang.

"I'm late for home ec." Peggy washed her hands and hurried out the door.

"Oh, no," Terri said. "That girl is gossip central."

I glanced at the swinging door. How long would my secret be safe? Five minutes? Ten? I might become "that pregnant girl" as soon as I walked out of the bathroom.

"Haven't you heard what they say about her family?"

I shook my head.

"Telephone, telegraph, tele-Richter." Terri smiled at me wryly.

"Peggy and I are becoming friends. And she seems honest. I think she'll keep her word."

"I hope you're right," Terri said in a tone that made it sound unlikely.

I heaved my bag onto my shoulder. "I'm late for gymnastics."

Terri's eyes widened. "You can't go to gymnastics. You're sick."

"I'm not sick, I'm—"

"Pregnant. Yeah, yeah, I know. And soon the whole school will."

I swallowed the lump in my throat. "I'll probably feel better soon. I can't go home. What would I tell my mom?"

"Tell her you caught the flu, something's going around the school."

I shook my head. "I'm a terrible liar. And I always feel bad about it afterwards."

"Then go to the nurse's office and lie down."

"I don't want her to know either."

"Let's go to the Sacred Acre," Terri said, referring to the smoking area. "We'll say we have a free period."

I grimaced. "It's fourteen degrees outside. And feels like two."

"Then let's blow this taco stand and go to the diner."

"Terri, I can't ditch every day just because I have morning sickness."

"We can get Belgian waffles," she said, wiggling her eyebrows.

Normally that would've been enough to tempt me. But today I'd lost my appetite. Of course, sitting in a restaurant sounded better than struggling through gym class.

Terri grabbed my arm. "We'll be back before second period."

❄

Terri leaned forward, her elbows on the Formica, aluminum-edged table. "Les, you're one of the few people with the body, passion, and training to become a truly great ballerina."

I fantasized dancing for the New York City Ballet and tingled all over.

"I'll support whatever decision you make." Terri waved her fork around. "But I don't want to see you throw all your dreams away, everything you've worked so hard for. You've wanted to be a dancer for as long as I've known you. Why should you give that up to change dirty diapers?"

I frowned at the gray-and-maroon checkered floor and tugged on my lip.

Terri took a bite of her waffle. "You're good, Les," she said between chews. "Really good. You actually have a chance to become a prima ballerina." She pointed her fork at me. "Unless you decide to have some jerk's baby instead."

I winced.

"When are you due?" she said, leaning back against the booth.

I played with the bananas on my plate. The powdered

sugar reminded me of the snow falling outside our window. "Sometime in August, I think."

"And when does NIU start?"

"The twenty-seventh. But I haven't gotten an acceptance letter yet."

"You're smart and talented. Of course you'll get in." She lowered her voice to a whisper. "But how are you going to take care of a newborn *and* go to college? You know how much work Miss Dixon said they were. And someone has to watch the kid when you're in class."

I cradled my glass of water. "Maybe I can start college a little late. Take off the fall semester—"

"What about summer intensives? The School of American Ballet is the best in the country."

"I don't know if I got in yet."

"But if you do?"

I rubbed the back of my neck. "That would be an incredible opportunity to miss."

"Of course it would. But if you don't take care of this soon, you'll be super pregnant by then."

I nibbled a salty piece of bacon and mulled over what she said. "I guess I won't be able to go."

She did a double-take. "Are you serious? You *need* to go, Les. I mean, get real."

A baby at a nearby table screamed and struggled to get out of his highchair, a poopy stench wafting over to our booth.

The infant's mom rubbed her forehead, shadows under her eyes.

I shuddered. "Maybe you're right."

"Of course I am." Terri grabbed her purse and picked up the check. "We can go to the clinic during school next week so your parents won't suspect anything. Want me to make the appointment today?"

I gazed at the little boy, who was now sucking on his bottle. "Give me some time to think about it."

"Time you don't have, my friend. Ms. Petipa's posting the leads tonight."

❄

"You're here early," Frankie said as I climbed into his Cadillac after school. "And you look like crap."

I flinched. "Thanks." I clicked my belt into place and looked out the side window.

"More trouble in paradise?" he said in a gentler tone.

I shrugged and pasted on a smile. "How's Diesel?" Frankie loved talking about his Siberian Husky with the ice-blue eyes.

"Diesel's fine." Frankie's gaze bored into me. "Quit tryin' to change the subject."

"We broke up."

"Is that why I saw him with his tongue down Sarah's throat?"

I groaned and closed my eyes.

"He isn't good enough for you. Never was."

"And now for Jefferson Starship," the radio DJ said, "and 'Count On Me.'"

"So," Frankie said, rubbing the back of his neck, "I've been meaning to ask you . . ." He cleared his throat. "Wanna go to the spring dance together? I know it'll be corny," he rushed to say, "but it might be fun too."

My cheeks blazed. Did Frankie *like* me? I ran a finger over the leather bench seat. "I thought girls were supposed to do the asking."

He lifted an eyebrow. "Planning on asking me?"

"I hadn't really thought about it," I stammered. "Hadn't really planned on asking anyone."

He took a long drag of his cigarette.

The smoke turned my stomach, and I tasted vomit. "Stop the car."

Frankie pulled over, and I jumped out and puked. He ran around the car and held my hair back.

I straightened, my knees shaky, and wiped my mouth. Frozen flakes landed on my nose.

He crossed his arms and grinned. "You could've just said no."

I laughed. "It's not you, it's . . ." I glanced at his Marlboro.

His eyebrows rose. "This?" He hurled it onto the ground. Stomped on it. "Never bothered you before."

That wasn't entirely true.

"Tired, nauseous, sensitive to smells—just like my cousin." His jaw dropped, and he staggered backwards. "You're pregnant."

The bitter wind blew the hair off my neck and left it bare and exposed. If he could guess, how much longer could I hide it from my parents? I avoided Frankie's eyes and nodded. No way would he want to take me to the spring dance now. No way would any guy.

"Oh, baby, I am so sorry," he said and pulled me close.

I burrowed into him and wept, all the tension of the last four weeks coming out at once. "You're beautiful," he whispered as he stroked my hair. I rested my head on his shoulder and breathed in and out to calm my heart and settle my stomach. Never had I felt so upset and so comforted at the same time. When I finally pulled back, he passed me his handkerchief. "Does Mr. Wonderful know?"

I wiped my face and shook my head. "Neither do my parents."

Frankie reached for another cigarette then seemed to think better of it. He paced back and forth. "I would suggest you guys get hitched, but you don't want to be stuck with that goon for the rest of eternity." He stopped mid-stride. "You know how my parents always expected us to get married?"

My breath caught. They did?

"Why don't we?" He put his arms out in a question. "I can get my mechanic's license. Work and support you and the baby."

Was this a pity proposal? That wasn't the fairy-tale romance I'd dreamed of. And I didn't want to be anyone's charity case. Even if I had to wait forever and a day, I wasn't going to settle for second best. "I don't know, Frankie. I'm not even sure I'm going to have this baby."

"Just think about it. You don't have to go through this alone."

Ms. Petipa reminded me of a cross between a pixie and a fairy godmother. She'd promoted me to junior apprentice at fourteen. Asked me to join our preprofessional company and play Clara for our annual *Nutcracker* production at fifteen. At sixteen, I got to play the Dew Drop Fairy and this year the Snow Queen, the most sought-after amateur role of all.

I was on the smaller side, at five feet four, 105 pounds and counting, but Ms. Petipa must be only four-feet-something and as trim as an adolescent. Judging by her face, heavy perfume, and dyed-red, over-processed hair, she was probably in her fifties, but she exuded more energy and zest for life than any of us. What would my fairy godmother say when she found out I was about to turn into a pumpkin?

"Focus on your turnout, Leslie," Ms. Petipa said, her hand on my thigh. "Engage your hips."

I rotated my legs so my knees and feet were turned out more. I glanced at the other girls in black leotards. Despite Ms. Petipa's favor, how could I expect to get the lead when I couldn't even get my turnout down?

"Plié. Tendu. Arabesque."

I stood on my right leg and lifted my left behind me, beads of perspiration on my forehead.

"Pull your ribs in, ladies." Ms. Petipa strode around the stuffy studio, her posture erect. She glanced at the clock that read 6:30. "That's it for today. I've chosen the leads for *Giselle* and will post the list outside the door directly."

My muscles twitched. What part did I get? Maybe I would just be in the corps this time. I shouldn't get my hopes up too much.

The paper went up, and the girls swarmed around the bulletin board like bees around a sunflower.

Butterflies in my stomach, I stood on my toes at the back of the crowd and arched my neck. I blinked. Was I seeing right?

At the top of the page, next to *Giselle*, was typed *Leslie Gardner.*

Warmth radiated through my body. Giselle. I was really

going to play her—the role I'd imagined dancing since I was a little girl.

"I'm Myrtha!" Terri yelled.

"Congratulations," some of our friends said and hugged us.

Other dancers slunk away, their shoulders drooping.

Sandra wrung her hands and ran toward the bathroom in tears.

I stared after her. What could I say? Sorry you didn't get the part and I did?

As I munched on raisins, Ms. Petipa motioned for me to follow her into the classroom. She closed the door behind us and smiled at me, but there was a twinge of pity in her gaze. "You could shine in this role, Leslie. It's perfect for you. However, I have to be honest. I almost didn't give it to you."

My stomach dropped. Was it because I'd tripped on the last night of *The Nutcracker*?

"I don't know what's been going on with you, but you need to focus. I've seen you daydreaming in class and you've seemed tired, almost lethargic at times."

I tugged on the bottom of my leotard.

"I put myself on the line casting you in this part instead of hiring a professional because of the promise I see in you. But you need to give it 100 percent. If I don't have your full commitment, I'll have to rethink my decision."

I had to have this part—it was the one I'd worked toward for years. "I'll give it my all, Ms. Petipa. You can count on me."

❄

Terri drove me home after practice, the heater blasting.

Outside it felt like Siberia. But inside her Chevette, it was starting to feel like the Sahara Desert. I unzipped my coat and pointed the vent away from my face.

"Can you believe it, Les? We got the two leads."

I smiled. "Our dreams are finally coming true."

"Remember when we used to pretend we were ballerinas

in the same company?" Terri giggled. "We always got the main parts."

I snacked on a sweet, red grape and envisioned us as the most amazing Giselle and Myrtha our company had ever seen, our performances moving the audience to tears. No matter how exhausted, I would work harder than ever to bring this ill-fated peasant girl to life in the most enchanting way possible.

"Tomorrow," the radio announcer said, "we're expecting a record-breaking snowfall in northern Illinois and northwest Indiana."

Terri turned up the volume.

"Fifteen to nineteen inches of snow are expected from midnight tonight until midnight tomorrow night, with another few inches on Sunday."

Terri turned right onto Cass Avenue. "You still having your birthday party tomorrow?"

An image of me standing on top of the Empire State Building just three days before leapt into my head. What if I'd jumped? Instead of celebrating my birthday, my family would be planning my funeral.

"Earth to Les."

I shook away the image of my broken body. "Sorry. If we do still have it, it'll probably just be my parents and Patricia and Heather, since they live down the block. I doubt anyone else will be able to make it through the blizzard."

14

Shannon: December 2014

It's the most wonderful time of the year," Andy Williams sang over Oakbrook Center's PA. "There'll be much mistletoeing, and hearts will be glowing, when loved ones are near."

I shivered.

"Remind me again," I said to Gabby, "why we decided to come to an outdoor shopping center in December?"

"Shannon!" someone called.

I turned.

It was Melvin Duffy, a social studies teacher at York. "What are you doing here?" he said, his ruddy face aglow.

"Christmas shopping. And you?" I took a bite of my soft pretzel, savoring the Parmesan and roasted garlic. Now that I was well into my second trimester, I couldn't seem to eat enough.

"Oh, the same." He raked a hand through his copper hair. "Took the day off because I had a dentist appointment. Hey, I've been meaning to ask you . . ." He unbuttoned his gray, striped polo. "We're reading *A Christmas Carol* in book club. Thought it would be appropriate since you guys are performing it next week." He glanced at Gabby and then back at me. "Anyway, I was wondering if you could drop by and share your thoughts. We meet Wednesdays after school. If you're interested, that is."

My stomach tensed. Between the play and Christmas, I didn't really have the time. And we were supposed to host a birthday party for Margaret, Wade's sister, next weekend. "Hmmm." I twisted the pretzel. "I appreciate your choosing that novella—it'll help prepare the students for the play when they see it—but things are really busy the next few weeks. Could I come in January? Will you still be discussing it then?"

"Well . . ." He adjusted his glasses. "We're actually finishing it next week—it's short, you know—but you could come next month if that's more convenient." He cleared his throat. "How's the first Wednesday after Christmas break?"

I checked the calendar on my phone. "That should be okay."

"Great. I'll meet you at your classroom and take you to where we meet. See you then." He was off before I had a chance to tell him I could find the room on my own.

Gabby looked sideways at me. "That was weird."

"He's a teacher at my school."

"Yeah, well, he's got the hots for you."

"Melvin?" I laughed and shook my head. "He knows I'm happily married."

"If you say so."

I took another bite of my pretzel and checked people off my Christmas list. "What should I get Wade?" I said, chewing the top of my pen.

Gabby's eyebrows squished together. "Who?"

I stared at her. "Wade."

Her eyes clouded.

"My *husband*."

"Oh, right," she said, snickering. "Of course. Junior moment."

"Junior moment?"

She squinted. "Freshman moment?"

"You mean *senior* moment?"

"That's it." She snapped her fingers. "Darn those idioms."

"Gabby, you can't be having senior moments already. You're only twenty-nine."

"Maybe we can find something for him in Abercrombie & Fitch," she said, heading toward the store.

"Okay," I said and followed. I stopped short at the entrance.

Travis was inside, looking at a hoodie on one of the racks, his baseball cap on backwards.

I rubbed my chin. Shouldn't he be in school? Maybe he had senioritis. I started to walk over to him but stopped mid-stride.

A sweet, skunky smell clung to his clothes.

Pot? I'd have to mention it to Wade and see if he could talk to Travis before he got into trouble. "Travis?" I put a hand on his arm. "It's good to see you. I heard you're sending out college applications soon."

He stared at my hand and jerked away. "Do I know you?"

My jaw fell open. "It's me, Shannon Henry."

He squinted at me.

"Wade's wife," I added.

"Who?"

"Mr. Henry. Your physics teacher."

"Lady, I'm sorry to break it to you, but I dropped out of Willowbrook, I've never had a teacher named Mr. Henry, and there's no way I'm going to college. I was lucky to make it through two years of high school."

I gawked at him. "But you come over to our house all the time. You play with Buster and the twins, eat dinner with us—"

"Lady, I don't know what you're smokin', but I have never been to your house. I don't know your husband." He swore. "And what kind of name is Buster?"

I staggered backwards. "He's . . . our dog," I whispered.

"Yeah, well, you must have me mixed up with someone else." He turned and pimp-walked out of the store.

Hands shaking, I called Wade's cell but he didn't pick up. I dialed his school.

"Willowbrook High School, Phoebe speaking. How may I help you?"

"Is Wade Henry in class or on break?"

"What year is he?"

"What year?" I glanced at Gabby who held up a pair of jeans, her dark eyes twinkling at her find. "He's a teacher," I said. "Not a student."

"Oh, I'm sorry, I'm not familiar with him. Is he new? Maybe part-time?"

I stiffened. "He's a physics instructor, the Science Department Chair, and he just won the Outstanding Teacher Award."

"Uh . . . Virginia Fenske won that award this year."

My chest tightened. "Virginia is a fabulous teacher, but my husband won the award. I attended the breakfast to honor him just last month."

"Ma'am, I'm looking at our website. Ms. Fenske is receiving the award."

During play practice that afternoon, I tried to put the strange encounter with Travis out of my head. Maybe he had mental problems Wade didn't know about. Or had a twin or a look-alike. But how could the receptionist not know Wade? Everyone knew—and liked—Wade, especially his students. He *had* won that award, no matter what Phoebe said. Maybe Ms. Fenske won last year and Willowbrook's IT guy hadn't updated their website with new pictures. In any case, I needed to focus on the rehearsal. Next Friday was opening night, and we still weren't ready.

"Let's take it from page 57," I said to my students. "And remember, Tiny Tim is dead."

Katherine, her dark hair under a bonnet for the part of Mrs. Cratchit, sat center stage at a wooden table and pretended to sew.

I made a note on my script and sipped my hazelnut coffee. Cradling the hot cup in my hand, I breathed in the aroma. Hopefully, it would soothe my nerves.

Ben strode onstage and kissed Katherine on the cheek, towering over her five-foot frame.

She set down her stitching. “You went today, then, Robert?”

“Yes, my dear,” Ben crossed over to the fake fireplace and prodded the logs. “I wish you could’ve gone. It would’ve done you good to see how green a place it is.” He stared off into space, as if remembering. “But you’ll see it often,” he said, turning back to Katherine. “I promised him I would walk there on a Sunday.”

“My little, little child.” Ben broke into over-dramatic sobs, and Katherine giggled.

“Ben.” I rose to my feet. “You’ve just lost your son. The little boy you loved more than anything else in this world. And no matter how much you wish and hope and pray, you’ll never get him back,” I said, a quiver in my voice. “Never. Never. Never.”

Ben gulped. “Sorry, Mrs. Henry.” He coughed. “My little child,” Ben said as if he meant it and picked up the crutch that no longer had an owner.

❄

The next day, Peggy’s kitchen table offered me solace as it had so many others in need of mothering. Gathering my thoughts, I peered out the window at her Christmas decorations.

Bright, oversized ornaments hung from the branches of her evergreen tree, and on the lawn Santa and eight reindeer prepared to go airborne.

“I’ve been reading about Down syndrome,” I said as I turned back to Peggy. “Children with Down’s often have heart problems, sleep apnea, thyroid dysfunction, frequent ear infections which sometimes lead to hearing loss.”

Peggy handed me a piece of garlic bread that looked like it had been dunked in melted butter. I’d come for a light lunch, but Peggy had gone all out. “Extra challenges do come with raising a child with Down syndrome.”

“Not to mention the major learning problems the child would likely never be able to overcome.”

“Learning does come harder for kids with Down syndrome.”

Peggy took her usual seat by the window. "But medicine and therapy have come a long way over the past thirty years, and people with Down syndrome can lead lives a lot closer to normal than you might think. They're even living longer now. Instead of only making it to age twenty-five, most of them live to be sixty or so now."

"That's good to know." I bit into the crunchy bread. *Mmmm.* Even better than I expected. Probably half a day's worth of recommended calories though. "What will happen when Wade and I die? Will the twins have to care for him?"

Peggy cut up the roast beef on her plate. "A lot of adults with Down syndrome can live on their own. Supported living programs are always an option once you and Wade are gone."

But how much would that cost? The amount of money we'd have to set aside would take from Katy's and Daniel's college fund or inheritance. "Even if he's able to live independently after we die, or in a group home, I'm afraid Katy and Daniel will feel cheated out of our attention while we're alive because this new child would need so much."

Peggy set down her fork and knife. "Katy and Daniel will love this child. Siblings of Down syndrome children often can't imagine their lives without such a special member of their family."

I squinted at her. "How do you know so much about Down's?"

"I researched it when I was getting my doctorate." Peggy sipped her water. "Plus, my niece's son has Down syndrome."

I raised my eyebrows. She'd never mentioned that before.

"When my niece first got the diagnosis, she was overwhelmed as she thought about everything her child wouldn't be able to do."

Finally someone understood.

"But life with Patrick has been less challenging and more joyful than my niece and her husband ever expected. When I visit, Patrick runs to hug me. Sometimes I think that kid loves better than ten 'normal' children ever could," Peggy said like a mother hen defending one of her chicks.

"I hate to say this . . ." I fiddled with my food. "But the doctor told us this child won't be like me and Wade. Is that true?"

"Oh no, no, no." Peggy shook her head and sucked in her cheeks. "This child will be different from you in some ways, but every kid inherits traits from their parents." Her expression softened, and she smiled. "Patrick inherited my niece's freckles and her husband's love for music."

I paused as I lifted a forkful of food to my mouth. Maybe our child would love science like Wade or the arts like me.

"Patrick just celebrated his seventh birthday last week. He got a new bike and learned how to ride it already. In fact," she said, "my niece just brought over a picture." She retrieved a photo frame from the living room and handed it to me.

A blond boy smiled at me from the top of a shiny bike. He had the happiest eyes I'd ever seen.

"He's adorable," I said, my eyes moist. What if his mother had chosen not to have him?

"Want more?" Peggy gestured toward my empty plate.

"Oh, no." I pushed it back. "It was delicious though. Thank you."

Peggy deposited the dirty dishes into the sink and set a piece of pie in front of me.

I opened my mouth to protest, but it did smell awfully good.

"Cherry," Peggy said. "Just pulled it out of the oven before you got here."

So much for trying not to gain too much weight this pregnancy.

"Sujeet Desai is Patrick's hero," Peggy said, sitting back down. "Have you heard of him?"

I shook my head.

"He plays seven instruments and has traveled to thirty states and eleven countries doing solo performances."

Seven instruments? I had enough trouble just learning the piano.

"He also earned a black belt in Tae Kwon Do and teaches martial arts. Four years ago, he married the love of his life." Peggy fixed her blue eyes on me. "Sujeet has Down syndrome."

I gasped.

"People with Down syndrome have become actors."

Corky from *Life Goes On* jumped into my head. When I was in middle school, my family and I watched that show every week. I started humming the theme song.

"Artists," Peggy continued. "Writers, musicians, and public speakers. Some go to college. Some even get married."

"Wow." My skin tingled. "I didn't think that was possible."

A goldfinch landed on one of the seventy bird houses hanging from Peggy's rancher.

I gazed at it as I enjoyed my fruit-filled crust, imagining all the things our child might be able to do after all.

Peggy moved her plate to the side and wove her fingers together. "I don't mean to be pushy, but you know I always say what I think."

I grinned.

"I want you to remember that this baby you're carrying is a *person* first of all. And *then* a child with Down syndrome." She handed me a book.

"Each Week of Your Pregnancy," I read.

"How far along are you?"

"Eighteen weeks."

Peggy took the book back and flipped through the pages. When she found the spot she wanted, she started reading. "Your baby's about the size of a bell pepper and is busy flexing his arms and legs. He's getting used to your heartbeat and familiar voices and will be startled if he hears a loud noise."

"Just like Mommy." I chuckled, remembering how I'd screamed in *Lady in the Water* when a sprinkler came on. Wade still teased me about it.

"If it's a girl, her uterus and fallopian tubes are in place."

I raised my eyebrows.

"If it's a boy, his genitals are noticeable." Peggy pulled her blazer closed. "He's developing his own unique fingerprints."

Like the unique snowflakes Wade's mom read about?

"And learning how to yawn and hiccup." She glanced at me. "Have you felt the baby move yet?"

I rubbed the back of my neck. "I'm not sure."

"Well, you will soon." Peggy set the book down. "More pie?"

I stared at my empty plate, and my face heated. How could I eat so much these days? "No thank you," I said, wiping my mouth. "It was really good though."

"I'll pack some for you to take home."

"Wade and the kids will love it." I rolled my shoulders back and crossed my ankles. "You never finished telling me the story about your friend from high school. What happened after she found out she was pregnant?"

Peggy grimaced. "I realized that's not my story to tell," she said after a moment. "If I get permission first, I'll tell you the rest. Or maybe she'll tell you herself."

My breath hitched. "Do I know her?" I stammered.

Peggy peered out her window. "Oh, look," she cried. "A cardinal."

15

Leslie: January 1979

On top of the ten inches of snow left over from New Year's Eve," the radio announcer said from my alarm clock, "we're looking at almost two feet of new snow between last night and tomorrow morning."

I pushed snooze and burrowed deeper under my rose-petal-pink bedspread. Guess my birthday party was canceled. Or at least postponed. And I wouldn't have to go to pointe class today or rehearse for *Giselle*, which was good. I needed a day to just lounge in bed, my present to myself. I wasn't really in the mood for celebrating, not with all these decisions hanging over my head. At least I could celebrate—on the inside—that I was still alive.

"Leslie?" Mom bustled into my room, bringing the spicy scent of carnations with her.

I pulled the covers off my head. "Yeah?"

"Happy birthday! This letter from NIU came for you." She handed it to me and perched on the side of my bed. "I just noticed it as I was sorting yesterday's mail."

I sat up and stared at the envelope in my hands. If I was accepted, how could I go? Unless I took Terri's advice.

It would be worse to be rejected. What would that say about my dancing?

"Well?" Mom lifted an eyebrow. "Aren't you going to open it?"

I tore the seal, wincing at the paper cut it gave me.

Congratulations! I am pleased to inform you of your admission to the School of Theater and Dance at Northern Illinois University for the fall semester, 1979.

"I got in," I said, breathing a sigh of relief. Now I just had to figure out the next part—how was I going to go?

"Of course you did." Mom smiled. "Now I know we've talked about this before, but are you sure you want to major in dance?"

I bit my lip, a bitter taste in my mouth.

"Why not minor in dance but major in something more practical?"

Like childcare? I skimmed the rest of the letter. The last two paragraphs jumped out at me:

The Intent to Register Form is enclosed for you to reserve your place in the fall class. You will also find a copy of 'Your Admission to Undergraduate Study,' which contains your Housing and Meal Plan Application. Please complete and return both forms with your housing deposit and advance payment postmarked no later than May 1, 1979.

We hope to see you on campus for one of our Spring Reception programs in April. You will receive a formal invitation to these events within the next few days.

At least I had three months to decide—baby or ballet school.

Mom read through the letter. "I'll write you those checks now so you can mail in the forms today."

Today? I gazed out the window at the swirling snow. How could I explain my hesitation without telling her the truth?

Mom followed my gaze. "At least fill out the forms. You can mail them once the blizzard passes."

I fingered the seam of my throw pillow. Could the blizzard last until April?

❄

"Leslie," Mom yelled from downstairs over the sound of laughing voices. "Everyone's here, and we're all waiting for you."

I reluctantly pulled myself away from the novel I was reading, *The Secret Woman* by Victoria Holt, and hurried down the steps into the dining room. Guess I wasn't going to get much alone time today. But at least I'd get to hang out with my niece and enjoy some good food, if the smell of fresh garlic was any indication.

"Happy birthday, Aunt Leslie," my niece Heather said as I pulled out a heavy walnut chair next to her. "I made you a card. Mommy said I can give it to you after lunch."

I smiled. "I'm sure I'll love it," I said, embracing her. *And I'm glad you're not putting it in my coffin.*

My sister, Patricia, passed me a plate of Italian sausage from across the table. "So," she said, "how does it feel to be eighteen?"

And pregnant? "Not much different than seventeen." *And pregnant.*

"If Leslie gets into the School of American Ballet's summer program," Mom said, "I was thinking of flying out with her the Friday before her classes start and making a weekend of it. Want to join us? We could shop, go out to eat, see some shows."

"Sounds great." Patricia handed me a dish of baked mostaccioli drenched in tomato sauce and mozzarella cheese.

I spooned some onto my plate and took a bite, the ground beef extra fatty today. A wave of nausea rolled over me. I swallowed a big gulp of ice water and breathed deeply to try to settle my stomach.

"So Les," Patricia said. "Are you getting excited? Just a few more months and you could be in New York City living your dream."

"Yeah." I stabbed a piece of sausage, feeling sicker by the minute. "That would be great." If I was going to have the baby, I needed to tell them soon. I didn't want them spending money on flights, hotels, and summer intensives if I wasn't even going to go.

Mom felt my forehead. "Are you feeling okay?"

"Just tired," I said, my fork trembling.

"Probably still recuperating from the crazy week we had." Dad helped himself to more pasta. "I don't blame you. I could use a nap right now."

"Your dancing really is incredible," Mom said. "Much better than the other girls in your company. How gracefully you move your arms."

"Plus, the expression you bring to ballet," Dad added. "Being a ballerina isn't an easy life, but I'm sure you could make it as a professional if that's what you really want."

Warmth radiated through my body. Dad had high standards and wasn't the flattering sort.

Patricia cut up the meat on Heather's plate. "When you were practicing for *Giselle* the other day . . . the part where she discovers the truth about the duke and his fiancé . . . you made me believe you were really in love and heartbroken." She arched a raven eyebrow. "Personal experience?"

I choked on a piece of spicy meat.

Mom frowned at Patricia.

"What? I'm just being honest." Patricia flung a stiff smile my way. "Now that Don's out of the picture, who are you going to the spring dance with?"

"I'm not sure I *am* going."

"Just because it didn't work out with Don," Patricia said, "doesn't mean you can't go with another guy. You should ask someone."

Dad reached for the bread basket. "I'm sure Leslie won't have any problem finding a guy to go with her. She's pretty, talented, and a nice person. And guys like good girls."

My cheeks burned. Would he still feel that way if he knew about the baby growing in my belly?

❄

As my family sang "Happy Birthday" Patricia carried a round cake into the dining room and set it down in front of me.

A ballerina danced atop pastel-pink icing swirled into rosettes.

The cake seemed to symbolize all my dreams. But today they seemed as childish as the plastic dancer with the perfect face.

"Don't forget to make a wish," Patricia said.

I wish I wasn't pregnant. I closed my eyes and blew out the candles, the scent of smoke lingering in the air.

"What did you wish for, Aunt Leslie?" Heather said.

I swallowed. "Uh. . ."

"She's not supposed to tell, sweetie," Patricia said, cutting the cake. "Or it might not come true." Patricia winked at me. "Tell me later?"

I focused on Mom and avoided Patricia's eyes.

Mom handed me a slice and then gave a smaller piece to Heather. "Why don't you give Aunt Leslie her presents?"

Heather's eyes lit up. She handed me a gift from my parents wrapped in paisley paper.

I opened it to discover a lavender bag with a silky cord drawstring. Ballet slippers were embroidered on the front. "It's perfect."

"Just like you," Dad said, tears welling in his eyes. "Well, practically perfect. We're so proud of you."

My eyes stung. If only he knew.

"Can I have a bag like that, Mommy?"

"Maybe when you start taking ballet lessons." Patricia smoothed Heather's hair. "There's no one Heather looks up to as much as Aunt Leslie."

I pasted on a smile for my niece. What kind of role model would I be if I had a baby out of wedlock?

"We thought you could use a new bag," Mom said. "For summer intensives and college in the fall."

I ran my hands over the luxurious fabric. Would I ever be able to use it for what it was intended? Or would it become a diaper bag instead?

"That's part one of your present," Mom said. "The other

part's a shopping spree. You've gotten curvier, and I thought you could use new clothes for your big summer in New York and your first year at NIU."

My face heated.

"Vivian," Dad said. "You're embarrassing her."

Patricia chuckled. "And I thought I was the only one with boobs in the family."

I took a bite of the strawberry cake and focused on forking off another piece. At least I'd gained one perk from being preg-nant—no more pancake chest. But how long would it take for them to discover why?

"This one's from me and Mommy." Heather handed me a book-sized present wrapped in lemon-colored paper.

I took the gift, thankful for the distraction, and unwrapped a suede journal.

"I thought you could use it to write down your stories," Patricia said. "When we were growing up, you were always sitting under the weeping willow tree making up fairy tales. I thought you were weird at the time."

I smiled. Patricia had always been the more practical one. More like Mom. I fit in with them about as well as a mermaid on a mountaintop.

Patricia's expression softened. "But now I miss hearing you talk about your characters and the adventures they went on."

"I just got back into it, actually," I said, meeting her gaze. "I'm taking a creative writing class."

Mom tucked a strand of black hair behind her ear. "Maybe after your ballet career is over and you settle down with a husband and children . . ."

I sipped my water. The children part might be earlier than they expected.

"You can write novels and children's books."

I thought about it a second and nodded. "I'd really like that."

Mom set her fork down, metal clinking against the side of the porcelain plate. "I have an announcement. As you know, your father got a raise with a promotion and my catering business has done well this year, so for our family vacation we're all going to a resort in Mexico."

Patricia brightened. "Mexico?"

"Don't expect something like this every year," Dad said. "But we thought we should do something extra to celebrate Leslie's graduation and the bright future ahead of her."

I bit my lip. My bright future was about to careen off a cliff.

"Don't worry, Leslie," Mom said. "We'll go after you're done with summer intensives, and before you start college so it shouldn't interfere with any of your plans."

❄

I was hurrying back upstairs to finish *The Secret Woman* when the doorbell rang. I jumped, and the presents I was carrying tumbled down the steps. Who could be at the door now, in the middle of a blizzard? Patricia was already talking about spending the night to avoid having to walk home.

"Can you get that, Leslie?" Mom called from the kitchen.

I picked up the journal and ballet bag and set them aside then hurried to the front door and peered out the square window.

Frankie stood on our doorstep, snowflakes on his mustache and a brown wool hat with ear flaps pulled over his afro.

"Frankie," I said, opening the door. "What are you doing here?"

"Happy birthday," he said, the smell of wood smoke clinging to his clothes. He stomped his boots on our welcome mat and handed me a present. "You might want to open that later."

I clutched it to my chest and peered behind me to make sure my family hadn't seen it.

"So," Frankie said, clearing his throat. "Let's have it. You coming with me to the spring dance or not?"

My mouth fell open. He still wanted to go with me?

He lifted an eyebrow. "Thought you got out of that one, didn't you?"

"No, it's just—"

"Don't tell me some other doofus already asked you."

I pulled Frankie back outside and closed the door behind us. Frozen flakes flew around us. What was I thinking coming out here without a jacket?

Frankie unbuttoned his coat.

"No," I said, eyeing his red nose.

"What, are you crazy?" He took off his coat and wrapped it around me. "I'm not going to let a pregnant woman freeze to death."

"Shh!" My eyes darted inside the house.

"They can't hear us," he said, waving my concern away. He paced back and forth, rubbing his arms. "So . . . you dragged me out into this blizzard to tell me what, exactly?"

"I'll be sixteen weeks pregnant by the spring dance," I whispered, my teeth chattering.

"And?"

"Well . . . almost four months pregnant isn't exactly how I pictured going to the dance."

He shrugged. "So you'll be a little rounder. No big deal."

"No big deal?" I stammered.

"I'll just strengthen the shocks on my car."

I glared at him. "I'm not going to be *that* big."

"So what's the problem?" he said, grinning.

I studied the snow piling up in our yard. "Springtime in Paris" was a far cry from the scene before me, but it would be here before I knew it. And with it, Don and Sarah dancing. Making out. Leaving together to do who knows what. "Frankie, I'm confused about so much these days. I just need a little time to think."

He nodded. "Okay. But don't leave me hanging," he said, jabbing his finger at me. "I'll have to beat the other girls away while I wait for your answer."

I remembered the letter I'd gotten from Northern Illinois University. "Guess what? I got into NIU."

"I can't believe you're acting surprised. I could have told you that five months ago. Congratulations." He gave me a hug and squeezed tight. He pulled away. "Casanova going there too?"

I swallowed. "He's headed to the University of Southern California. He wants to be an actor."

"Yep. He's Mr. Responsibility."

"Frankie, that's not fair. He doesn't know about . . . you know, yet," I whispered.

"Would it make any difference if he did?"

I blew out my breath. "I don't know."

Frankie jerked his head toward our driveway. "Need help with the snow? I can clear your roof, your driveway, and your sidewalks. Just bring me a shovel and I'll get started."

I raised my eyebrows. "You're going to shovel our roof in the middle of a blizzard?"

"Best to stay on top of it."

"How about you come back tomorrow, after it stops snowing?"

He tipped his hat. "See you tomorrow then, birthday girl."

I handed him his coat and watched him walk away, his long legs striding over the snow drifts.

Remembering the present in my hand, I hurried upstairs and plopped down on the cushioned bench at the foot of my bed. I ran my hand over the wrapping paper—a little girl and a little boy at a birthday party. My eyes moistened. How many times had Frankie and I played together as children?

Careful not to tear it, I peeled off the paper and my jaw dropped.

It was a book of baby names.

Did Frankie think I was going to *keep* this child?

On the cover of the book, storks delivered babies in white sheets. If only that were how babies were made and storks only delivered them to mothers who were ready.

"Here are those checks," Mom said, marching into my room.

I shoved the bright-orange book behind the bench, the wrapping paper crinkling as loudly as my heartbeat. "Thanks." My hands trembled as I took the ticking time bombs. If I didn't mail them in soon with my Intent to Register Form, Mom would notice when she balanced her checkbook next month.

One month to decide.

Baby or ballet.

16

Shannon: December 2014

Fidgeting in the patient chair, I peered at my phone. Where in the world was Wade? He should've been here a half hour ago. I texted him again—*B here soon?*

Dr. Beck knocked and strode into the room. "How are you?"

About to meet a child I'm not ready for. Without my husband.

"Fine," I lied.

She closed the door and sat on the stool, her close-set eyes fixed on me. "Have you and Wade come to a decision?"

I rubbed my arms to combat the chill in the room. "We're probably going to keep the baby but haven't decided for sure yet."

"I don't want to rush you," she said, her posture stiffening. "But you should make up your mind soon—the sooner the better. If you choose to terminate, after all, we should schedule the abortion." She cleared her throat and looked at her clipboard. "I have a cancellation at 3:30 today. We could do it then or as soon as you decide."

My stomach tightened.

"On the other hand, if you want to continue with the

pregnancy or want more information before making a final decision, we can do the ultrasound now and take a look at how the fetus is developing."

More information was always good. "Let's do the ultrasound."

Wade hurried into the room and tipped an imaginary hat.

I breathed a sigh of relief.

"Sorry I'm late. Traffic was horrible. There was a train, and this guy in front of me—"

Dr. Beck glanced at her watch.

"Sorry. What did I miss?"

"We were just about to do the ultrasound," I said.

Dr. Beck led us down the hall to another room where a tech we'd met before sat behind a monitor. "Sit back, please," she said and started pushing buttons on a keyboard. She was pregnant too and further along than me. She must've been eating only carrots because, besides her small belly, she seemed as trim as a high school track star.

I wished I'd devoted more time to getting back into shape after Lily was born. On second thought, no. I wished I'd spent every waking moment snuggling with her, kissing her warm cheeks, basking in the glow of each sweet smile she sent my way.

"Honey?" Wade raised his eyebrows.

I looked around.

Everyone was waiting for me.

"Oh. Sorry." I scooted backward on the exam table, the paper crinkling beneath me.

The tech lifted the bottom of my turtleneck and smoothed cool gel with a medicinal scent over my stomach. "Bones look white on the scan," the soft-spoken tech said and turned the monitor toward me.

I strained my neck to see.

"Liquids black and soft tissue gray and spotted." She ran the transducer over my womb, making it sound like we were in the middle of a wind storm.

I stared at the screen. Was our little one sucking its thumb?

"Is that the baby's heartbeat?" Wade said.

"Mm-hmm." The tech zoomed in on the heart. Her brows knit, and she enlarged it.

The hair on my neck stiffened.

Dr. Beck exchanged a look with her then turned her attention to us. "This is the fetus's heart." She pointed at the monitor. "Four chambers, the atria and the ventricles, and the four valves. There's the blood flowing."

Globs shrunk and expanded over the organ.

"Unfortunately . . ." Dr. Beck let out her breath.

I held mine.

"There appears to be a large hole in the center. There is an opening between the two pumping chambers known as a ventricular septal defect, as well as between the two collecting chambers known as an atrial septal defect."

My chest felt like brick after brick was being pressed on top of it. I couldn't breathe.

Wade took a seat on the end of the patient chair and squeezed my leg as if to say, "We're in this together."

Dr. Beck perched on a stool and looked back and forth between us. "As we discussed earlier, almost half of children with Down syndrome are born with a heart defect. Atrioventricular septal defect, which is what it looks like your fetus has, is the most common form of congenital heart disease for kids with Down syndrome. AVSD is caused when tissue fails to join in the heart during the embryonic stage."

"Is there anything we can do?" I said, a quiver in my voice.

"I can refer you to a fetal cardiologist who'll give you a fetal echocardiogram to determine the severity of the problem. Children with atrioventricular canal defects usually need to have surgery by the time they're six months old."

I pictured a surgeon slicing into our baby's chest.

"When they also have Down syndrome," Dr. Beck said, "they may need surgery even earlier to prevent lung damage."

My mind revisited Lily's four-month birthday. She'd stopped breathing while I slept. If we had this baby, would I even make it through one night?

"Do you want to know the sex?"

My hands trembled. Knowing might make our decision

even harder. On the other hand, I liked to be prepared. I glanced at Wade.

He leaned forward, his eyes bright.

I nodded at Dr. Beck.

"It's a girl."

I handed my file to a gray-haired receptionist.

"Do you need to make another appointment?" she said.

I frowned. The question was, an appointment for what? A checkup or an abortion? Either way, we needed to decide. The sooner the better, Dr. Beck had said. "Umm . . ."

"We'll do that later." Wade led me to the elevator and pushed the down arrow. "Red, what's going on in your head?" He lifted my chin.

When the doors opened, I stepped on and leaned against the hand rail.

"Talk to me," Wade said as the elevator closed.

"She's going to need surgery. What if we lose her in the operating room? What if we lose her before that?"

Wade swallowed, his extra-large Adam's apple bobbing. "That could happen." He put his hands on my shoulders. "Or it might not. Chances are everything will go smoothly."

Chances are hadn't worked out too well before.

Ding. The doors opened.

Classical music greeted us as if this were just another trip to the doctor's office, just a normal ultrasound for a normal baby.

We stepped onto the slate tile floor, and a phone rang at the information desk.

Wade gestured toward the cafeteria in the corner. "Want to get something to drink?"

"Don't you need to get back to school?"

"That's not what's important right now."

I eyed all the people talking and laughing and shook my head.

Wade escorted me past the cloth-covered chairs and cozy

fireplace and out the automatic glass doors. We hurried along the brick path to the parking lot, the wintry air nipping at our faces.

"So." Wade grinned. "A girl."

I smiled weakly. "I love daughters," I whispered. "But we just lost Lily six months ago. Will this daughter even make it to her six-month birthday?"

"Oh, Red." Wade put his hands on my cheeks. "I wish I could get inside your head and help you find joy again."

I turned aside and brushed away a tear.

He squeezed my hand. "We're going to get through this."

Dark clouds moved toward us.

"We are," he said, his grip tightening. He exhaled and leaned against our minivan. "What do you think about keeping her? I know it'll be hard—I'm not trying to minimize that—but I think we can deal with this."

I shivered. "*Deal* with this?"

"You know what I mean." He wrapped an arm around me. "Of course most of the burden would fall on you, like it has with the twins, but I could help out more."

His phone rang and Darth Vader's theme song played, the Imperial Army advancing on us.

"Oh shoot," Wade said. "That's my student teacher—I forgot we were supposed to go over her progress review at lunch today." He silenced his phone. "You going to be okay?"

"Go." I kissed him. "I love you, darling."

"I love you more." His eyes lingered on mine a moment. Then he jumped into his sedan. "We'll talk later."

I climbed into our Odyssey, plopped my purse onto the passenger seat, and popped a piece of raspberry gum into my mouth.

The dashboard gleamed and the carpets appeared freshly vacuumed.

That was odd. Our car hadn't looked this clean since we'd first bought it. Had Wade gotten it detailed?

As I lay in bed that night, the silence felt like the hush before a hurricane. If only I could shake off these fears, this madness that was twisting me in knots. Tangling my mind. Playing tricks on me with increasing frequency.

Somewhere in the darkness an owl hooted.

Its lonely call made me shudder. I got out of bed, drew aside our bedroom drapes, and peered out the window.

Clouds streaked the black sky like a horde of ghosts passing by. Shadows crept over the yard and the roof of Rebecca's white-sided house.

I closed the curtains like a child who covers his face and thinks he's hidden.

But the shadows remained.

Waiting.

Watching.

Creeping ever closer.

I climbed into bed with Wade and burrowed into his warm body, as if that could protect us from danger.

He put his arm around me. "Everything okay?"

I breathed in his manly scent, trying to capture it in my memory. Just in case.

"Red?"

I sighed. "I just . . ." I sat up and studied his face. "I just feel like . . . something terrible's about to happen to you."

"Oh, no," he sighed. "Have you been watching one of those movies where the husband dies again?"

I shook my head.

"A book?"

"Not this time." My vision blurred. "I'm just scared to lose you." I bit my lip to keep the tears at bay, but a salty drop reached my tongue. "Please don't die, my love," I whispered.

He kissed me on the forehead. "Not planning on going anywhere, Red. I'm right here."

"But what if these hallucinations—or whatever you want to call them—become real?" I ran a hand over his stubbly face as if it were the last time I'd ever touch him. "What if tomorrow I wake up and you aren't here?"

17

Leslie: February 1979

I hurried outside with a spring in my step, clutching the letter from the School of American Ballet. The thermometer I passed read nineteen degrees, but it felt more like five with the wind. I shivered and ran down the sidewalk

I froze. Where was Frankie's Coupe de Ville?

In its place sputtered a small, brown sedan that smelled like exhaust fumes and looked like a worn-out wren compared to the tangerine eagle he usually drove.

I opened the passenger-side door, the metal cold against my hand, and climbed in. "Where's your car?"

"You're sittin' in her."

My breath caught. "What happened to the Cadillac?"

"I needed money for something more important."

What could be more important to Frankie than his car? "Like?"

He winked. "That's for me to know and you to find out."

I clicked my seat belt into place, my stomach fluttering. Could Frankie be saving up for an engagement ring?

He pealed out of the driveway and headed down York Street.

I remembered the envelope in my hands, and my heart started drumming. Of all the girls who'd competed in cities across the country, I'd made it. "Guess what?" I waved the letter in front of Frankie.

He raised an eyebrow. "You're trying to knock me out with a piece of paper?"

"I got into the summer intensives program!"

He scratched his cheek.

Not quite the reaction I was going for.

"I thought you couldn't go because of the baby."

I slipped the envelope inside my book bag. "I could go if . . ."

He narrowed his eyes. "If what?"

"Well . . . you know."

"If you have an abortion?" He braked for a red light. "Is that what you want?" He glanced at me. "Or is that just what Terri's talked you into?"

I played with a strap on my book bag.

"By the way," he said, "you can't avoid my question forever. Or pretend I didn't ask."

Did he mean the spring dance or getting married? Better to assume he meant the dance. "Frankie, I'm flattered you still want to go with me. But I'm just not—"

"You just don't like me like that." He put his hand up. "I get it. Only jerkwads get to be more than a friend."

"Frankie, that's not—"

"Just tell me you're not waiting for him. If I don't deserve you, he certainly doesn't."

The light turned green.

An elderly woman caught in the middle of the road hurried the rest of the way across.

Frankie slammed on the gas. "Tell me you won't take him back."

"Probably not. But he is the father of my child, if I decide to—"

"Just because he can make a baby doesn't make him daddy material. See how quickly he ran off on you?" Frankie glared at me. "Is that the kind of nimrod you want raising your child?"

❄

In movies class birds flew free, signaling the end of *The Diary of Anne Frank*.

I closed my eyes, haunted by the image of Anne's life snuffed out before she could even go to high school or get married. My stomach rolled. My life might be snuffed out, too, in a different way.

Mr. Marek flipped on the lights, and I blinked and rolled my shoulders back.

He leaned against his desk and crossed his ankles, his triangle-shaped face scanning the room. "Thoughts?" he said, one bushy eyebrow raised.

Terri raised her hand, her citrusy Charlie perfume extra pungent today. "How could the Germans do something like that? I mean, to kill so many people just because of their race, their ethnicity."

"Good point, Miss Trombelli," Mr. Marek said. "But what about our own history of slavery just a century ago? Or the Dred Scott case where the Supreme Court ruled that blacks were inferior, didn't deserve the rights whites had, and could never become U.S. citizens just because of the color of their skin?"

I made a note about the Dred Scott case in my spiral notebook.

"That was a long time ago," Terri said. "Before any of us were born. I can't imagine Americans doing something like that today."

Peggy draped her periwinkle blazer over the back of her chair. "It's easy for us to point fingers at other nations, other generations, while doing things that are just as bad ourselves."

Terri frowned. "As bad as the Holocaust or slavery?" She snickered. "I find that hard to believe."

"Today, in this country," Peggy said, "we target the youngest and most defenseless for extermination."

Terri squinted. "What are you talking about?"

"Roe vs. Wade, when the Supreme Court decided unborn children were less human than the rest of us."

I put a hand on my belly then quickly removed it, my knuckles whacking the cold metal chair.

Terri huffed. "That's different."

Peggy stared at her. "How is an unborn child any less human than a Jew or black person? We all started out where they—"

"What about the mother's rights?" Terri's face turned as red as a persimmon.

"Do mothers have the right to kill their children once they're born? That's not a right, that's—"

"When it's inside a woman," Terri said, her voice rising, "it's part of her body. A woman should have the right to decide what she does with her own body."

"Even if it means killing another human being? Unborn babies aren't diseases to get rid of, like Nazis thought Jews were. They're children."

I ran a finger over the names etched in my desk. Had I been thinking of the life growing inside me as a disease, something to get rid of? Was I about to snuff out the life of an innocent child?

The dismissal bell rang as if separating boxers at the end of a match.

"Good discussion, ladies," Mr. Marek said, a twinkle in his eyes. "Tomorrow we'll begin watching *Roots* and see if that mini-series generates as much discussion as today's film."

❄

I trudged down the stairs, my eyes on the green-speckled tiles, as couples exchanged cards, bears, and roses. Their fragrance reminded me of the long-stemmed flowers Don gave me after *The Nutcracker*. I quickened my pace to the exit. If I could just get out of here, I'd be done with Valentine's Day for the year.

"Hey Leslie, got a sec?" Peggy slammed her locker shut and strode toward me.

"Actually, I'm kind of in a hurry."

"I just wanted to ask if you have plans tonight. If not, want to do dinner? My treat."

I chewed my lip. She probably wanted to find out about the baby—whose it was, why I'd slept with him, why we hadn't used birth control every time. "I've got technique class then pointe and variations in Westmont."

"Tomorrow night?"

"Technique class again and then rehearsal for *Giselle*."

"And I thought I was busy," Peggy said, shaking her head. "Friday?"

"Technique then pointe and variations again." I shifted my books to my other arm. No one seemed to know I was pregnant besides Frankie, Terri, and Peggy, and she'd known for a month now. Maybe I could trust her. "We're done early on Fridays though."

"After that week, I should hope so."

I laughed. "We get out at 6:30. Should we meet you somewhere?"

Peggy tilted her head. "We?"

"Terri and me. We ride back together."

Peggy glanced at some passing students then fixed her gaze on me. "I was hoping to talk to you alone."

"Alone?" I gulped. "Okay."

"Pick you up at seven?"

"I may be a little late."

"I can wait." Peggy started to go then stopped. "Can I ask you a question?"

I nodded.

"Did you make a decision about . . . you know what yet?"

I rubbed a hand down my jeans. "No."

"Don't. Not until after we talk."

I nodded again, more slowly this time. What had I gotten myself into?

After Peggy left, someone put a heart-shaped box of candy on top of my books then hurried away, their hand tingling the hairs on my arm.

I glanced over my shoulder and Frankie winked, his grin as roguish as ever.

I ran my hands over the silky bow, opened the box, and

pulled out a truffle. I sank my teeth into the dark chocolate, and raspberries filled my mouth.

Maybe Valentine's Day wasn't so bad after all.

❄

Terri pulled a yellow jumpsuit over her black leotard, zipped it up and moved closer to me, away from the ears of the other dancers. "What does Peggy want to talk to you about?"

"I don't know." I stepped into pleated pants. "But I think it has something to do with the baby."

Terri rolled her eyes as she peeled an orange. The smell freshened up the musty room.

She handed me a slice and I popped it into my mouth, but the juice stung a paper cut on my hand.

"I cannot believe she had the nerve to compare abortion to the Holocaust," Terri said. "I mean, of all the—"

"I actually thought she had some good points."

Terri's jaw dropped. "You're not serious."

Ms. Petipa stuck her head into the room. "I'm locking up in five minutes, ladies."

Terri grabbed her coat. "Don't let Peggy guilt-trip you," she said when our director walked away. "You need to get rid of it and move on with your life. *Giselle* will be here before you know it, and you definitely don't want to be pregnant for that."

I pictured myself in costume on opening night, puking on stage at the climax of my performance.

Terri dropped her voice to a whisper. "Ms. Petipa's catching on to you."

My eyes darted to the empty doorway where she'd just been standing. "I wanted to disappear when she asked me if I'd been eating junk food. Am I showing already?"

"You don't look pregnant. Yet." Terri looked at me pointedly. "Just like you gained a couple pounds, especially in your boobs and belly. But I wouldn't worry about it. As soon as you have the abortion, you'll be back to normal in no time."

I sank back in the chair and sighed.

"So it's settled?"

I frowned. "I don't know."

"I'm sure it'll be quick and painless, and then you can get on with your life. Remember, it's just a bunch of tissue."

❄

"You're probably wondering why I wanted to talk to you," Peggy said from the other side of the diner's booth.

My stomach tensed. Peggy didn't waste any time beating around the bush. But no matter how hard she pressed, I wasn't going to let her talk me into—or out of—anything.

"I just finished a paper for child development class on prenatal development, and I wanted to share what I learned and give you a way out."

I leaned forward.

"How far along are you?"

I glanced at the other diners who were sitting too close for my comfort. They seemed preoccupied. At least for now.

"I'm not sure," I muttered.

"When did your last period start?"

I sipped my hot tea and thought back, the dark sweetness calming me. "The Friday before Thanksgiving."

Peggy pulled out her wallet calendar and counted. "You're thirteen weeks pregnant."

I lifted my eyebrows. "That far along? But I just found out I was pregnant in December."

"This is counting from your last period like doctors do. The baby's actually only around eleven weeks old."

Our fifty-something waitress set a fried fish platter in front of Peggy and a chicken salad sandwich in front of me. "Anything else I can get you ladies?" She pushed up her oversized glasses with her wrist.

"No, thank you." Peggy cut off a piece of her filet and dipped it in tartar sauce. As she chewed, she flipped through index cards with writing on them. "Your baby's about the size of a peach."

I took a bite of my toasted triple-decker sandwich and tried to imagine a baby that small. Maybe Terri was right and it was just a bunch of tissue.

"And he has his own unique set of fingerprints."

I choked on a piece of bread.

"Here." Peggy handed me my glass. "Drink some water."

I swallowed the cool liquid then took a deep breath. "I'm fine. Really."

Peggy scooped up some coleslaw and glanced back at the card. "He's forming teeth and vocal chords."

That didn't sound like tissue. I took a bite of my chicken salad, the celery crunching between my own pearly whites.

"If it's a girl, she already has over two million eggs in her ovaries."

I sat back against the uncomfortable wooden booth. "She has . . . ovaries?"

"She already has all the organs you do. In fact, the baby's been squirming around in your uterus five or six weeks now."

That meant he'd been moving inside me when I auditioned in New York City, almost jumped off the Empire State Building, and celebrated my eighteenth birthday in the middle of the blizzard. He'd practiced every routine with me as I prepared for *Giselle*. I put a hand on my abdomen.

Peggy laughed. "You won't be able to feel him kick for several weeks."

I took another bite of my sandwich, a whiff of dill floating up to my nose. "I didn't realize it had developed so much already."

Peggy put her elbows on the table and wove her fingers together. "Leslie, please don't abort this baby. I know it'd be hard for you to raise this child on your own. . . ."

That was an understatement.

"But there are other options. My aunt and uncle have been trying to have a child for years but haven't been able to. I'm sure they would love to adopt your baby."

"Is this the aunt who had a miscarriage?"

Peggy nodded and took a drink of her milk. "Aunt Dawn's a nurse, lots of fun to be with, and amazing with her nieces and nephews. I know she'd make a wonderful mom to your son or daughter."

My throat closed, and my eyes watered. My *son* or *daughter*.

Was that what was growing inside me? I ran a hand through my hair. "What about her husband?"

"Uncle Gary's terrific too. Steady. Hard working. Great sense of humor."

At least my baby would have good parents if I gave it up for adoption. I hadn't thought of that before.

"Why not give your little one life and at the same time bless someone else with the gift of a child, one they would never be able to have on their own?"

"That does sound amazing, but—"

"Want to meet them? I could set something up."

This was all happening too quickly. And I'd promised myself I wouldn't let Peggy talk me into anything tonight. I stared at the linoleum floor a moment then met her piercing blue eyes. "Staying pregnant would mean missing summer intensives at the School of American Ballet—something I've been looking forward to for months. And it would make dancing as Giselle next month a lot more difficult, if not impossible."

Peggy wiped her mouth. "Don't other ballerinas take off a few months here and there for injuries and things like that?"

"Not usually this early in their career. Besides, depending on when the baby comes and how difficult the delivery is, I might have to miss weeks or even months of college, especially my dance classes."

Peggy ate a french fry then offered me the rest on her plate. "You could deliver early. But even if the baby comes later, couldn't you postpone your dance classes a semester or start college late?"

"Maybe," I said, enjoying the greasy goodness of the fried potatoes. "But even if all those things worked out, having this baby means everyone will know I'm pregnant—my parents, teachers, classmates. What will people say? They'll think I'm a—"

"You can't control what people say." Peggy reached across the table and squeezed my hand. "You can only control what you decide to do. Your parents will be upset and disappointed, but I'm sure they'll forgive you and love you just as much as they always have."

I pushed my food around my plate. "I hope you're right."

"I usually am," she said, chuckling. "Just think about it. What's a few months of embarrassment and lost opportunities compared to a lifetime of blessings?"

18

Leslie: March 1979

I embraced the cold commode, my head in its avocado mouth, and threw up the salty crackers I'd nibbled on last night to try to settle my stomach. I wiped my mouth and sat back on my heels as rain pounded on the window. I should be sleeping before the opening night of *Giselle*, not dealing with morning sickness. I wanted to slap myself for being so stupid, so careless. How was I going to perform tonight?

Exhaling, I leaned against the tub and gazed out at a sky as foggy as my future. Would I become the prima ballerina I'd always dreamed of? Or would I have to bag groceries just to make ends meet, hoping not to run into old friends from high school?

I shook my head. I needed to try to go back to sleep and give my performance every ounce of my energy. Maybe I'd feel better by tonight. But would it be enough to dance the most difficult routine of my life?

"Leslie." Mom knocked on the bathroom door.

I jumped. "Yes," I said, my heart racing. Had she heard me puking? I flushed away the evidence, but the smell lingered.

"Those checks I gave you two months ago for NIU."

My throat constricted. I pulled my blue-gray robe snug around me.

"They still haven't cashed them," Mom said. "You did mail them with the forms, right?"

I closed my eyes and rubbed my forehead "Not yet," I whispered.

"What?" she called through the door.

I cringed. "Not yet," I said louder. "But I'll do it soon."

"Leslie," Mom said in her I-can't-believe-you tone. "The deadline is May first, and the spring reception for new students is in a few weeks. Why haven't you mailed them?"

I'm not sure I'm going to college in the fall. I'm not sure if I'll accomplish anything besides disappointing you.

"Leslie?" Mom rapped harder. "Did you at least fill out the forms? If you did, give them and the checks to me and I'll mail them today. This isn't something you can put off."

❄

Dressed in a medieval peasant dress, I stepped out of Giselle's cottage onto a stage made to look like the Rhineland of the Middle Ages, the piney scent of rosin in the air. Goosebumps rose on my arms. This was it. My chance to prove I was meant to be a professional ballerina. As light and lively music played, I skipped across yellow leaves in a series of ballottès. Would I trip again?

The carrot-topped guest artist playing Duke Albrecht disguised as a peasant sauntered onstage and tried to kiss my hand.

I pulled away, my head down, and hurried toward my little house, my long tutu swaying with the music.

He captured my hand and led me to a wooden bench where we sat side by side.

It felt good to be pursued, even if this was just pretend. And I was suddenly glad I'd just brushed my teeth, the taste of cinnamon still on my tongue.

He leaned over to kiss me.

I jumped up and ran away, a flutter in my stomach. I picked a daisy and danced around with it, holding it up in the air. Plucking off one petal, I beamed as if to say, "He loves me." I plucked off another petal and frowned. I counted the remaining petals.

He loves me not.

Was this really happening? Was I really dancing with a pro?

❄

I was breathless by the time I finished the village festival dance. Never had I felt so alive.

A senior playing the gamekeeper Hilarion barreled toward me bearing a sword. Dark eyes flashing, he pointed at the duke and pounded the sword.

Furious at Hilarion for revealing his true identity, the duke pulled the sword out of its sheath and charged after him.

All of us danced, but I channeled the emotions I'd experienced in my relationship with Don. At the end of the number, finally able to express my own broken heart, I bolted across the stage toward the duke, my hair wild, my heart racing.

Hilarion caught me in his arms, his body a warm wall.

I pulled away and tottered toward the front of the stage. Reenacting the petal scene I'd danced earlier, a whisper of a smile caressed my lips. I tore off the last imaginary petal and shuddered, staring at my hands.

He loves me not.

The duke rushed over and lifted me in the air.

I shook my head and moved away. One of my feet landed on the sword. I grabbed it and tore around the stage, chills rushing over me as the music climaxed. I pointed the sword at my heart and pretended to pierce myself with it, then dropped it, the metal clattering on the wooden stage. I clutched my chest and flew around the stage. Finally, I collapsed into the duke and slipped through his arms onto the black stage.

He picked me up, but I was as limp as a dead daisy.

Backstage, wearing a white dress with a tattered hem, I popped a Clementine slice onto my tongue. The sweet juice refreshed both my mouth and my spirit as I watched the second act. The first had gone off without a hitch, but could I nail the ending?

After the Wilis killed Hilarion, I pulled a gauzy veil over my face and ran onstage. Standing in front of the duke, I stretched out my arms to protect him.

Terri, as Myrtha the queen of the Wilis, turned away, her chin high.

I danced to buy the duke time, my tea-length tutu swirling around me.

The duke lifted me upside down and twirled me.

My stomach flipped and I almost gagged, but I clamped my mouth shut just in time. *Leslie, today you aren't a pregnant high schooler. You're a forsaken village girl. Or rather the ghost of one.*

As we ended, I felt as airless as the spirit I was playing. I slipped offstage and breathed a sigh of relief.

My heart still doing grand jetés, I pulled a light yellow tunic over my head and bit into a Golden Delicious apple. I'd danced better than ever tonight. What if my dream of becoming a prima ballerina was still within reach?

"You were incredible," Terri said, buttoning her silk blouse.

"And you were such a convincing Myrtha, you terrified even me."

Terri shot me a mock-evil look and chuckled. "You couldn't have been a more shy and innocent Giselle." She tilted her head. "But, wait, that's what you're like anyway."

If only the innocent part were still true.

Terri sighed. "You love this, Les. You really need to schedule the you-know-what soon, before you start"—she dropped her voice to a whisper—"showing."

I glanced at my rounding stomach and exhaled. What if I

hadn't started feeling better this afternoon? I would've missed a completely magical evening.

"I can't bear to sit by and watch you let your dreams go down the toilet. Let me make an appointment for you next week."

I rubbed off some of my stage makeup. "Can we cancel it if I change my mind?"

"Sure. But why would you?"

"Remember what Peggy said in Mr. Marek's class? She also said—"

"Forget Peggy. She thinks she knows what everyone should do, but this doesn't concern her. I don't want to start college in the fall without you. We're supposed to be roommates and take classes together and everything." She winked. "Maybe date some cute guys."

I studied the dusty floor. What guy would want a girl with a baby? "Maybe I can just start a semester or two late."

"How do you know you'll ever go if you don't go this fall?" Terri zipped up her black leather boots. "What if you start waiting tables and decide it'd just be easier to keep doing that instead of pursuing your career? Especially since you'll be so out of shape from, you know, and not dancing."

I frowned. Would I ever get my body back after having a baby?

"And after college we can join the same company, rent an apartment together, marry some famous male dancers or some Prince Charmings who come to a performance and fall in love with us the first time they see us dance."

Could my Prince Charming have been in the audience tonight? Smiling at my daydream, I glanced at my watch. "Oh my goodness." I jumped up. "I gotta go. Frankie's waiting—he's giving me a ride home tonight." I put on my shoes and hurried into the auditorium.

Frankie stood at the front of the crowd, wearing a hunter-green plaid shirt. "That whole thing was retarded, backwards, obviously written by an idiot woman."

I felt like a cold fist punched me in the gut.

"No, baby, I mean . . . you were great." He hugged me to

his side then released me. "But why did Giselle choose the lame playboy prince over the manly hunter who brought her ducks and stuff?"

I shrugged.

"How 'bout a little mercy for the guy who really loved her? What happened to that, huh?" Frankie shook his head. "Just remind me never to watch *Giselle* again."

"It's just a story, Frankie."

"Yeah, well, the story seems too much like real life to me.

An elderly lady's strong perfume made my stomach turn. I moved a couple feet away from the crowd.

"Excuse me, Miss Gardner?" A slender man with a European accent held out his hand. "I'm Bence Vàradi from the Chicago Ballet."

I shook his hand, my palm sweaty. Was he a talent scout?

He jerked his head toward the stage and smiled. "Nice work up there." He handed me a textured business card. "Your technique is excellent, but your musicality is what really dazzled me. The way you expressed the role and related it to the music makes me think you'd make a wonderful addition to our company."

"Thank you," I said, warmth coursing through my body.

"We're looking to add a new dancer or two to our company this summer, starting in June. Would that be something you'd be interested in?"

My heart sank. I'd be six or seven months pregnant by then. I stole a glance at Frankie before turning back to Mr. Vàradi. "Would it be okay to start later, say in September?"

He frowned. "We'd like plenty of time to get you acclimated and to prepare for *Swan Lake* in October."

Swan Lake? If there was a ballet I'd dreamed of dancing in even more than *Giselle*, it would be the one about the princess turned into a swan by a sorcerer.

Mr. Vàradi scraped a hand through his dark, receding hair. "Is there a reason you couldn't come in June?"

I bit my lip. At least one of the reasons might be acceptable. "I've been accepted into the School of American Ballet's summer intensives program, and that doesn't end until July 27th."

"I see," he said. "Ms. Hall, our head artistic director, may be fine with you coming in late July, especially considering the special training you'd be receiving in New York, but September would in all likelihood be too late. You'd probably have to join us as soon as your summer program ends. Is that possible?"

I rubbed my fingers over my thumb, groping for a valid excuse. "Our family's going to Mexico for a vacation in August."

He studied me. "Sometimes we have to make sacrifices to get what we really want. Do you really want to be a professional dancer?"

"More than anything."

"Then why don't you take a few days to think about it? In the meantime, I'll share what I saw today with our director, let her know about your scheduling conflict in June and July, and see if she's interested in offering you a position with us. If she is, I'll give you a call."

I forced a smile. "That would be wonderful," I said and scratched my number on the back of one of his cards. As he walked away, I imagined myself starring in *Swan Lake* with the Chicago Ballet. I beamed like a little girl who just discovered she's a princess.

Only one little thing stood in my way

19

Leslie: March 1979

I unpacked boxes, the unfamiliar carpet digging into my bare knees.

The doorbell rang.

I hurried to the front door and peered through the moon-shaped window.

A ruddy-faced delivery man stood outside.

I opened the door, and he barreled into the kitchen and set a high chair down.

What was going on?

Before I could say anything, two more men carried a white crib upstairs. Another followed with a bassinet and stuffed animals.

"I don't need these," I said to the first guy.

He consulted a piece of paper. "That's not what my instructions say."

"Please. Just take them away." I raced upstairs to stop the other men—they had set up the crib in one of the bedrooms.

I opened my mouth to protest but froze when I saw what was lying in the crib—the most adorable baby I had ever seen. I picked him up and he cooed.

Tears trickled down my cheeks as I held him close and inhaled the sweet scent of milk and baby powder. "Rock-a-bye baby," I sang, a hitch in my voice, "in the treetop. When the wind blows, the cradle will rock. When the bough breaks, the cradle will fall, and down will come baby—"

"You're right. You don't need these." A raven-haired man snatched the infant out of my arms.

"I need these! I need *him*!"

I reached for the boy. The man jerked away. I lunged for him. He ran down the stairs.

"I need him! I want him!" I stumbled down the steps and shot out the front door. But I was too late.

The delivery truck sped away, nothing but fumes left behind.

I woke up screaming, my arms aching for the child I'd lost.

❄

Later that morning, Terri peeled off her black leather boots and perched cross-legged on my squeaky bed. "Don and Sarah broke up."

I touched my throat and curled up in my velvet armchair. I'd thought I was over him, but was I? "How come?"

"She wanted to go back to Phil."

So Sarah missed Phil, but Don didn't miss me.

"Now Sarah's going to the spring dance with Phil, and Don's going to have to go stag. That or ask someone else. Rhonda's always had a thing for him. Maybe she'll ask him."

I bit into one of the deviled eggs Mom had made yesterday, the mustard, mayonnaise, and minced onions melting in my mouth.

"You're not going to ask him, are you?"

I shook my head.

"And if he asks you?"

I glanced at the *Giselle* program on my nightstand. Could I forgive Don if he asked me to, like Giselle had forgiven Duke Albrecht? Would forgiving him mean I should get back together with him? He *was* the father of my child, even if my feelings had dwindled over the past few months.

"Just say no," Terri said. "He doesn't deserve another chance."

I remembered my dream, and a chill rushed over me. "I had a nightmare," I said and told her every detail.

"Must've been the pizza you ate last night," Terri said.

I put a hand on my stomach. "I think it had something to do with my baby."

"Your *baby*?" Terri leaned forward. "Les, it was just a dream. You can't let some late-night junk food ruin your future."

I tried to scrape a spot off the armrest. Was that all it was?

Terri planted her feet on the floor. "You've got plans, Les. Big plans. And having a baby right now's not going to work." She reached for an egg and leaned back in bed, as if it were settled.

I bit my lip. "Is a baby supposed to work around my plans?"

"Les, all your years of training have been leading to this point—summer intensives at the School of American Ballet, college at NIU, then dancing with a company. Preferably the same one as me," she said, her mouth turning up in a smile.

I had dreamed of that for so long. Still dreamed of it, in fact. I lit the candle on my dresser and closed my eyes. The lavender scent drifted over me as I pictured the future Terri described. How many ballets could I star in? How many roles would I play? What costumes might I wear? My skin tingled just thinking about it.

"By the way," Terri grabbed my arm. "A scout from Chicago Ballet talked to me yesterday. They might offer me a position with their company."

"He talked to me too!"

Terri's eyes brightened. "What if they hire both of us?" she yelled, pulling me onto the bed.

We squealed and bounced on the mattress, like we'd done as little girls. Were our childhood fantasies really about to come true?

❄

"Leslie, someone's here to see you," Mom yelled after Terri left.

I dried and put away the last plate in the kitchen cabinet and hurried to the front door.

Don stood there in a black vinyl coat.

My heart stopped.

"Hi, Les." He gave me the once-over. "You look great."

Great? I didn't have on a stitch of makeup, and my outfit wasn't doing anything for my rounding figure.

"Can I take you out to dinner tonight?"

I raised my eyebrows. As if we were still dating. As if he hadn't left me for another girl. "I don't think that's such a good idea."

Don stared at our doormat a moment then raised his head, his eyes glassy. "I know I messed up, Les, and I'm asking you to forgive me. I don't know if you heard or not, but Sarah and I broke up."

I tucked a strand of hair behind my ear. "I heard *Sarah* broke up with *you*," I whispered, glancing behind me to make sure Mom and Dad weren't in earshot. "Because she wanted to go back to Phil."

"Can we at least talk outside?"

I peered behind him. "Isn't it raining?"

"Just drizzling."

I grabbed a hat, raincoat, and umbrella from the closet and took a seat on the concrete steps under the overhang.

Don sat beside me, his sandalwood cologne closer than I liked. "Sarah did want to go back to Phil," he said. "But I also wanted to come back to you, and she understood that. We both made a mistake and now we want to be with the people we belong with." He took my hand. "I've missed you."

And they expected all would be instantly forgiven? I frowned and pulled my hand away. What about all Phil and I had gone through?

Don searched my eyes. "Phil was thrilled to get Sarah back. I guess I was hoping for the same response."

Dampness seeped into my bones. He expected me to be *thrilled*?

"Even though I know I don't deserve it." He watched the cars swishing by on York Street. "Les, you might not believe me, but I never stopped loving you. Never got over you."

"Then why did you leave me and start dating Sarah?" I said, a sour taste in my mouth.

He rubbed his hands over his corduroy pants. "I had feelings for her, but I think that was because you didn't seem as into me anymore with all your ballet and stuff."

"You knew the extra practices were just until *Giselle* was over."

"I guess I thought you'd always put ballet before me. Before us."

I let out my breath. Was he right? Had I put ballet before him? "Ballet's been a huge part of my life since I was a little girl."

"I know," he said, gazing into my eyes as if he were my biggest fan.

"And I have to make time for it if I ever hope to become a professional. Just like you make time for the school plays. But that doesn't mean I didn't have time for you."

"I understand that now," he said, putting his arm around me.

My whole body tensed. Was the chill from the rain spitting on my hands or in my heart? I put a few inches of cement between Don and me.

"I'm gonna see your name in lights one day."

I rubbed my arms to warm them. Maybe if I didn't have this baby . . .

"I heard you got accepted into the School of American Ballet's summer program." He lifted his hand to give me a high-five.

I met his hand halfheartedly. "I'm not sure I'm going."

Don's eyes widened. "Why not? I mean, sure, I'll miss you and wish you were gonna be here the whole summer, but isn't this what you've always wanted? I was planning to visit you. Go to the Empire State Building—"

"Something came up."

"Something came up?" Don tilted his head. "What could've come up that's more important to you than this? You talked about it for months."

I chewed on my nail. This was as good a time to tell him as any. "I'm not sure how to say this. I guess I'll just tell you. I'm—"

Mom opened the door. "Lunch is ready."

My breath caught. What if she'd come out a few seconds later?

"Don, you're welcome to join us too." She smiled at him then leveled her eyes at me. "Don't be long. We're all waiting."

"I'll be there in a minute," I said as she closed the door.

Don took my hands in his. "What is it, Les?"

"I gotta go," I said, standing.

Don scrambled to his feet. "Let me take you out for dinner tonight—how's Kon-Tiki Ports sound? You can tell me then."

Kon-Tiki Ports, where we'd gone on our last date.

"I've got something I want to talk to you about too."

If I went with him, he might consider us back together. But somewhere away from the house would be a better place to tell him about the baby. *If* I told him about the baby.

"I promise you won't regret it," he said.

What was the harm? Didn't he deserve to know? "Just dinner. Nothing more."

❄

"Tonight or Never," our middle-aged Asian waiter said as he set my drink before me.

I sipped the non-alcoholic rum flavored with lime and honey. Every time I touched the goblet, I remembered what I had to tell Don. Tonight or never.

"And Tiger's Milk." Our waiter put a mug of hot eggnog in front of Don then hurried off to a neighboring table to take their order.

"I have something for you." Don handed me the thin,

rectangular-shaped present I'd been wondering about since we got there.

I unwrapped it to find a framed poster of Margot Fonteyn and Rudolf Nureyev in the second act of *Giselle*. Dressed in layers of white tulle, Margot stood on pointe, her arms crossed over her chest. She gazed down at Rudolf, who knelt beside her, his hand on her arm as he begged for forgiveness.

"Thank you," I said, a lump in my throat. Maybe Don and I could still have that fairy-tale romance I'd dreamed of. Maybe we could raise this child together.

"I came last night," he said, reaching across the shiny black table for my hand.

My pulse raced. He'd come to my performance?

"You've never looked more beautiful." He beamed at me. "And I finally see now. I've been an idiot—the biggest idiot that's ever walked this earth. I hope I'm not too late."

An image of Frankie grinning at me on Valentine's Day after his hit-and-run candy drop-off popped into my mind.

Don glanced at the poster. "I was going to give you that at the spring dance, but I figured celebrating your acceptance into the School of American Ballet is as good a time as any." He took a sip of his eggnog. "Speaking of the spring dance." He laid his hands on my arms. "Wanna go with me?"

I thumbed the corner of the poster. "I don't know . . ."

Our waiter dropped off our appetizer. "Cantonese egg rolls," he said with a flourish.

"Thanks." Don put one on his plate. "Already got another date?" he said after the waiter left.

I bit into the deep-fried pork and cabbage, the smell turning my stomach. "Frankie asked me."

"Frankie? The gearhead?"

Frankie, who drove me to school every day, who had trudged through a blizzard to shovel our snow, who had offered to marry me knowing I was pregnant with someone else's baby. Don's, to be exact.

"Did you tell him you'd go with him?"

"Not yet."

Don rubbed his chin. "So what's the holdup?"

"I'm not sure I want to go."

"Why not?"

A woman in a Chinese dress played an erhu as I sipped my frosty drink. Tonight or never. "I have to tell you something."

He searched my eyes. "Anything."

I gripped the slick red booth as if I were on a roller coaster about to plummet four hundred feet. "I'm pregnant."

Don's eyes shot out of his head. "What?" His face paled, and he loosened his collar. "How? When? Is it mine?"

I stiffened. What kind of girl did he think I was? "Who else's would it be?"

Don shook his head. "I don't know. I'm sorry. I guess I just wanted to make sure." He drew in a breath then released it. "How long have you known?"

I revisited that fateful day I'd taken the e.p.t. test. "Since December."

"December?" He gulped. "That was three months ago. Why didn't you tell me earlier?"

Like when he'd told me he liked Sarah? Or that they were dating? Or maybe when I spotted them kissing in the school hallway? "You were . . . preoccupied."

Don ran his hands through his wavy hair. "What are you going to do?"

What was *I* going to do?

"I mean, I want to be a dad one day," he whispered. "Sometime in the future, the *distant* future. But I'm moving to California in August. And you're going to NIU."

The waiter stopped by. "Everything okay with your meal?"

I glanced at my barely-touched egg roll, forced down another greasy bite, and nodded.

"Let me know if you need anything else," he said and left Don and I alone.

Silence hung between us like a muggy mist.

I circled the goblet with my finger. "I could give the baby up for adoption. Peggy's aunt and uncle haven't been able to have children."

"You told *Peggy*?"

"She overheard Terri and me talking about it in the school bathroom."

"Who else did she tell?"

"No one, I think. Except maybe her aunt and uncle."

Don's eyes widened.

"She promised."

"Peggy's great, but I'm surprised half the school doesn't know by now."

I took another sip, my hands trembling.

"This is why you might not go to New York." Don clasped my hand in his. "Les, I don't want to see you give up your dreams."

Tears sprang to my eyes.

"Look, I've got a little money saved up and could pay for . . ." His eyes darted to the table next to us then back to me. "An abortion. If that's what you want."

Was he really concerned about me? Or how a baby would disrupt his life?

"I'll stop and get you the cash before I drop you off."

20

Shannon: December 2014

"Your card was declined," the grocery store cashier said.

I frowned. "Can you try it again? My husband always pays the bills on time, and we haven't put many Christmas presents on it yet or made any major purchases recently."

She swiped it again. "Still not working. Do you have another card?"

I handed her the Citibank Photo card I'd had since high school with the picture of me at fifteen. *Boy, do I look young.* I really needed to update that and change my last name on the card to Henry.

The cashier peered at the picture then back at me. She swiped it. "This one works."

The machine printed out the receipt, and I signed it and grabbed my bags out of the cart.

"Have a nice night."

"You too." I hurried across the parking lot, Arctic wind stinging my face.

Pizza from a nearby restaurant spiced the air. I breathed in the scent, and my stomach growled. I should treat my students to Little Caesars tomorrow night. Their Crazy Bread was always a hit.

Where was our minivan? I knew I'd parked it in this aisle, right next to the black SUV. I zipped down the rest of the aisle and checked the cars on either side.

No sign of it.

My chest tightened. Must be pregnancy brain again. That or someone had taken it.

I flew through the rest of the parking lot, my fingers turning into icicles and the bags growing heavier with each step.

No blue Honda Odysseys.

I called the police.

"911. What's your emergency?"

"Someone stole my minivan."

❄

Five minutes later, a black squad car pulled up to the curb where I was waiting.

A stocky policeman stepped out. "Good evening, ma'am. Officer Schmitt." He shook my hand, his grip firm. "Sorry about your car. Let's see if we can find it. I need your ID and the make, model, color, and plate number of your vehicle."

I handed him my license. "Thank you so much for coming. It's a blue Honda Odyssey, 2010." We'd gotten it the year the twins were born. "I don't remember the plate number."

"Where'd you park?"

"Over there." I pointed toward the end of the row.

He opened the back door of the car. "It's freezing. Get in. We'll check the area for broken glass—a sure sign it was stolen."

I climbed into the back seat behind the Plexiglas barrier.

After checking the spot I showed him and not finding anything suspicious, Officer Schmitt drove through the rest of the parking lot.

No blue minivans.

A red Toyota Corolla now occupied my former spot. The

officer parked and started filling out the police report, looking up my registration. After a moment, he cleared his throat. "Um, Miss Lennox?"

I blinked. Why was he using my maiden name? "It's Mrs. Henry now."

"You should get your license updated." He thumbed his ear. "Your registration says you own a Toyota, and the license plate number matches that one right there."

He gestured toward the shiny Corolla parked in my former spot.

My mouth fell open, but no words came out. I had never seen that sedan.

"Forgot which car you took today?"

My muscles tensed. "That's not ours. We don't own a Corolla."

"Your registration begs to differ," Officer Schmitt said.

I couldn't blame the officer for how the situation looked. *He must think I'm crazy.*

"Want me to try your key?"

I got out of the car, the cold air shocking me, and fumbled inside my purse. I pulled out a keyless remote. My breath caught. It didn't belong to our minivan.

"Ma'am? Are you okay?" Officer Schmitt came and stood beside me. I could almost see the wheels spinning in his head.

I handed him the key that would either prove I was right or that I'd totally lost my mind.

He hit the unlock button.

Beep-beep.

"That's impossible."

"I can drive you to the station, if you're not feeling well. You can call a friend to pick you up from there."

My car or not, I needed a way to get to work tomorrow. "Oh, no, that's all right. I can drive myself."

Officer Schmitt crossed his arms and tilted his head as if he were weighing the evidence against me. "Are you sure you're okay to drive?"

"I'm fine. Nothing a little rest won't solve."

"Might be a little more than that," he said. "I've had a lot of sleepless nights in my line of work, but I've never forgotten which car was mine."

I took a deep breath and forced a smile I hoped would appear sane. "Officer, my husband's always playing pranks. I'm sure this is just another one of his tricks. That or pregnancy brain."

He cocked an eyebrow. "You're pregnant?"

"Yeah," I said with a lopsided grin. "Explains a lot, huh?"

"Not really."

I had to convince him I was playing with a full deck. Our play opened tomorrow, and I needed to get to school early. My students were counting on me. "Actually, come to think of it, my husband told me to expect an early Christmas present today. And he knows I love Corollas. I'm sure this must be his way of surprising me." My acting ability was coming in handy, but I cringed inside. I hated lying.

Officer Schmitt studied me for a long moment. "Do me a favor," he finally said. "Make sure you go straight home and get some rest."

❄

Bing Crosby sang "White Christmas" as I drove home in the unfamiliar sedan that still had that new car smell.

I checked the clock on the dashboard. 9:13. Thank God the twins were spending the night at Gram and Grandpa's house. I hated to miss tucking them into bed, but I needed to talk to Wade. Alone. Hopefully he wasn't still at the movies with his sister.

Maybe he *had* gotten me this car for Christmas. Not that we usually bought each other such expensive gifts, but he could've traded in his Fusion. Of course, I'd still have to yell at him for spending so much money. I loved the car, but I didn't need it, and we could've used the money for those ballet lessons Katy had been asking for.

My mind revisited the day I'd seen the flat screen television in place of our big-box TV. This was getting scarier every day. Would Wade even see this sedan? He might insist it was the same minivan we'd always had. I shook my head. Of course he'd see the sedan. The police officer had.

I pulled into our driveway and grabbed the groceries and the mail on my way into the house. I set the bags on the counter and opened the fridge.

The gallon of milk resting on the top shelf was full.

I could've sworn it was almost empty this morning. I put the new gallon behind the old one and shut the French doors. Oh, well. Between the four of us, both would be gone in no time.

I put the food away and washed and ate some strawberries. If only I'd gotten whipped cream too. Picking up our electric bill, I squinted at the name typed on the front: *Shannon Lennox*. Our utility bills always came addressed to Wade and Shannon Henry.

I tossed the envelope aside, making a mental note to ask Wade about that too, and glanced at another bill from our dentist. It was also addressed to Shannon Lennox. *This makes no sense*. I'd gone to that orthodontist before marrying Wade, but I'd updated my information after we got married. Wade and the kids had been going there for years.

I flipped through some holiday sales flyers then picked up a card addressed to Gabby Diaz. It was an old friend of hers who must not have updated Gabby's address since she moved out years ago.

I set it aside for Gabby and peered at the last card.

A return label with my parents' address filled the top left corner, but the handwritten address in the center screamed at me.

Miss Shannon Lennox.

My stomach clenched. I could understand computer glitches at companies or an administrative error, but I couldn't fathom why my mother would address our family Christmas card just to me, and use my maiden name at that. I would have to call her. But not tonight. Tonight I needed to sleep. Tomorrow was a big day.

I set the mail aside and trudged into the pantry to refill Buster's bowl.

No sign of his food on the shelves.

I groaned. I should've grabbed more at the store.

He might still have enough in his bowl for tonight and tomorrow morning. I walked back into the kitchen.

No sign of his bowl either. Or Buster.

Now that I thought about it, he hadn't barked and jumped on me when I'd come in.

"Honey," I called, heading upstairs. "Did you take Buster to your Mom's when you dropped off the twins?" I peeked into the bathroom then stepped into our bedroom. "Wade?"

He must not have gotten back from hanging out with Margaret.

I texted him. *Darling, I'm home. Will you b back soon?*

Who is this? he texted back.

I grinned and shook my head. *I miss u. R u on ur way home?*

You have the wrong number.

He was taking this too far. *Wade?*

I don't know anyone by that name. Stop texting me.

I called him, my hands trembling.

No answer.

Maybe he wasn't answering because he was still in the theater, but I had to try one more time. Tapping my fingers on my dresser, I called again.

No answer.

I tried Margaret's cell.

"We're sorry," an automated voice said, "you have reached a number that has been disconnected or is no longer in service."

I hung up. I felt for my wedding rings but felt nothing but skin. I stared at my left hand.

Bare.

My adrenaline spiked. *Where did I leave them*? I darted into the master bathroom. Maybe I'd taken them off when I'd exfoliated my hands the night before.

I searched the floor. The sink. The medicine cabinet. No rings.

I plopped down on the toilet seat. The diamonds came from my grandmother's twenty-fifth wedding anniversary ring. I could never replace them. I leaned back against the toilet.

Only one towel hung on the hooks behind the door.

Maybe I'd put the rings in my jewelry box. I rushed back into the bedroom and opened the rosewood drawers. I slammed each one shut when they failed to produce my beloved bands.

Tears pricked my eyes. What was wrong with me today? Must be all the stress getting ready for opening night. I'd read somewhere that stress could make you absentminded.

Maybe I'd taken off the rings when I washed all those greasy pans this morning. I ran downstairs.

No jewelry around the kitchen sink or anywhere on the gold countertop.

They must be in our room. I hurried back upstairs and hunted under our bed and in the top drawer of my nightstand.

Nothing but dust and a carpet that needed vacuuming.

I sneezed.

The house always looked a wreck right before a play. At least it didn't look nearly as bad this year as it usually did.

I forced myself to rest against the side of the bed and take some deep breaths. I was not losing it. I was just stressed and exhausted. Everything would be all right. Breathe in. Breathe out. Everything had an explanation. I'd feel better next week when I was on vacation. I'd wrap presents, mail Christmas cards and bake chocolate chip cookies with the twins, festive music playing in the background.

I forced myself to think about something else. I still had Christmas shopping to finish too. What should I get Wade besides those jeans Gabby helped me pick out?

My phone beeped, and my belly fluttered. Was it him? I read the message and sighed.

Melvin was texting for my help with a fundraiser to save the rainforests in Argentina. Maybe Gabby was right and he did have a crush on me.

No, that couldn't be right. Melvin knew I was happily married.

My eyelids grew heavy. It was getting late, and I needed to get some sleep before opening night tomorrow. I brushed my teeth, washed my face, and changed into red silk pajamas, an early Christmas present from Gabby. As I climbed into bed, I glanced at Wade's nightstand. We still hadn't found our wedding picture, and Gabby said she hadn't touched it. Where could it be? Could I really have become that forgetful?

Sirens sounded in the distance and sped ever closer until they seemed right outside.

I remembered all those shows I'd seen where policemen came to the house of someone who'd died. My heart started pounding. I hurried to the window and peeked out.

In Rebecca's driveway, the flashing lights of several cruisers and an ambulance warned something terrible had happened.

21

Leslie: March 1979

I rubbed the cash Don had given me like a grotesque version of the security blanket I had clung to as a child. It promised freedom, a life unencumbered by shame or the demands of an infant. The chance to be a dancer.

I never imagined I'd have an abortion. What if Peggy was right and this fetus—this *baby*—was already a little person? How could I live with myself if I killed my own child?

One thing was certain—I needed to decide soon.

The phone rang as I pulled on jeans and a sweater. Who could be calling this early in the morning?

"Leslie," Mom yelled from downstairs. "It's a Mr. Váradi from the Chicago Ballet."

I clasped my hands to my chest, suddenly super awake. Was he going to offer me a position in his company? I hurried down the steps into the living room. "Hello?" I said as I picked up the receiver.

"Hi, Leslie. Bence Váradi here. I talked to Ms. Hall, our head artistic director, and we'd like to offer you a position with our company."

Warmth flooded my body. It was really happening. I was going to become a professional ballerina!

"Miss Gardner?"

"Yes, I'm here," I said, my heart galloping like a racehorse bearing down on the finish line.

"I spoke to Ms. Hall about your scheduling conflict this summer, and she's fine with you not joining us until the end of July. However, she said August or September would definitely be too late. Could you join us right after your summer intensives program?"

I glanced at my belly. "I guess so."

"Fabulous," he said, his accent stronger than ever. He went over rehearsal times, salary, benefits, and minimum health standards. "Are you ready to sign a contract?" he finally said.

I sank onto our mustard-colored couch, rubbing the back of my neck. "I should discuss it with my parents first." I glanced at Dad who was sitting on the other side of the end table.

He smiled.

"I've also been accepted into Northern Illinois University's School of Theater and Dance."

"Talking to your parents is perfectly understandable," Mr. Váradi said. "But don't take too long to get back to us. If you're not going to join us, we'll need to find another dancer. Can you give us your final answer one week from today?"

One week to decide my future—coed, teen mom, or professional ballerina. I swallowed. "Sure."

"So?" Dad said as I hung up.

I leaned back and grabbed a sunburst pillow to cover my expanding lap. "Chicago Ballet offered me a position with their company."

"Wow." He nodded, a gleam in his eye. "That's quite an accomplishment."

"That's great, honey," Mom called from the kitchen, the aroma of steamed ham drifting into the living room. "But what about college? John, don't you think she should get her degree first?"

Dad tapped a pencil against his newspaper. "That might

be wise. Prepare for life after ballet." He studied me. "But it's up to you. What do *you* want?"

I tangled my fingers in the soft yarn on the crocheted pillow. "I'm not sure. But I've got until next Tuesday to decide."

❄

At a red light on our way to school, Frankie whipped off his aviator sunglasses and stared me down. "Are you going with me or not?"

I fooled with the car door. Should I go with my friend, who'd always been there for me? Or the father of my child, who betrayed me but wanted me back? Either way, Frankie was right—the dance was five days away and I needed to decide.

The light turned green, and Frankie stepped on the gas. "Someone else asked me."

My stomach hardened. Wait. Was I . . . jealous? "Who?" I said, trying to sound casual.

"Cheryl Richardson."

"Cheryl Richardson?" I pictured the busty brunette. "She's cute."

"I'd rather go with you."

Before I had a chance to respond, the Austin Allegro sputtered to a stop, and Frankie jumped out and lifted the hood.

I followed, stuffing my hands into my pockets to protect them from the cold.

"You can stay in the car," he said, tinkering under the hood. "I'll have us out of here in no time."

"I don't mind. I like the fresh air."

"Yeah, I know the car stinks. I gotta replace the clutch."

So that's why it smelled like burnt newspapers. I studied the snow still lining the road. "Remember when we got stuck in that snowdrift on the way home from Terri's party?"

"How could I forget?" Frankie said, his head buried in the engine. "You were in high heels and a skirt and got the ridiculous idea of trying to help push the car out."

"I was supposed to be home by midnight."

"I think your parents would've understood."

"But you have to admit," I said, sighing, "the snow was breathtaking. It made it all worth it."

"Breathtaking is one word for it." Frankie wiped his hands on his charcoal shirt, a red Cadillac printed on the front.

"Why'd you say you sold the Coupe again?"

"I didn't." Frankie slammed the hood of the Allegro shut. "Dang, I'm good." He jumped back in the sedan and started the ignition. "I guess you heard Sarah finally realized what a turkey Don is and broke up with him. I may be just a gearhead, but I know how to treat a girl better than that moron."

I clicked my seatbelt. Had Frankie ever had a girlfriend? "I made a decision about the spring dance," I said, suddenly realizing I had.

"You're not going with Casanova, are you? I'd rather see you go with a lame-footed frog than that doofus."

Where did Frankie come up with these things? "He did ask me two days ago."

Frankie groaned. "Of course he asked you. Sarah dumped his stupid butt and now he's scrambling for a date. Maybe he even realizes what an idiot he was for letting you go. That doesn't mean you should go with him."

"Doesn't it?"

Frankie's jaw dropped. "You can't be serious."

"I'm not," I said, smiling. "I'm going with you."

❄

I ran my hands over a satin dress on the department store rack that looked like something a princess might wear. Could a pregnant princess pull it off?

"Try it on," Terri said, grabbing the hanger.

I found an open fitting room and pulled the coral pink gown over my head.

"Need me to zip you up?"

I yanked open the curtain, and Terri pulled up the zipper, my flesh catching. "Ow!" I said and rubbed my back.

"Sorry." She grimaced. "You've gained weight."

Struggling to breathe, I studied my appearance in the mirror. Where my flat stomach used to be was a rounding pouch, overly emphasized by the embroidered, form-fitting fabric.

"What do you think?" Terri said.

My body felt as heavy as it looked. "I can't go to the dance looking like this." I turned around so Terri could unzip me then slumped onto the triangular bench.

"We'll get one that's looser in the middle."

"I don't know. Maybe I should sit this one out. It's not worth it."

"No way, José. I'll be right back."

As she headed back to the racks, I peeled off the dress and examined my belly in the mirror. Time was ticking. I couldn't hide this pregnancy much longer. I was surprised I'd been able to hide it this long.

A few minutes later, Terri handed several dresses over the curtain. "One of these should work."

I tried on the first one, a lacy frock that hung on my body like the drapes in our living room. I stepped out of the fitting room and frowned at Terri. "I feel like a frumpy curtain," I said with a weak smile.

She laughed. "Unfortunately, I have to agree."

I tried on the next, a floor-length lavender dress with a ruffled square neckline. I tied the ribbons around the empire waist and did a twirl, the skirt flaring out. "This one has potential," I said as I opened the curtain.

"That's so you," Terri said, her eyes lighting. "And it screams 'Springtime in Paris.'"

"Springtime. Yeah, right." I chuckled. "Is it still supposed to be in the twenties on Saturday?"

"That's the high. Lows are expected to be in the single digits."

"Great," I said, shivering. "I hope they pump up the heat in the gym." I examined my figure in the mirror from every angle. Besides a slight swell, it wasn't obvious I was pregnant—I just looked a little bloated. "I think this is the one," I said. "But I'll try on one or two more, just to be sure." I pulled off the dress, put on the next one, and stepped back out. "Did I tell you Frankie proposed?"

Terri's eyes widened. "What? No, you did *not*. When?"

"A couple months ago. When he found out I was pregnant."

Terri flung out her arms. "A couple *months* ago? And you're just telling me *now*?" She huffed and shook her head. "We've really got to work on your failure to communicate huge news like 'I'm pregnant' or 'my boyfriend proposed.'"

I decided the spaghetti-strap gown I had tried on was a no.

"Is there anything else you need to tell me?" Terri said.

"Well, Bence Váradi called this morning and offered me a position with their company."

"Les! Are you kidding me? Why didn't you tell me?"

"I'm sorry, I was planning to. I just . . . hadn't gotten around to it. I was hoping he called you too."

She ran a hand through her dark, feathered hair. "Not yet."

"He might've called after you left for school. He called me really early. Maybe your mom will have a message for you when you get home."

"I hope so," she said, blowing a strand of hair out of her face. "So?" Her eyes twinkled. "Did you accept his offer?"

"I told him I had to think about it, what with NIU and everything." I gestured toward my belly.

Terri's mouth fell open. "You told him you were pregnant?"

"Of course not," I said, changing into a pretty polka-dot dress.

"So you're telling me someone handed you your dream life on a silver platter and you told him you had to think about it?"

I stepped out of the fitting room. "My mom wants me to go to college first."

"And your dad?"

"Said it was up to me," I said. "Mr. Váradi gave me a week to decide."

"College is one thing, but having a baby is another. Can you even afford to raise a child right now?"

I closed the curtain, the cloth a measly barrier between us.

"You don't have a job," Terri said. "You don't have any money saved. You'd have to quit school, start working full time."

Where would I work? The only thing I was trained to do was dance.

"Either that or beg your parents to fork out money."

I slipped out of my dress. Could I really ask my parents to support my illegitimate child? I hadn't even summoned up the courage to tell them I'd had sex, much less that I was pregnant.

"Don't let Peggy—or anyone else for that matter—make you feel guilty. It's *your* body, so it's *your* choice."

Was it? I pressed a hand to my abdomen. Sometimes it seemed like everyone *but* me was going to decide my future. Mom was telling me to go to college. Peggy said to give my baby to her aunt and uncle. Don and Terri wanted me to have an abortion, although for different reasons. Don probably didn't want the responsibility, while Terri just wanted us to dance together. I pulled on my street clothes and let her in.

She plopped down on the bench. "So. Tell me about Frankie's proposal. Details, Les, details."

"Well, for starters," I said, pulling on my boots. "He's not my boyfriend, or at least wasn't then. And I didn't tell you earlier because I thought it was a pity proposal, like 'Don's obviously not going to marry you. Guess I should.'"

Terri stared at me. "Les, guys don't propose out of pity."

"They do if the girl's pregnant."

"Not when she's pregnant with someone else's child."

I pressed my lips together as I hung up the last dress. Maybe she had a point.

"Now if *Don* proposed," she said, crossing her legs, "you might assume he was offering to marry you out of some sense of obligation. But the baby isn't Frankie's. He just has the hots for you. Has for a long time."

My cheeks flamed.

"A proposal from Frankie might even tempt *me*," she said in her Farrah Fawcett voice. "Not that I want to settle down anytime soon."

I tried to smooth my tousled hair. "You think I should've said yes?"

"Of course not. You're too young to get married and have kids. But you could at least start dating him. There'll be plenty of time for marriage later." She grabbed the dress we'd decided on and headed for the cash register. "Are you excited about going to the dance with him? A lot of other girls asked him."

A *lot* of other girls? "He mentioned Cheryl."

Terri nodded. "I figured. I overheard her in the cafeteria describing him as a stone cold fox."

I guessed he *was* really good looking under all that hair.

"And she's not the only one. But of course he only has eyes for you," Terri said in a sing-song voice.

"Did I tell you my parents are planning to take us to a beach in Mexico in August?" I said as the saleslady rang up my purchase.

Terri's eyes widened. "Ooh. Can I come?"

I sighed. "I don't even know if I'm going." I turned away from the cashier and lowered my voice. "I'll be eight or nine months along by then. Can you imagine me going into labor on our family vacation?" I cringed. "I'd rather die than tell them I'm pregnant, but how much longer am I going to be able to hide this?"

Terri gripped my arm. "Get rid of it now," she whispered, "and you won't have to tell them. You won't have to tell anyone. It's time to take care of this and move on with your life."

I leaned against the counter and let out my breath. "Maybe it is."

"I know it is." Terri grabbed the bag and pulled me toward the exit. "Let's make the appointment now—no more stalling. We can call from a pay phone on our way to the movie theater."

"Movie theater?" I stopped mid-stride. "We've got jazz and technique classes tonight."

"We'll tell Ms. Petipa we're sick."

I gave Terri my are-you-serious look.

"Hey, for you at least, it's actually true."

"Not really. My morning sickness is practically gone. And it's not really sick—"

"Same difference."

"What about our parents? What are we gonna tell them?"

"That we worked really hard getting ready for *Giselle*, and now we need a break. Just one night off." She skipped down the stairs to the main level of the mall. "Believe me. They'll understand."

❄

"I'd like to make an appointment for a friend," Terri said into the pay phone.

I sagged against the cool glass booth. It would feel good to finally be free of this burden.

"She's fifteen weeks pregnant."

A frazzled-looking woman led a little boy out of the mall across the parking lot, one eye on the overcast sky.

"Two o'clock in the afternoon next Tuesday?" Terri put one hand over the receiver. "Does that work?" she said to me.

That was the same day I needed to get back to Bence Váradi about the company position. "We don't have school that day," I remembered.

"So you won't miss any classes."

"But my parents will wonder where I am."

"Just tell them you're going to my house."

I studied the black clouds advancing on us and nodded.

"She'll be there." Terri hung up. "It's all settled," she said, looping her arm through mine. "One week from today, you'll be a free woman."

A cold breeze blew by, leaving goose bumps on my arms. Why didn't I *feel* like I'd be free?

22

Shannon: December 2014

I stared at the empty space in the bed next to me. Wade still wasn't home? I glanced at the clock. 7:56 a.m. I sat up, running through the horrible events of last night. Rebecca had been beaten by an unknown assailant and was now in the hospital fighting for her life. The police were looking for her fiancé Eric.

Sinking back onto the pillow, I remembered that a few weeks before Wade mentioned he and Margaret might go to their parents' cabin in Wisconsin for a couple days. I hadn't realized it had become a definite plan, but maybe he'd forgotten to tell me.

Or I'd forgotten he told me.

I shook my head. Pregnancy brain was really becoming a problem. Between Rebecca's assault, the Down syndrome diagnosis, and all the last-minute play preparations, I was starting to lose my mind. Not to mention all the literal things I'd lost recently . . . like what had happened to our minivan?

I hopped out of bed and scratched my neck. If Wade was in Wisconsin, why didn't he remind me when I'd texted him last night? He should have known I was worried. As much as

I loved his sense of humor—life was never dull around him—sometimes he took things too far.

Lumbering to the bathroom, I plopped onto the cool toilet seat.

Something felt off. Smelled off. Like hot copper. I peered at the toilet paper.

Blood.

My throat constricted. I dropped the scarlet tissue into the water and put a hand on my stomach. It was flatter than it had been in months. Years, even. Was I having a miscarriage?

I put a tingling hand to my forehead. Maybe it wasn't that serious. After all, I'd read that lots of women experience light bleeding during pregnancy. But why was my stomach smaller?

I wiped again.

More blood.

I wrestled a pad out of the back of the cabinet and grabbed my phone from the nightstand.

"OB-GYN Associates, Norma speaking," an older woman said. "How may I help you?"

"Is Dr. Beck there?"

"I'm sorry, she isn't in yet. Can I take a message?"

I lowered myself to the edge of the bed. "I'm spotting, and my stomach's flatter. I think I had a miscarriage."

"I'm sorry to hear that," Norma said like she meant it. "Let me get a nurse for you."

I scooted back against the headboard and tried to slow my breathing. I stared at the corner of my nightstand. Where was Lily's picture?

"This is Jill," a younger woman said. "How far along are you?"

I searched around the bed.

"Ma'am?"

"Sorry," I said, forcing myself to stop and focus. "Nineteen weeks."

"And your name? I want to pull your chart."

"Shannon Henry."

"Bleeding can be caused by a lot of things in your second

trimester," Jill said over the sound of a metal drawer opening. "How much blood is it?"

"Just a little."

"Not enough to fill a pad within an hour?"

I tugged on my bottom lip. "I don't think so."

"And how long have you been spotting?"

"I just noticed it now."

"Any pain or cramping?"

"Not really," I said, putting a hand on my stomach.

"Any contractions or other labor symptoms like nausea, diarrhea, or back pain?"

Contractions? Wasn't it too early for those? "No."

"You said your last name's Henry?"

"Yes."

"I can't find your chart for some reason. Maybe someone else pulled it. In any case, Norma's telling me there was a cancellation at 3:30 today. Does that time work for you?"

I'd have to make arrangements for the kids to stay late at school if Wade was still away, but this appointment couldn't wait. "That's fine."

"Great," she said, too perkily. "We'll put you down for 3:30. However . . ." Her tone grew serious. "If the bleeding increases or you have any cramping, go straight to the emergency room."

❄

I was beginning to hate the sight of doctors, or at least the sound of them.

Lily didn't make it.

Your baby has Down syndrome.

Staring at the overcast sky from behind the glass doors of the school, I sipped my ginger and ginseng tea that promised to be stress-reducing—it wasn't working—and breathed in the scent of cinnamon and orange peels. What would Dr. Beck say today, "Yes, you did have a miscarriage"?

A student opened the door next to me and frigid air rushed at me.

I shivered and glanced at my watch. Only an hour left until I needed to leave, and I still had to get some things ready for opening night tonight. Would my students remember their lines? Would we have more problems with the sound system? My brain couldn't handle any more questions. I sighed and trudged into the auditorium.

Ravi grinned at me on his way out. "See ya tonight, Miss Lennox."

Dizziness circled me. Miss *Lennox*? "It's Mrs. Hen—"

The doors swung shut.

I shook my head. Ravi was always goofing around. He probably discovered my maiden name and decided to use it to get a laugh. Too bad I wasn't in a laughing mood.

I dragged myself onto the black stage. Where was the costume I'd been hemming earlier for our not-so-tiny Tim? If he—or I—had misplaced it, we might not be able to find it in time.

After searching longer than I had time to, I finally found it in an unswept corner behind the stage curtain. I shook off the dust, smoothed out the wrinkles, and hung it on the rack downstairs.

Tiny Tim's crutch clattered onto the cement floor.

I picked it up and leaned it against the wall. What had happened to my own special needs child? Just when I was beginning to fall in love with her, I'd lost her.

Just like I'd lost Lily.

I sank onto a folding chair, tears rushing into my eyes. Had I caused this miscarriage with all my worrying about the Down syndrome diagnosis plus all the stress of the play? Maybe God was punishing me for not wanting her at first, or at least not being sure if I wanted her.

I wiped my nose and called the friend who'd always been there for me.

"This is Gabby Diaz," her voicemail said. "If you have ice cream or dark chocolate or want to take me out to dinner, please leave a message at the beep."

"Hey Gabby," I said, my voice scratchy. "Sorry for calling so many times. I guess you broke your phone or dropped it into the toilet again."

I smiled despite myself. Gabby could go through phones quicker than a baby could go through diapers.

My smile disappeared. Baby diapers. Would I ever get to change this baby's diapers?

❄

"I'm Shannon Henry, here to see Dr. Beck," I said to Norma, who was sitting behind the desk.

"We still haven't been able to find your file. Could it be under another name?"

"Maybe Lennox, my maiden name?"

Norma flipped through some hanging folders. "Here it is. Did you get married recently? I'll have to update our records."

I shook my head slowly. "I've been married seven years. Maybe you filed it under the name on my credit card? My Citibank card's still under my maiden name. I keep meaning to update it but haven't gotten around to it."

"No problem," she said, shrugging her shoulders. "I'll update it now. In the meantime, have a seat. A nurse will call you back shortly."

I sank into a black leather chair and pressed my hands to my stomach. Wade needed to know what was going on. Why couldn't I get a hold of him? Maybe he wasn't getting reception in Wisconsin or forgot to bring his phone. I tried dialing my in-laws again but just got the busy signal.

Half an hour later, a nurse appeared and led me to the back where she checked my weight and blood pressure. I changed into a hospital gown and climbed onto the patient chair in a room that reeked of medical disinfectant. Crossing and uncrossing my arms and legs, I waited, hoping for the best but fearing the worst.

Someone knocked.

"Come in," I called.

Dr. Beck opened the door and did a double-take. "Shannon." She smiled. "It's you. I was surprised when the nurse told me a Mrs. Henry was here to see me." She took a seat on the rolling stool. "Congratulations. When did you get married?"

I squinted at her. "I've been married seven years now. You've met my husband Wade multiple times. Don't you remember?"

She rubbed her chin.

"Never mind," I said. "I think I had a miscarriage."

"I'm sorry to hear that." She scooted closer. "How far along were you?"

"I would've been twenty weeks on Monday."

Her mouth fell open. "Why didn't you come in earlier?"

"It just happened this morning," I said, my throat thick. "I called as soon as—"

"No, I mean why haven't you been coming to see me every month? Did you just find out you're pregnant?"

My head jerked back. "I've been coming to you since I was eight weeks pregnant."

Dr. Beck stood and paced. "Miss Lennox—"

"Henry."

"Right." Dr. Beck flipped through my file. "Our records indicate you haven't been to our office since several months ago when you got a Pap smear."

I opened my mouth, but no words came out.

"There's definitely no record of you being pregnant." She studied me a moment and then sat back down. Her expression softened. "Could you have gone to another office?"

"Another office?" I stood, my legs wobbly. "You did my ultrasound here just last Saturday."

Dr. Beck staggered backward. "Our techs do the ultrasounds, and I don't remember seeing the report."

"You helped with this one since our daughter has Down syndrome."

Dr. Beck's face went white. "Now *that* I would remember." She reached for the doorknob. "Can you wait here a moment?" She scurried away as if her feet were on fire.

The room spun—walls, posters, and instruments whirling around me. I dropped my head into my hands and tried to breathe. I had to get out of here. Had to talk to Wade.

Fumbling for my clothes, I stumbled onto the cold floor. I dressed and dashed out before anyone came back. Had I imagined this pregnancy to help me get over losing Lily? But how had Wade imagined it too?

❄

Minutes later, I pulled into the preschool and made a break for the bright red awning.

Dr. Beck was wrong. I'd find our ultrasound pictures and bills from my prenatal visits and march back in there to prove I was pregnant. Or at least had been.

I stepped into the building and stopped in my tracks.

A blonde girl sat at Camila's desk.

I ran a hand through my hair. "Is Camila sick today?"

"She's visiting her family in Brazil. I'll be covering for her the next few days."

I exhaled. Everything was as it should be here. I hurried down the hallway past the mural of zoo animals and imagined wrapping my arms around my babies in just a few moments. Only a day or two had passed since I'd seen them, but somehow it felt like an eternity.

"Deck the halls with boughs of holly," Miss Jing sang as she helped the kids make snowflakes out of Play-Doh, the smell of salt and flour permeating the air. "'Tis the season to be jolly." She spotted me standing at the door and brushed a strand of black hair out of her face. "May I help you?"

"I'm looking for the twins. Are they in the bathroom with Mrs. Morales?"

"The twins?"

"Katy and Daniel. Their grandma dropped them off this morning."

"Um . . ." Jing stood. "Let me see if Mrs. Morales can help you. I think there's been a misunderstanding."

"Did Wade pick them up?"

Jing looked confused. "I'll be right back," she mumbled and disappeared into the bathroom.

I twirled my hair. Had something happened to them?

Maritza strode toward me. "I'm Mrs. Morales. May I help you?"

My chest tightened. Why was she introducing herself? "Where are Katy and Daniel?"

"I'm sorry, Ms.—"

"Maritza," I stammered. "You know me."

She lifted her eyebrows. "I'm afraid I don't remember meeting you. Maybe you can refresh my memory?"

"I drop my kids off here every day!"

Maritza's eyes widened.

"Jing, tell her," I said. "The twins have been coming here since August."

"Ma'am." Maritza moved toward me. "We don't have any twins in this—"

"How can you say that? You know and love my kids. Katy loves to play dress up and Daniel loves board games, and just a few weeks ago you called me when Daniel fell and you thought he might have broken his arm."

"I'm afraid that's not—"

"Stop it!" I pounded my fist on the door. "Where are my children?"

The preschoolers gawked at me.

I leaned over the door. "Emma," I said, reining in my voice. "You know Katy. She spent the night at your house last weekend. Remember?"

Emma's eyes were huge saucers. She shook her head.

"But—"

Maritza moved between us. "Ma'am, I'm going to have to ask you to step into the office. I can't allow you to scare the children."

"Scare the children?"

"Maybe you have the wrong preschool and I can redirect you to the right one? Did you mean to go to the Children's Academy in Lombard?"

"No! I did not—"

"Is there someone I can call for you? A friend or family member who can come pick you up?"

"Maritza, I know you," I said, my voice shaking with each word. "I can't believe you're acting like we've never met. I know your husband."

"I'm very sorry." Maritza's eyes flashed to the parents coming down the hall. "But you need to step into the office, or I'll have to call security." She reached for the phone on the wall.

I staggered to the side and wrung my hands. I couldn't get arrested, not when I needed to find Katy and Daniel. I ran past the other parents and grabbed my phone out of my purse.

No messages from Wade or Gabby. I dialed Wade's parents. Busy signal.

I threw back my head and wailed. *Where are my children?*

A bearded man and his son stopped mid-stride, their eyes wide. "Can I help you, miss?" the man said.

Heat flushed my face. I shook my head. I must be having a nightmare, like all the others. This couldn't be happening.

I pinched myself. It hurt.

I scrambled for my keys. No luck.

I knelt and dumped everything in my purse onto the floor. Coins spun in all directions.

A wide-eyed teacher and little boy hurried past me.

I grabbed my keys, shoved my wallet into my bag, and bolted to my car. I turned on the ignition and froze. Where was I going?

I tried my in-laws again. No answer. Maybe they were on their way to my house.

I sped home, dialing Wade's number with my free hand for the sixth or seventh time that day.

"Lady," a gruff male voice said. "You need to stop calling."

I gasped. It wasn't Wade.

"Like I told you last night," the stranger said, "you've got the wrong number."

I gritted my teeth. "I think I know my own husband's phone number. What did you do with him and why do you have his phone?"

He snorted. "Lady, I don't know your husband from Adam. This number's been mine for six years." He swore at me and hung up.

I hunted for Officer Schmitt's card in my purse, my eyes

darting between the passenger seat and the truck in front of me. I held up the card and almost rear-ended the truck. At the next stop light, I punched in the numbers.

"Villa Park police station," a young man said.

"I'd like to report three missing persons."

23

Shannon: December 2014

I flung the door open and charged into our house.

Gabby was curled up on the sofa with a bowl of ice cream watching TV. "Shannon, so glad you're home," she said. "You gotta look at this guy in this movie. He looks like someone I see every day on the L. Could be his twin."

"Gabby," I breathed. The pressure melted off my shoulders. "Thank God you're here. You won't believe what just happened."

She sat up. "What?" She turned off the TV and fixed her eyes on me. "Did you get in a car accident or something? Are you okay?"

"I'm fine," I said, looking around. "But where's Wade? Is he home?"

She squinted. "Who's Wade?"

My legs went limp. I grabbed the armchair.

Gabby rose. "You look terrible."

"He's my husband, of course," I stammered.

Her gaze clouded. She rubbed her forehead. "Your . . . *husband?*"

My whole body started shaking.

Her eyes grew wide. "What's going on? You're starting to freak me out. I think you need to sit—"

Adrenaline coursed through me. I raced upstairs to the twins' bedroom. "Katy! Daniel!"

"Shannon, wait," Gabby said, on my heels. "What are you doing?"

I shoved open their door.

Gray walls and a black bedspread with a white lily pattern had taken over their room.

I spun around. "Where are Katy and Daniel's beds? What happened to their stuffed animals and Winnie-the-Pooh bedspreads? Who did this?"

Gabby's mouth fell open. "Winnie-the-Pooh? What are you talking about? My room's looked like—"

"*You* don't live here."

She blinked. "I don't live here?"

"Of course not," I said, lifting my hands.

"Please come sit down. Take it easy." She put a hand on my forehead. "Did you hit your head? I'll call 911."

I jerked away. "No, I did *not* hit my head."

"It's okay. You're going to be all right."

I collapsed on the bed and took a deep breath. "You think I've lost my mind too, don't you?"

Gabby sat beside me and put a hand over mine. "I don't know," she said in an uncertain tone. "But you're scaring me. Tell me what happened."

"I went to the preschool to pick up Katy and Daniel."

"I don't want you to smack me or anything," Gabby said. "But who are Katy and Daniel again?"

My knees wobbled as I got up.

"For crying out loud, calm down, Shannon. I'm your friend who's trying to help you. Whoever they are, I'll help you find them."

"*Whoever* they are?"

She gripped my shoulders and shook me. "You have to snap out of this. I'm not your enemy, and I'm trying to understand, but you're not making any sense."

I jerked away. "My kids are missing," I said, digging my

fingernails into the palms of my hands. "And I can't find Wade. I need to find them."

Gabby whirled and punched the door. "Is this some kind of sick joke or something?"

If she didn't believe me, no one would. I burst into tears.

"Okay, Shannon. Not a joke," she said and hugged me tightly.

I tensed.

"But I really don't know what you're talking about. You're not married. You don't have kids."

I reeled and gripped the headboard to draw strength. When had everyone gone insane? "You were the maid of honor in our wedding," I said, my breath coming in short bursts.

She looked frightened.

I needed to get to my in-laws' house. Maybe the twins were still there. I hurried downstairs into the kitchen.

"Where are you going?" Gabby hounded me. "Let me come with you. It's not safe for you to drive when you're acting like this."

I slammed the door and dashed to the car. A blast of wind choked me. I must be having a nightmare again. Either that or I *was* losing my mind.

"Wait," Gabby yelled.

I jumped into the sedan and started it, the new car smell punching me in the nose.

"We wish you a merry Christmas," a choir sang from my dashboard. "We wish you a merry—"

I silenced them then flipped on my headlights. In ten minutes, I'd be at my mother-in-law's. Even if she didn't know where Wade and the kids were, at least she wouldn't think I was crazy.

Gabby banged on the window. "Open the door."

I stared at my best friend. She didn't know who Wade was. *Why do I remember who she is?* With one last look at her, I put the car in reverse and backed out of the driveway.

A school bus swerved, blasting its horn.

I gasped and slammed on the brakes. Taking a deep breath, I checked my rearview mirror and looked over my shoulder before inching onto the glassy road. I shifted to Drive and swung left onto Division Street.

Barren elm trees outlined in white stood on both sides, spindly skeletons of what had been, silent sentinels of what was to come. Snowlike white ashes landed on my windshield and then just as quickly disappeared.

❄

I pulled into the driveway of the familiar brick home, grabbed my purse and hurried to the door, snow crunching under my boots. I rang the doorbell and paced back and forth. "God, please let them be here," I cried.

A man with dark eyebrows and gray, receding hair opened the door. "Can I help you?" he said in a deep voice.

He must be one of Dad's friends or a relative I'd never met. Maybe Mom's literary agent. "Is Leslie here? She's not expecting me."

"She's upstairs getting dressed—we're about to go out to dinner with some friends."

"I need to talk to her." I brushed past him and made a beeline for the stairs.

He blocked my path. "Why don't you wait in the living room?" His mouth tilted up, but his eyes frowned. "If you give me your name, I'll let her know you're here."

I pursed my lips. Who did this man think he was? "Shannon," I muttered. Perching on the edge of a charcoal couch, I blinked at the purple pillows. What had Mom done to her living room?

The stranger in the starched suit headed for the stairs but paused and turned back to me. "I'm sorry, I didn't introduce myself." He held out his hand. "I'm Vince Neuman, Leslie's husband."

I gulped for air.

"Are you okay?" he said, his brow creased. "You look pale."

I shook myself out of my stupor. "There must be some mistake," I said, wobbling to my feet.

"Mistake?" He pursed his lips. "What kind of mistake?"

"You're Leslie's *husband*?"

"For over twenty years now."

I narrowed my eyes. "Frank's her husband."

Vince's posture stiffened. "You must have the wrong house. My wife only has one husband and that man is me."

"I've been here countless times!"

Just then, Leslie appeared on the stairs. She wore a pencil dress, her hair up in a bun, and peered at me with bloodshot eyes.

"Honey," Vince said, offering her his hand. "This lady is looking for a Leslie, but she has the wrong Leslie and the wrong house."

"I was looking for *you*, Mom."

Her head jolted back. "I'm afraid there's been some mistake," she said in a hoarse voice. "I don't know you."

My mouth fell open. "What do you mean, you don't know me?" The words rushed out. "I'm your daughter-in-law."

"My husband's right," she stammered. "You must be in the wrong house. We don't have any children."

24

Leslie: December 2014

I studied my reflection in the antique makeup mirror, a hollowness in my chest. My fifty-three-year-old skin looked washed out, especially against the unforgiving black of my dress. At least the dark color made me look trim. That and never having had children helped, I supposed.

But somehow it didn't seem like a fair exchange. What I wouldn't give to have a son and a daughter, maybe even some grandchildren to read to and snuggle with. Terri was expecting her third any day now.

The doorbell rang.

I picked up the cigarette lying in the crystal ashtray and inhaled, smoke curling through the air. Vince would get the door. It was probably just the UPS guy with a shipment of costumes for my studio.

I put on my pearl Audrey Hepburn earrings, just one of many gifts from Vince. He was such a generous provider. I should be happy.

But something always seemed missing. What was the meaning of my life, my real purpose? Besides entertaining people for a few hours, how had I made the world a better place? I had driven myself so hard. For what?

Looking in the mirror again, I sighed. The gray eyes a former boyfriend once compared to misty mountains looked as dingy and lifeless as the ashes I flicked off the end of my Virginia Slims cigarette. I closed my eyes and pinched the bridge of my nose. Maybe I was just getting old. I should be grateful I had a dutiful husband.

I slipped on black pumps, popped a piece of mint gum into my mouth—Vince despised smoky kisses—and headed for the stairs. It sounded like he was arguing with someone, an assertive edge to his usually warm voice.

I tiptoed down a few steps to see who was here while remaining out of sight, but the last step creaked and Vince spotted me.

❄

"Of course you have children," the striking redhead said.

I gripped the banister, the oak slippery against my hands.

"I'm sorry, miss." Vince moved toward the woman, his eyes declaring he meant business. "But I'm going to have to ask you to leave."

She was clearly in no condition to leave. "It's okay, honey." I attempted a smile. "Let's try to get to the bottom of this . . . misunderstanding. The poor girl's beside herself." If only she really were my daughter-in-law, and I could alleviate her concerns. Heal whatever was broken.

"My name is Shannon Henry," she said, her jaw set. "And I'm married to your son."

Now I knew she was out of her mind. "I don't have a son," I said, in the gentlest tone possible. "And my married name is Neuman. My maiden name was Gardner."

"Yes! Your maiden name *was* Gardner. But your name changed to Henry when you married Frank thirty-five years ago."

Goosebumps rose on my arms. Did I know this woman? She knew about Frankie and the feelings I'd once had for him.

Feelings I still struggled with from time to time. Memories I still daydreamed about. "Frankie and I are just friends, have been since we were kids," I said, but I wondered if Vince suspected anything.

"Okay, miss," he said, leading the woman toward the door. "You need to go now."

"Mom!" She broke free. "How can you not know me? How can you not know Wade, your own son?"

A chill raced up my spine. Did she say *Wade*?

"What about the twins? You adore them. What happened to you and to this house?" she said, her eyes wet. "And who is this man?"

"I'm sorry, but I don't know what you're talking about. Although I've always liked the name Wade." I remembered the baby names book Frankie had given me all those years ago. "I might've named my son that . . . if I'd ever had one."

She stepped toward me. "You *do* have a son."

My vision blurred. How I wished she was right.

"I know you, Mom." The woman reached for my hand. "I know you were born and raised in this house and later inherited it from your parents when they died in a car accident."

I pulled away. I must be having a nightmare. How else could this stranger know what happened to my parents? Unless she was a friend of the family. But why would she pretend to be my daughter-in-law?

"I know you were a dancer when you were young, but you gave it up after high school. And what about your daughter, Margaret?"

"Margaret?" I stammered. "That's what I always wanted to name a girl. After Margot—"

"You *did* name your daughter that."

"No, I didn't," I said, my muscles tense. I needed to make this woman understand. "And I didn't give up dancing after high school." I scanned the photographs on the wall: me as Swanhilde in *Coppèlia*, the winter fairy in *Cinderella*, and the Snow Queen in *The Nutcracker*. "I joined a company after I graduated and was a principal dancer for years. When I retired at thirty, I started my own studio." I peered at a picture of me as Giselle my senior year. "What . . . year . . . was your husband born?"

"1979," she whispered. "August 31, 1979."

A week after my baby had been due.

25

Shannon: December 2014

Leslie sank to the steps, as if I'd just told her someone had died.

"Don't listen to this woman." Vince sat beside her and wrapped his arm around her. "She doesn't know what she's talking about."

Seeing another man being intimate with my mother-in-law was giving me the creeps.

"I got pregnant in high school," she said softly, her eyes fixed on me. "But I never had the child."

Fear gripped the deepest part of me. She was lying—she had to be.

"I . . ." Tears pooled in her eyes. "Had an abortion."

I shook my head. "You couldn't have."

"I did," she said gently. "And because of complications caused by it, I was never able to have children."

"That's not possible," I spat out. "You had the baby—a son. I met him ten years ago, married him seven years ago. He's an amazing husband, a gifted teacher, and a wonderful daddy to our children."

Leslie winced. "Grandchildren too?" She wrapped her arms around herself, and Vince drew her close and kissed the top of her head.

I cringed and wanted to leave but felt my phone in my coat pocket. "I'll show you a picture," I said, realizing I'd been carrying proof with me all this time. I pulled out my phone and flipped through the photos: Gabby, my family, some of my students. My fingers turned to ice. Where were the pictures of Wade and the kids? "I don't know what happened to them," I muttered, flipping through the photos again and again.

"Honey," Vince said to Leslie, barely loud enough for me to hear. "This woman obviously needs help."

Leslie bit her lip.

"Miss," he said turning to me, "I can assure you my wife is telling the truth. She has no children or grandchildren." He stood and put a hand on her shoulder. "And now, if you'll excuse us, I'd like to talk to my wife. Alone."

I wasn't going anywhere. Not until I got more answers. But my legs couldn't hold me up any longer. I staggered into the living room, dropped onto their loveseat, and cradled a pillow in my empty lap. Next to me, a crimson poppy bowed its head and stared forlornly at its lifeless petals that had fallen onto the ebony end table. "Did I just dream the last ten years of my life?" I said after a moment to no one in particular. "The *best* years of my life?"

The grandfather clock struck six o'clock.

"Wade is . . . my dearest love," I whispered. "My best friend. My heater. My hero. I always criticize him for little things, stupid things, really," I said, glancing at Leslie. "But I can't imagine anyone more perfect for me. Or a better father for our children."

A tear tumbled down Leslie's cheek.

"And Katy and Daniel . . . and Lily." I rubbed my wrist where my charm bracelet used to be. "They're gone," I cried, my shoulders heaving. "My babies are gone." I curled into a tight ball, swallowed up with sadness.

Wade's body would warm me. Wake me.

Katy would burrow into my chest saying, "Mommy."

Daniel would wrap his arms around my neck and squeeze.

I straightened and gripped the armrest. "This can't be happening. This must be one of those nightmares where I lose Wade but wake up to find him lying right beside me, safe and sound. He'll fold me into his arms and kiss my head." I started pacing. "We'll laugh about this in the morning. Katy and Daniel will come running into our room, bouncing on our bed, asking me to make them pancakes." I slapped myself, and my cheek stung. "Wake up!" I smacked myself harder. "Wake up!"

26

Leslie: December 2014

Vince closed the door behind the woman who claimed to be my daughter-in-law with the finality of a funeral director closing a coffin.

I rose from the stairs and headed for the wine rack in the china hutch. The bottle of Pinot noir might just be able to help me forget. For tonight at least. I pulled it out, relishing the cool smoothness of the glass.

Vince snatched it from me. "It's time you laid off the booze." He motioned toward the living room. "Come on," he said, his voice gentler. "Let's sit down and talk."

He led me to the loveseat where the stranger had just been sitting, my head dizzy with echoes of her words. Had I really killed her husband thirty-five years ago? My own child?

"Are you okay?" He patted the seat next to him.

I sat and fingered the snowy pearls around my neck, a gift from my father the first day I danced with the Chicago Ballet. Had the sacrifice been worth it?

"Leslie?"

I stared at the poppy the woman had been so fixated on, the scent of sweet death in the air. I wiped the gray pollen off the table, but the dust clung to my fingertips. "I never got to watch my baby take his first steps," I whispered, a knot in my belly. "Read him stories. Play with him at a park. Hear him play an instrument or act in a school play—"

"Wait a minute." Vince held up his hand. "You really believe this woman knows your children?" He locked eyes with me. "The children you never had?"

"How else could she have known what I would've named them?" I searched his eyes. "I've only shared those names with a few people."

"It must've been a lucky guess . . . or a coincidence . . . or maybe someone you told shared them with her."

"Like who?" I raised my eyebrows. "You?"

"Of course not."

"Terri?"

He lifted his hands, palms up. "Who knows where she got them?"

I studied the photos on the fireplace mantle: Terri and I in *Swan Lake*, Vince and I at our wedding, and some of my dance students after our production of *The Sleeping Beauty*. What I wouldn't give for some pictures of children and grandchildren.

Vince followed my gaze.

"I never got to congratulate my son on his first job. Or hear him announce he and his wife were expecting. Be there for the birth of their first child—or children, if the woman's right and they had twins."

Vince shook his head, his face tight.

"I never got to be a grandma . . . and will never have the chance to be." I squeezed my eyes shut. "I killed the only child I'm ever going to bear." I said, my voice breaking. "How could I take his life to save mine?"

Vince squeezed my shoulder. "Honey, you can't—"

"Part of me died during that procedure." My mind returned to the day of the abortion. "I think I've always known, somewhere deep inside, what that procedure really was."

"You did what you thought you had to do at the time," Vince said, rubbing my back.

"I cried every day for years," I said, a lump in my throat. "I didn't know if I'd ever be able to stop crying." I walked over to the window where some carolers were making their rounds.

Candles lit the blackness around them.

"Sleep my babe," they harmonized. "Lie still and slumber, all through the night."

"Lie still and slumber," I sang to my lost child. "All through the night."

The telephone rang, its shrill call jolting me back to the present.

"That's probably Frank and Cheryl wondering where we are." Vince reached for the phone on the end table. "I'll tell them we'll have to reschedule."

I nodded. There was no way I could eat anything tonight.

"Neuman residence," Vince said. After a moment, he put his hand over the mouthpiece. "It's Terri. She said she has something she wants to tell you. Should I tell her this isn't a good time?"

I hesitated a moment then took the phone.

"I know you guys are about to go out, but I just had to tell you I'm a grandma again," she squealed. "Danielle had her baby, a perfect little boy. Six pounds, ten ounces, and nineteen inches long."

I don't know how, but I got the word out. "Congratulations."

"I won't keep you—I know you need to go—but I'll be over soon with lots of pictures. Wait till you see all the clothes I got him. I bought out the store."

As soon as Vince began to snore, I snuck down the stairs.

My foot missed a step.

I bumped my way down to the front door and froze, my ears pricked and my bottom throbbing.

The dark house was silent except for the grandfather clock playing "Waltz of the Flowers."

I struggled to my feet and crept into the living room, took out the bottle, and poured myself a glass with trembling hands. Crimson splashed onto the crocheted tablecloth Vince's mom had made. His very *particular* mom. I ran into the kitchen, grabbed a rag, and tried to rub out the wine. *Oh, no. That made it worse.* Groaning, I threw the rag into the sink and hid the stain with a placemat. Tomorrow I'd figure out how to clean it.

Why had I listened to Terri and had an abortion? I knew she loved me—she'd only been trying to help me all those years ago—but now she was a grandmother, and I was . . . nothing. Not a mom. Not a grandmom. Not even a very good wife. Being a dancer and later an instructor hadn't proven as fulfilling as I'd thought it would.

I swirled the burgundy liquid around in the bottom of the glass, longing to lose myself in its depths. Cherry and strawberry aromas filled my nose along with the fainter scent of damp earth.

Shivering, I pulled my robe tighter around me. Maybe the wine would warm me, both physically and emotionally. At least for awhile.

Guilt jabbed me in the stomach. Vince didn't want me drinking. I shook the thought away. He didn't understand, didn't even believe the woman was telling the truth. But I knew.

I downed the fruity spirits to escape the images that still terrorized my soul, then poured another glass and peered at my aching stomach. The abortion had happened over three decades ago, but sometimes I could still feel the pain as clearly as the day it happened, like a phantom leg lost in a war. Instead of nurturing my baby in the safety of my womb, I had let a doctor tear him to pieces.

"What have I done?" I whispered. If only I could forget the sound of that machine.

27

Shannon: December 2014

I awoke with my heart racing but sighed in relief. It was only a dream. Just like all the others. Wade and the kids were . . . I rolled toward his side of the bed and reached for him.

Cold sheets met my hand.

No.

I sat up and leaned against the headboard. A wrought iron frame jabbed my back. What had happened to our bed? It was smaller now too, a double instead of a queen. I stared at the blood red drapes hanging from the unfamiliar canopy then jumped out of bed. Cold wood met my bare feet, sending a chill from the soles of my feet up my legs. Who had changed everything about our bedroom, and how had they done it without me noticing?

I rushed to the twins' room to smother them in kisses and assure myself everything was all right. I flicked on the light.

Gabby was lying in the bed. Gabby from my nightmare.

I gasped and staggered backward. Could the dream have been real?

I shook my head. Impossible. I must still be sleeping.

Awakened by the light, Gabby blinked and stretched. "What's going on? Is everything okay?"

She was real. Entirely too real.

This couldn't be happening. Wade and the kids must be away on a trip. His clothes must still be in our room. They had to be.

I ran back to our closet and tore through the skirts, blouses, and dresses.

No suits or ties, not even the Jedi robe I'd bought him for his birthday.

Had he moved his dress clothes to the highboy? But why would he put his button-down shirts in there? They would get wrinkled. And we both knew how much he hated ironing.

I yanked open the drawers, flinging out bras, leggings, tank tops.

None of Wade's pants, polos, or sweaters. Not even one holey sock.

Tears stung my eyes. How I longed to smell just one sweaty shirt.

Gabby stepped into the room. Her eyes darted to the clothes strewn all over the floor. "What the hey? Are you reorganizing your closet again? At 5 a.m.?" She leaned against the door frame. "What happened to you last night? Are you okay?"

I brushed past her down the hall into the nursery. I couldn't listen. Not if she was going to lie again.

"Shannon, please calm down," she said, on my heels.

I flipped the light on in the baby's room, longing to breathe in my daughter's things.

Metal shelves, a glass desk, and dark purple walls punched me in the stomach. The air rushed out of me. I wheeled on Gabby. "What have you done? Why are you changing everything? Where is my family?"

"Oh, no . . ." Gabby swallowed and shook her head. "You're doing it again."

I put a hand on my belly.

Flat abs mocked me.

I flew downstairs to the living room.

The zebra rug Gabby had been trying to get us to buy

screamed at me from under a glass coffee table with sharp corners. Gone was the cushy ottoman we'd bought when the twins started walking. And in the center of the table sat an oil reed diffuser, the odor of linen smothering the room.

Our fragrant balsam fir had been replaced with a fake excuse for a Christmas tree covered with breakable blue bulbs. Where were the mismatched ornaments? What about the special ones we put in the twins' stockings every Christmas Eve?

Speaking of stockings, where were the embroidered ones Aunt Darlene made us? Instead, store-bought stockings hung from the mantle.

And in the place of the skiing snowman in the corner stood a floor vase filled with sticks—the one Gabby had showed us in that magazine.

But perhaps most terrifying of all, on the wall hung the flat screen television I'd seen on Thanksgiving Day. Our big-box TV, lovingly marked with Katy and Daniel's fingerprints, had vanished. Again.

I shot into the kitchen. Buster's bowls must be around here somewhere.

Nothing. Not even one blasted piece of dry dog food.

The fridge! I always taped the kids' drawings to the front.

Stark white except for a flowery memo pad, Gabby's interior decorating card, and a few inspirational magnets.

Where were the kids' Christmas lists? What about the magnetic letters we always left messages with? Or the cross-eyed reindeer Katy and Daniel made in preschool?

I dashed to the sink.

Clean.

Sparkling.

Empty.

I jerked opened a cabinet.

Chip-free mugs. Matching black glasses.

I picked one up. I could see my face in it.

Gone were the plastic tumblers, the Star Wars mugs, the cups with straws.

"Shannon." Gabby put a hand on my shoulder. "There's nobody else here. It's just us, honey."

The glass slipped from my hand and shattered into a thousand pieces.

❄

After Gabby coaxed my crumpled body off the floor, I dragged myself upstairs to our bedroom. *Our bedroom.* I choked at the thought. It wasn't our bedroom anymore. And if Gabby—and everyone else but me—was right, it never had been.

I sagged into the wrought-iron settee by the window and stared outside at the falling snow, trying and failing to make sense of everything. What was it Mom had quoted from that *Snowflake Bentley* book?

"I found that snowflakes were masterpieces of design," I could still hear her read after Thanksgiving dinner, the smell of pumpkin pie wafting in from the kitchen. "No one design was ever repeated. When a snowflake melted . . . just that much beauty was gone, without leaving any record behind."

How could she not remember me and the kids, after all the weekends, holidays, and vacations we'd shared? Summer trips at the dunes in Michigan. Mother's Days. Father's Days.

Birthdays. I would never look at another the same. I remembered Katy's and Daniel's faces as they opened their presents. The chocolate fudge cake Margaret made with Spider-man rescuing Snow White. Singing "Happy Birthday" and blowing out the candles. I could still picture the flickering flames. Now their lives had been blown out. As if they'd never been.

I ran my hands over the sleek, onyx music box my parents had given me when I'd completed my masters in theater. I opened it and the tune of "I Dreamed a Dream" from *Les Miserables* filled the room.

My eyes pricked. Was there really no record of Wade or the twins . . . except my memories? And could I even call them memories if no one else shared them? How had I imagined our entire lives together?

Our wedding. The birth of each child. Hearing "mama" for the first time.

Each snuggle, each kiss, each night under the covers.

Where did my life go? Where did *their* lives go?

Gone. Like the snowflakes that melted on my windshield.

❄

"I hate to bring this up now," Gabby took a seat at the industrial-style kitchen table we'd apparently bought. "But you do realize you missed opening night."

I sighed as I slipped into the metal chair. "That had occurred to me."

"I tried calling in an excuse for you, but no one answered at the school and I didn't have your principal's or assistant director's number."

"Thanks for trying, Gab." Maybe tea would help soothe my soul as it had so many times before. I filled up the teapot with water, set it on the stove, and turned on the burner.

"There's something else." Gabby locked eyes with me. "Something terrible."

More terrible than losing my family?

"Rebecca died at the hospital."

I gasped, my hand flying to my chest. "What?" I stammered. "Are you sure?"

Gabby nodded, and I sank into the chair. Closing my eyes, I covered my face with my hands. Just when I thought my heart couldn't break anymore. I laid my head on the table, my only escape from a world gone all wrong.

My phone rang—the vintage ringtone indicating Mom was calling.

I groaned. Why couldn't everyone just leave me alone? A thought occurred to me. That's exactly what *had* happened. But maybe Mom was the one person who would believe my story. I answered the phone, a glimmer of hope on the horizon.

Mom expressed her shock and sympathy when I told her about Rebecca. Then she launched into the real reason for her call. "You spend too much time working with those kids at that high school. You need to get out more, meet people your own age. How do you expect to get married if you spend all your time with teenagers?"

I lowered my head, a new wave of grief rushing over me. She didn't remember Wade and the kids.

"Shannon? Are you there?"

"Yes, Mom," I managed, "and I meet plenty of people my own age at school."

"Who? Not that Melvin guy, I hope."

The social studies teacher Gabby thought liked me?

"No one can say he didn't bend over backwards to make a good impression on your dad and me when we came out to visit, but he was nervous just shaking my hand. And his handshake was limp and weak. You can tell a lot about a person by their handshake, you know."

The red teapot shrieked.

I moved it to a cool burner, poured hot water into a mug, and stuck in a tea bag. The scent of jasmine filled the air. I tried to force down some health-nut bread as Faith Hill sang "Where Are You Christmas?" from the living room TV but ended up forcing back tears instead.

"You need someone more gifted, dynamic, and talkative," Mom was saying.

Gifted.

Dynamic.

Talkative.

Just like Wade.

I trudged into the bathroom and tried to tame my disheveled hair. I should look at least halfway presentable for the play tonight. Even if I didn't *feel* presentable. Even if I never wanted to leave the house again. I owed it to my students. They'd worked so hard.

"If you married Melvin—"

My jaw dropped. *Married Melvin*?

"You would be the shining star in his universe, and he would never leave you. But I think you're settling for safe because you've been hurt in the past. And I want you to be with someone you're actually *excited* to be with."

My thoughts wandered back to my dating days with Wade,

his crazy proposal, and the months leading up to our wedding. Even after seven years of marriage, life had never gotten boring.

"Isn't there a singles group you can join? You're not getting any younger, you know."

"Thanks, Mom," I said, plucking out several gray hairs. They seemed to be multiplying these days.

"If I don't tell you the truth, who will?"

"Look, Mom, I really gotta go. Tonight's the second performance of *A Christmas Carol*, and I need to get to school to set up." I decided not to mention the fact that I'd already missed opening night. That would bring on too many questions. Questions I didn't have the strength to answer.

"See, this is what I'm talking about. It's a Saturday night, and what are you doing? Spending it with a bunch of kids."

"It's my job, Mom."

"I know, but there's more to life than your job."

At least there *was*.

"Before you go, Dad and I have been meaning to suggest eHarmony to you."

The online dating service?

"One of our friends found his fiancé through them. We would pay for it. Consider it a Christmas gift."

I swallowed a huge lump in my throat. All I wanted for Christmas was my family back.

"What do you think?" Mom pressed.

If only I could explain I was already married. Or at least felt like I was.

"Just think about it," she said. "You don't have to decide today."

After I hung up, I listened to my voicemails from yesterday. Peggy. My assistant director. Even some students wondering where I was and what they should do about some technical difficulties.

I glanced at the clock. One hour before I needed to leave. One hour to come up with a good reason why I'd missed opening night.

Peggy strode into the auditorium. Her blue eyes flashed. "Where were you last night? And why haven't you returned any of my calls?"

Oh, no. Here we go.

"It's not like you to not show up—especially for opening night—and then not even respond to your voicemails. We were all shocked by your absence."

"I had a . . . family emergency."

"Must've been pretty serious."

"Very."

"What happened?"

Maybe Peggy would remember. I glanced at my students who were hovering around and then pulled Peggy aside and lowered my voice. "Do you remember me being . . . pregnant?"

"Pregnant?" She pursed her lips. "I didn't even know you were dating anyone."

I squeezed my lips together. She had no memories of them either.

"Did you finally agree to go out with Melvin?"

So he *had* been asking me out. I shook my head.

"I always thought his feelings were one-sided." She clutched my arm, her nails digging into my skin. "But you're pregnant?"

"I thought I was . . . but . . . it turns out I'm not."

She crossed her arms and narrowed her eyes. "So you walk out on your students who have been preparing for this play—looking forward to this play—all semester?"

My chest tightened. How had I let so many people down? "Some of my family members went . . . missing."

Her eyes widened. "Missing? Who? Did you find them?"

I bit my lip. Peggy was a family friend. She knew Wade and the twins. She had to. Maybe she just needed to be reminded, like Gabby had that day we went shopping. "Do you remember . . . Wade?"

"Wade?" Peggy's brow furrowed. "Doesn't ring a bell. Is he your brother?"

I choked on a sob but tried to turn it into a laugh. Did no one remember my wonderful husband, my precious children? I looked up at the ceiling and blinked back tears. "So . . . you don't remember me having any . . . difficulties . . . this year?" *My daughter dying? My unborn child having Down syndrome?*

"You mean with the Cooper brothers?"

If only high school pranksters were the worst of my problems. "No. I mean . . . you don't remember me . . . losing anyone?"

She frowned. "Not that I can recall. Did one of your parents die?"

"No."

"Grandparents?"

"Never mind. It doesn't matter anymore," I lied.

"But you still didn't answer my question," Peggy said. "Who is missing?"

❄

Fog drifted along the bottom of the dark stage as the play came to a climax.

I fidgeted in my itchy seat. When could I get out of this musty theater and away from all these people? How many more fake smiles would I have to muster before I could finally be alone? Alone with my memories. They were all I had left.

Thunderstorm sound effects echoed throughout the theater.

Cloaked in black, Suresh stood in the middle of a cemetery pointing at a tombstone.

Andrew, who looked like Scrooge in his gray wig and aging make-up, trudged toward the grave, trembling.

"Good Spirit," Andrew said, falling on the ground before Suresh. "Assure me I yet may change these shadows you have shown me, by an altered life. Oh, tell me I may sponge away the writing on this stone."

28

Leslie: March 1979

"You need to get up." Mom rapped on my door. "Your sister'll be dropping off Heather any minute. I'm working on breakfast, but I still have to shower. Can you watch her for a little while?"

"Sure." I threw on my baggiest pair of painter pants to hide my expanding waistline and made a beeline for the bathroom to wash my face and brush my teeth.

The doorbell rang.

I dabbed concealer under my eyes to cover the dark circles and ran downstairs.

"Aunt Leslie!" Heather tied her arms around me and squeezed.

"She's been driving me crazy asking when she's going to see you," Patricia said. "She just had to wear her tutu today."

I knelt in front of my niece.

"Of course, she wants to be a ballerina too," Patricia said. "So I guess we'll be spending some big bucks on ballet lessons, like Mom and Dad did with you."

I cringed thinking of all the time and money Mom and

Dad had spent on my dancing over the years. What a waste if I dropped out now.

"I'll see you a little later," Patricia said as she hurried out the door.

Heather and I followed the smell of bacon into the kitchen. She took one look at the scrambled eggs and wrinkled her nose. "Not eggs again."

"You know you love my eggs," Mom said. "I put cheddar cheese on them, just the way you like."

I picked out the crispiest piece of bacon and took a bite as I prepared a plate for my niece.

"Aunt Leslie's going to watch you for awhile, and then we'll go to the toy store." Mom pulled off her apron and headed for the stairs.

After Heather gobbled up her last forkful of cheesy eggs, we curled up in Dad's brown Naugahyde recliner, rain pattering on the window next to us.

My stomach growled. I put my hand on it. I guess the baby didn't like bacon and eggs. Heather stared at me with her chestnut eyes. "My teacher rubs her tummy like that, too, but she has a big belly. She has a baby inside her."

The phone rang, its shrill call a welcome interruption.

I took a deep breath and picked it up. "Gardner residence."

"Leslie?" It was Peggy. "I was just wondering how you're doing and if you've had time to think about things. I don't want to push you, but I'd really like you to meet my aunt and uncle. It might be good to get their perspective before you make such an important decision."

I played with the phone cord and glanced at my niece. Could she hear what Peggy was saying? "They're free this afternoon."

I tugged at the collar of my turtleneck, suddenly feeling hot. What if I got their hopes up and then decided not to have the baby?

"Unless, of course, you're thinking of keeping the baby and raising it yourself."

Mom might pick up one of the extensions to make a call. I had to get Peggy off the phone.

"I'm really not sure what I'm going to do," I said quickly. "But I guess I can meet them so we can talk about how everything would work if I do decide to . . ." I struggled for the right words.

"Good," Peggy finally said when I failed to finish my sentence. "You'll see they're wonderful, loving people."

"Honk when you get here, and I'll come outside. You don't need to get out of the car or anything." I couldn't have my parents asking Peggy any questions.

"I'll pick you up at noon."

I hung up, a glimmer of hope in my heart. What if this was the answer I'd been looking for? A way to save both my life and my child's? Of course, if I did give my baby up for adoption, I'd be super picky about who I'd let raise him. Would Dawn and Gary be good enough parents?

I hung up, avoiding eye contact with my niece. What had I just agreed to?

Mom strode into the room. Had she heard?

"Who was on the phone?"

I cleared my throat. "Just a friend from school," I said as nonchalantly as I could. "We're going to hang out later."

"Only if you clean your room first. It looks like a bomb went off in there."

"She's not coming here. We're going out."

Mom put on her watch. "I thought you had the dance tonight."

"Peggy and I are just doing lunch. I should be back with plenty of time to get ready."

Thunderstorms always made me want to stay curled up in bed with a novel, where the prince was always that—a prince. Where the enemy was as obvious as a witch or a dragon and relatively easy to slay. Where the right path was clear and the voices drowning out your own could be drowned out themselves.

I turned the page of the book I was reading and pulled my

blanket over my feet. Why did I tell Peggy I'd meet her aunt and uncle? It would be so much harder to say no now.

Seven minutes to twelve, a car beeped.

Oh, no. Was that Peggy already? I dragged myself out of bed and pulled aside the curtain. Sure enough, her dark blue Chevy Impala sat in our driveway, motor running. I ran down the stairs without saying good-bye to Mom and Heather, grabbed my raincoat, and hurried to the car.

❄

I pulled my lavender dress over my head, zipped it up, and tied the ribbons around the empire waist.

I needed to make a decision. Now or never. Tell my parents I was pregnant or go through with the abortion on Tuesday.

After spending time with Gary and Dawn, I knew that aborting my baby or abandoning my dreams weren't my only options. I could give the child to them. They seemed like they'd be wonderful parents, and I wouldn't have to raise the baby myself.

But could I do that? Know that my own flesh and blood was out there living its life apart from me?

I had liked Dawn from the moment I met her, which would only make things harder if I decided to say no. She had an easy smile and a laugh that lifted my spirit. She and Gary had been high school sweethearts who just celebrated their tenth anniversary. Gary was a man of few words who seemed as loyal as they come.

"Nothing would make us happier than to be parents," Dawn had said.

And nothing would make me unhappier, at least at this point in my life. I put a hand on my stomach. Why had it been so easy for me to get pregnant and so hard for this loving couple who had been longing for a child for ten years? Sure, they didn't have much money, but what they lacked in finances they made up for with big hearts.

I checked my makeup one last time.

"If you decide to bless us with your child," Dawn had said as I left, "you'd be more than welcome to visit. Or, if you'd rather not do that, we could send pictures and updates through the mail or through Peggy."

They would raise the child but I could still see him, either up close or from afar. So why was I holding back?

I twirled in front of the mirror. I was already sixteen weeks pregnant. If I didn't have an abortion soon, I would be as plump as a pumpkin.

The doorbell rang. It must be Frankie. With one last look, I hurried downstairs to meet him. But it wasn't Frankie who stood at the bottom of the stairs talking to my mother. At least not the Frankie I was used to.

The Frankie who turned at my footsteps and whistled at me was a wrangler from one of my romance novels about to lead me off into the sunset. Or lasso me, I wasn't quite sure. Either way, a hunk with a capital *H*.

He tipped his head, but instead of his unruly afro he sported a short crop of dark-brown curls that made me want to run my fingers through them. His tan, chiseled face was now clean-shaven, making his roguish grin even more dangerous. And he'd exchanged his usual jeans and T-shirt for a corduroy three piece suit the color of a dusty street in the middle of a shoot-out. Looked like I was the one about to be shot. Right through the heart.

He ran a hand over his square jaw. "Like it?" he said, seeming all too aware of how devastatingly handsome he looked.

My heart did a pirouette. *More than you can imagine.*

❄

Hand in hand, Frankie and I stepped through a flowered archway into the school gym and entered "Paris in Springtime."

I was determined to forget about Don, the pregnancy, and the decision I still had to make. Tonight I was Cinderella at the ball.

I took in the street-side cafe, the canopy overhead, and the painted murals on the walls.

Girls in long dresses danced with their dates, bouquets in their hands, as the Ralph Berger Orchestra played on a stage across from us.

I spotted Sarah and did a double-take. She was wearing the first dress I'd set my eyes on at the department store—a satin gown with huge sleeves, a tiny waist, and an embroidered bodice. And she looked beautiful in it, just like I imagined the princess bride must look in William Goldman's novel.

At least Sarah wasn't here with Don. Instead, Phil held her close, beaming like a little boy on Christmas.

On the other side of the room, Don winked at me as he spun Rhonda around.

Frankie led me to the refreshments table and handed me a drink and a slice of cake topped with a daisy.

I sipped the punch, the 7UP tingling my tongue as the orchestra started playing Andy Gibb's "An Everlasting Love."

"Ready to get down, Twinkle Toes?" Frankie cocked his head.

I nodded and downed my punch, catching several girls checking out Frankie.

He captured my hand and led me to the center of the dance floor, his grip firm and possessive. Wrapping his other arm around my waist, he searched my face, a smile skipping over his. He spun me around and dipped me, and then his mouth met mine. Gently at first, like winter's first flakes coming to rest, then intensifying to a burning blizzard of swirling, dizzying, snow, sparking every nerve in my body. "I love you, Leslie Gardner," he said, his breath hot on my ear.

My knees went weak. My heart felt like it would come out of my chest with all its pounding. Had I just given it away a second time?

Frankie lifted me and led me in one routine after another, spontaneous—and ridiculous—moves thrown in at every turn. I laughed, not caring how loud I was or what anyone else thought. I only wanted to be with him—this man who knew me like no other—dancing until my feet could no longer carry me.

When the music slowed, I studied him, treasuring every detail to remember forever.

29

Leslie: March 1979

The airplane shuddered.

A red haired stewardess grabbed the top of my seat. "Everyone, please sit down and buckle your seat belts."

I tightened mine and clutched the armrests, every bone in my hands popping out.

Next to me, a woman about Mom's age peered out the window. "Those mountains are awfully close," she said, clenching her pearls.

I stared past her at the jagged peaks.

Magnificent and dreadful. Like meeting a lion in the wild.

Oh God, please don't let us crash.

The stewardess deposited a toddler in my lap. "Please take care of him for me."

He hugged a stuffed dog with a spot over one eye, its head tilted as if to say, "Won't you love me?"

I unhooked my belt, pulled it around us, and clicked it back into place. For some reason, being with him felt right. More right than anything had ever felt.

"Thank you." The stewardess struggled to stay on her feet. "You have no idea how much he means to me." She hurried to the front of the plane and strapped herself into a pull-down chair.

I wrapped my arms around the little guy and squeezed him tight, a flutter in my stomach.

He stuck two fingers into his mouth and settled in as if he belonged with me. As if he'd always belonged with me.

A jolt thrust us backwards.

The tail of the plane tore off, sucking passengers outside. Their cries filled the air then vanished.

The boy clung to me, his whole body trembling.

Wind clawed at my hair.

Backpacks, briefcases, and duffel bags toppled around us.

We all became strangely silent, as if by holding our breath we could escape our fate.

But my heartbeat thrashed in my ears.

The window next to us shattered. Glass shot into the woman's thigh. She screamed and grabbed her leg.

The boy wailed.

I wanted to wail too, but I had to remain calm to assure him everything would be all right. "I've got you," I said, trying to shield him from the wind.

The middle-aged woman clenched her teeth and whimpered.

The jet slammed into the ground.

My jaw smacked the seat in front of me, my seat forced forward by the ones behind.

The plane shrieked to a stop, metal screeching on the floor as the rows piled up in front.

I spit out blood. Tasted iron.

The woman beside me slumped in her seat, her mouth open, her eyes hollow.

I looked in my lap—the boy was gone!

I clambered out of my seat, my muscles sore. "Where's my son?" I yelled. Black spots clouded my vision as I waded through the smoke, the smell of burning plastic in the air.

A beefy man with a black mustache sneered. "You're too young to have a child. What are you, a tramp?"

"I just had him," I cried. I pushed past the man and

climbed through the wreckage, casting aside seats and luggage. If I could find him, I'd protect him forever. I'd shower him with kisses every day of my life.

I heaved aside the last bag.

Underneath it lay the boy's stuffed animal. Covered in blood.

My chest ached and my body went cold.

Where is my son?

❄

I woke Tuesday morning with a start and took in my pink bedroom. The sun was rising behind the blinds, and I could hear the traffic on York Street. "Just a nightmare," I whispered and relaxed against my pillow.

But why had I called the boy my son?

I shivered and pulled the collar of my purple pajamas tight around my neck. Had the dream been about my unborn child? The little guy did have Don's hazel eyes.

I pulled out Bence Váradi's card and ran my fingers over the textured surface. If I had the baby, I couldn't accept the Chicago Ballet position. And, worse, I might never dance professionally, something I'd longed for since I was a little girl.

A knot formed in my stomach.

Baby?

Or ballet?

I caressed my belly and tears rushed into my eyes. How could I exchange my child's life for even the most glittering of fantasies? Didn't he deserve to have dreams of his own?

I had to cancel the appointment Terri had made for me. There was no other choice.

I glanced at my alarm clock. 5:37. The clinic would be open in a few hours. If I could just get the number.

I snuck downstairs and grabbed the directory out of the kitchen cabinet.

I locked the door to my room and thumbed through the phone book, the pages thick with the scent of ink and paper. Where had Terri made the appointment? I skimmed through several clinics, not seeing any names that sounded familiar. I didn't want to have to call her to find out because I knew she'd try to talk me out of it. I flipped to the next page.

Women's Health Services.

I breathed a sigh of relief. That sounded right.

Since we didn't have school, I set my alarm for 8 a.m. and tried to go back to sleep. When I woke, I'd cancel the abortion and tell my parents I was pregnant.

Come what may.

❄

"Love will find a way," Pablo Cruise belted from my radio.

I listened until the song ended and then turned off the music. Would I really find a way through all this mess? Time alone would tell. But for now, there was something I had to do. Two somethings, in fact.

I locked my door and dialed the number from the phone book. Hopefully Mom and Dad wouldn't overhear my conversation

"Women's Health Services," a female voice said. "How may I help you?"

"I'd like to cancel an appointment."

"*Cancel* an appointment?"

"Yes," I said more confidently than I felt.

"Name, please."

"Leslie?" Mom rattled the door knob. "Why is your door locked? I want to show you something."

I held my breath. My arms started shaking.

"Are you still there?" the receptionist said.

"Just a minute, Mom," I called. I turned back to the phone. "Leslie Gardner," I whispered into the receiver. "I was supposed to come in at 2:00 today."

"Unfortunately, miss, we require twenty-four hours notice to cancel an appointment. Otherwise, you have to pay a fee. Are you sure you want to cancel?"

I ran my hand over the silky straps of my first pair of pointe shoes.

"Leslie?" Mom called again, her voice strident.

"Yes," I said into the phone. "I'll come in later to pay the fee." I hung up before I could change my mind and hurried to the door.

Mom held up a white, frilly dress. "What do you think? I got it for you for Easter Sunday."

"It's beautiful," I said. And it was. But it went better with the innocent image Mom had of me than the truth. "Mom. I need to tell you something."

"What?"

"You might want to sit down."

Her dark eyes narrowed as she lowered herself onto the bed. She spotted Mr. Váradi's card and lifted her eyebrows. "You decided to accept their offer? I still think you should go to college first, but your dad says it's up to you."

If only that was what I needed to tell her. I took a deep breath and forced out the words. "I'm pregnant."

Her face blanched. "You're *what*?"

"Pregnant," I repeated as if she hadn't heard me the first time.

She clutched her chest. "Are you sure? Maybe you have the flu."

"I took an e.p.t. test."

She stared at me incredulously. "How could you do something like this? You and Frankie just started dating."

"It happened before that. With Don." Bile crept into my mouth. Why had I surrendered my body, my purity, and as it turned out, my dreams to someone I'd only known a few months?

"But you and Don broke up in January. And you're just telling me now? How long have you known?"

"Three months," I mumbled.

"Three *months*?" Mom shook her head. "Leslie Amanda, I cannot believe this. I thought we raised you better than this."

I studied my hands, my face ablaze.

"What are you going to do? You can't go to summer intensives. No wonder you didn't want me to book the flights."

I swallowed hard.

"I'm assuming you're going to give it up for adoption?"

"That is an option," I said, finding my voice. "My friend's aunt and uncle said they would adopt it."

Mom exhaled and sagged against the bedpost. "That's a relief," she said. "A *small* relief."

I fiddled with a button on my pajama top. How would I feel if someone else raised my child? I met Mom's eyes. "I'm not sure that's what I want to do. I mean, isn't this baby my responsibility?"

Mom put her arm around me. "Leslie," she said, her tone more tender. "Though I can't imagine my grandchild being raised by strangers, you have your whole life ahead of you. Having a baby right now would change everything."

My eyes watered. "I know," I said, a hitch in my voice. "But—"

"We'll discuss it with your father," she said briskly and stood. "But I'm not telling him." She leveled her eyes at me. "*You* are."

"Telling me what?" Dad stepped into the room, the scent of cigars clinging to his shirt and tie.

I peered into eyes that were proud of me for perhaps the last time.

❄

After I called Mr. Vàradi and turned down his offer, I noticed the pale pink music box Frankie had given me for Christmas. I ran my hands over the gold and violet butterflies and gently opened the box.

The ballerina pirouetted to a melancholy melody from *Swan Lake.* After a few minutes, the music slowed and faded out before the song was over.

The notes not played haunted the air.

Hot tears spilled down my cheeks. *I might never dance again. At least not on a stage.*

My hands trembled as I closed the box and buried it on a shelf in my closet behind the journals where I used to write stories.

I looked around my room—the *Giselle* program on my dresser, the Margot Fonteyn poster on the wall, the pointe shoes tied around my bedpost. I looked out the window at the gray sky and licked away a salty tear. *Is my life over?*

The phone rang, bringing me back to the present.

"Guess what?" Terri squealed when I picked up the receiver. "Chicago Ballet offered me a position!"

I swallowed the lump in my throat. "That's great," I said, trying to infuse my voice with excitement. Terri had worked hard for this.

"Did you accept the position they offered you yet? Dancing together in the same company is going to be so much fun."

I glanced at the empty space on my dresser where the music box had stood. "Actually, I wanted to talk to you about that."

"Why don't you fill me in on all the details when I pick you up for your appointment?"

I squeezed my eyes shut. "I canceled it, Terri."

"You what?"

"I canceled it. I can't go through with it."

"Oh no," she groaned. "More bad pizza?"

I sighed. "It's more than that, Terri. I can't kill my—"

"We've talked about this, Les. It's just a bunch of tissue. And no one has to know."

"*I* would know. And I already told my parents."

Terri gasped. "Why? What did they say?"

I winced, remembering the disappointment on Dad's face. "They want me to go stay with my grandma in Michigan right after graduation so people don't find out and then give the baby up for adoption."

"So you're not going to be here this summer?"

I sank onto my bed and clutched a velvet pillow to my stomach. "I'm thinking about keeping it. And if I do, there's no reason to go away to hide the pregnancy."

"You're thinking about *keeping* it? Les, you cannot be serious. What about college?"

I took a shuddering breath. "I'll probably take the first

semester off since I'm due the twenty-fourth of August and classes start the twenty-seventh. But I plan to take at least some classes in the spring semester."

"Who's going to watch the baby while you're at school?"

I shrugged as if Terri could see me. "Maybe my mom?" Not that it seemed likely right now.

Silence reigned on the other end of the line.

I untied my pointe shoes and kissed them one more time, the smell of sweat and old medical tape bringing on a rush of memories.

"Why are you doing this?" Terri said. "We had so many plans. Plans that were working out perfectly."

Another tear slid down my cheek as I packed the shoes away with the ballerina box. "If I could go back and change what I did with Don—or even dating him in the first place—I would. But I can't. And I'm not going to make someone else pay for my mistakes."

"It's not your fault. You were just being a normal teenager."

I let out my breath. "It's time for me to grow up."

The clock on my nightstand ticked away the seconds.

"It's not too late to make it to your appointment," Terri finally said.

I sat up straight and put a hand on my stomach. "It's always been too late."

❄

I pulled out the baby names book under my mattress and climbed into bed. If I was going to keep the baby, I needed to pick out a name. Two of them, in fact, since I didn't know whether it was a boy or a girl. I bit into a tart Granny Smith apple and flipped through the girls' section first.

One name popped off the page.

Margaret.

I underlined it with my finger. If I had a girl, I could name her after Margot Fonteyn, and maybe she'd grow up to be a prima ballerina too.

I skipped ahead to the boys' section and scanned the pages, several names catching my eye.

Brent.

Justin.

Nicholas.

Wade.

"Wade," I said out loud, liking the sound of it. But would my family expect me to name the child after them? Dad had been named after his father, I'd been named after my grandmother, and Patricia had been given Mom's middle name.

The doorbell rang.

"Leslie, it's Frankie," Mom yelled a few minutes later.

Frankie? What was he doing here? I checked myself in the mirror over my dresser. Bloodshot eyes and a puffy face. Great. I wiped away runaway mascara and put on lip gloss. After I pinched my cheeks like Scarlett O'Hara in *Gone with the Wind*, I tried out a smile and hurried downstairs.

Frankie had on the same corduroy suit he'd worn for the spring dance.

I glanced at my jeans. "Were we supposed to go out tonight?"

"You look beautiful," he said. "Let's go. I have a surprise for you."

"A surprise? What kind of surprise?"

He cocked an eyebrow. "You do understand the concept of a surprise, right?"

I grabbed my coat but punched him in the arm on my way out.

He ushered me into his cramped car like I imagined Prince Charming must've ushered Cinderella into their wedding carriage. "Remember that house that caught fire a few months ago?"

I nodded, picturing the smoke and fire engines.

"I want to show you something." He backed down our driveway, drove a few blocks down the street, and then turned into the driveway of a small brick house with red shutters.

"Wow," I said. "It looks great. Where's the fire damage?"

"Let's check it out." He got out of the car and pulled out a key.

My breath caught. "Is this one of the houses your Dad was hired to remodel?"

Frankie winked at me and opened the door.

I followed him into a spacious room with gold shag carpet and breathed in the smell of fresh wood. Sunshine poured through the windows and bathed me in a warm glow.

"The living room and dining room," he said.

"Nice. Lots of light."

He led me upstairs through three rooms with unpainted dry wall. "The bedchambers," he said as if he were a British butler. "And the powder room," he said in the same voice.

The basement had been made into a family room with a fireplace and wood paneling. Back on the main floor, we walked through a large, eat-in kitchen and out a sliding glass door into a tiny backyard.

"So." He spread his arms. "What do you think?"

"Your dad did a fabulous job."

"Not my dad. Well, he helped a little—mainly advice—but most of the work was done by these two guys," he said, holding up his fists.

I squinted at him. "You're working for your dad now?"

"Nope," he said. "Bought the house and remodeled it myself."

"You bought it?" I stammered. "But how could you afford it?"

"Remember the Cadillac?"

I gasped. "You sold the coupe to buy this place? But why?"

Frankie led me to a rose bush fragrant with deep pink blooms. "I planted this bush because a dozen roses aren't enough for you." He got down on one knee.

I staggered backwards. Frankie was proposing. For real this time.

"Every year," he said. "This bush will bloom to remind you that my love and commitment to you will never die." He pulled a small jewelry box out of his pocket and opened it. "My heart and this house are yours. If you'll have them."

I could hardly breathe. Frankie had sold his most treasured

possession—his 1974 Cadillac Coupe de Ville—to buy me this house. Knowing I was pregnant with someone else's child. And then he must've spent almost every night and weekend working on it. Repairing the fire damage. Putting up new walls. Installing new flooring. All so he could provide a home for me and my child.

As I gazed into the chiseled face of my best friend, he pulled out the most exquisite diamond ring I'd ever seen. A princess-cut stone beamed at me from the center while daintier gems sparkled from the band.

My mouth fell open. "How did you afford this too?" I whispered.

"My granny left it for me when she died." He took my small hand into his calloused one. "Now, will you quit asking questions and let me pop the only one that matters?" he said, cracking a smile.

"Only if you'll get on with it," I teased.

"Leslie Gardner." His brown eyes twinkled with the diamonds. "Will you marry me?"

Just then, as if he'd cued them, a flurry of snowflakes started falling from the sky. One landed on our entwined hands as if to bless our union.

But before I said yes, I needed to tell him what I'd decided to do. I put his free hand on my belly. "Are you ready to be a dad?"

"No," he said and kissed my forehead. "But I will be."

30

Shannon: December 2014

As I set up for the final performance of *A Christmas Carol*, Peggy pulled me aside. "I want to introduce you to someone." She led me into the buzzing school lobby toward a teen girl with Down syndrome. Peggy pulled me close and lowered her voice. "I told her mom you were asking some questions about Down syndrome the other day."

My breath caught. Did Peggy remember I was pregnant? I was about to ask when she started making introductions.

"Shannon, this is Andrew's cousin Jennifer and her mom, sister, and best friend," Peggy gestured toward the girl with Down's then nodded at a forty-something woman and two attractive girls next to the popcorn machine.

The fake butter smell turned my stomach—like it had when I was pregnant.

"Jennifer was elected homecoming queen of her high school this year," Peggy was saying.

My eyes widened. Homecoming queen? That explained the tiara gracing the top of her honey-ginger hair.

I shook Jennifer's hand. "Is that your crown?"

"Yeah." She adjusted her wire-rimmed glasses. "I like it so much I wear it all the time."

"You never take it off?"

"Not even when she sleeps," her mom said.

"I was so surprised when they called my name."

"I wasn't." Jennifer's friend slipped off her purple coat. "It's your attitude about life—you're always willing to try new things and you're always smiling, even when you're down."

"You're super friendly too," the slender girl with braces said. "Everyone loves you. Of course that doesn't stop us from fighting sometimes."

Jennifer playfully punched her sister in the arm.

"With a little love and encouragement," their mom said, "children with disabilities can do amazing things. Jennifer can hear a song at church and come home and play it on the piano without any sheet music."

"Oh, Mom." Jennifer rolled her eyes.

"That is amazing," I said, a lump in my throat. What might my daughter have accomplished if I had only believed in her enough to give her a chance? Was that why I had lost everyone?

"Honestly, she's been such a blessing to our family." Her mom pulled me aside. "It was hard finding out she had Down syndrome, but I wouldn't go back and change a thing if I could."

Neither would I, I realized, if I could just have my baby back. What unique blessings might God have had in store for us?

The girls excused themselves to find their seats, and I turned to Peggy to ask her the question kindling in my soul.

Just then, my assistant director handed me a hot cup of French vanilla coffee. "Thought you might need this," she said as I sipped it. "But it's time to start. And there's a problem with the mics."

"Spirit," Andrew cried, his lapel microphone screeching.

I winced.

"Assure me I yet may change these shadows you have shown me, by an altered life." He fell on the ground before the black-cloaked figure of Suresh. "Oh, tell me I may sponge away the writing on this stone."

The sound guys struck a dissonant chord, and the theater blacked out.

A few moments later, a spotlight rose on Andrew who was clutching a bedpost, his eyes squeezed shut. He opened them and gasped, his hand flying to his chest. "I will live in the Past, the Present, and the Future." He scrambled out of bed. "The shadows of the things that would have been may be dispelled. They will be. I know they will."

I tapped my foot on the floor, my palms sweaty. Could the shadows in my own life be dispelled?

Andrew fiddled with his sleeping gown. "I don't know what to do," he cried, laughing like a lunatic. "I am as light as a feather, I am as happy as an angel, I am as merry as a schoolboy. I am as giddy as a drunken man. A merry Christmas to everybody," he shouted. "A happy New Year to all the world."

Church bells rang throughout the theater. Their merry clanging gave me goose bumps.

Andrew opened a window on stage right and stuck his head out. "What's today?" he called to a red-scarfed boy walking by.

The boy stopped mid-stride. "Eh?"

"What's today, my fine fellow?"

"Today?" The boy pulled his Bible against his chest. "Why, Christmas Day."

"It's Christmas Day," Andrew said as if to himself. "I haven't missed it."

Scrooge had a prize turkey delivered to the Cratchits' and bustled through town wishing everyone "Merry Christmas." Then the cast ran onstage for curtain calls.

The audience whistled when the Cooper brothers appeared, howled when Ravi danced onstage to Bhangra music, and rose to their feet when Andrew bowed.

I leaned back in my seat, a lightness in my chest. The play was a success. All the long hours had been worth it. I stared at my feet. Or had they been, if they'd meant less time with my family—my family that I would never see again?

Peggy strode onstage, carrying a handheld mic and a snowdrop bouquet. "None of this would've been possible," she said into the microphone, "without our drama director extraordinaire, Mrs. Henry." She motioned toward me, and my students started cheering.

I hurried onto the stage, a flutter in my stomach. Something seemed different.

Peggy handed me the flowers.

I reached out to accept them and spotted my charm bracelet back on my wrist. "Wade," I said, tears springing into my eyes. I fingered the twins' charm. "Katy. Daniel." I stared at my belly.

Round!

My baby kicked. My precious little baby kicked!

"Mrs. Henry?" Peggy lifted an eyebrow.

"Yes," I yelled. "Yes, I am!"

Peggy's eyes widened.

"I have to go." I ran back to my seat and grabbed my purse. "Katy, Daniel, I'm coming! I'm coming!"

People gasped and murmured, but I didn't care. I dashed to our minivan—our heavenly, blue Odyssey with Cheerios ground into the seat and carpet—and sped home, dialing Wade's number.

"Hi. You've reached the cell phone of Wade Henry."

It was him! It was really him!

"I'm sorry I'm unavailable to take your call. Please leave a message, and I'll get back to you as soon as I can. Have a great day."

"I will!" I giggled, tears tumbling down my cheeks.

Minutes later, I pulled into our driveway, leapt out of the car, and flew into our wonderfully messy house, toys scattered all over the floor. I fell headlong into Wade's arms. "I love you," I cried, squeezing him tight. "Oh, how I love you."

"I love you too, Red," he said slowly. He held me at arm's length and searched my eyes. "Are you all right?"

"Yes! You're here. You're all here!" I knelt before Katy

and Daniel and smothered them in hugs and kisses, Buster joining in with his own slobbery smooches. Could I ever let them go?

Wade stooped beside me. "Honey? Are you sure you're all right? Did something happen?"

"You wouldn't believe me if I told you," I said breathlessly. "But I'll tell you anyway. One day. But, for now . . ." I put a hand on my belly. "We're having a baby!"

"Yes, we are," Wade said, his eyes moist.

Daniel's head jerked back. "A baby?"

"Yes." I laughed. "A baby sister."

"A baby sister?" Katy squealed. "We can play house together."

I drew the kids close and snuggled against Wade's warm chest. "I couldn't ask for a better husband."

"I don't know." He squinted at me. "I still think you got the short end of the stick."

❄

After I finally convinced myself Wade and the kids were real and not going anywhere, I celebrated with a piece of chocolate applesauce bread Rebecca—dear, sweet, very alive Rebecca—had brought over. Apparently, Wade had stepped in when Eric started getting rough with her the night before. As a thank you, Rebecca had brought over the dessert. If she only knew she owed him her life. I bit into the bread, the butter, cinnamon, and chocolate chips melting in my mouth.

That's when I saw Buster's head stuck in the trash can, food scraps strewn across the floor, and the sink and counters overflowing with dishes.

"Thank you God for every blessed bit of it," I whispered, never meaning anything more. "Buster, get out of there! We have a birthday party to prepare for!" I clapped my hands together and rallied the troops. "Everyone will be here in an hour for Aunt Margaret's party, and nothing's ready. Not dinner, the cake, the house—"

Wade caught me in his arms. "We'll help you with all that,

Red. We can order Chinese for all I care. But first, can you look in your stocking?"

A smile played on my lips. "But Christmas isn't until next week."

"Who cares?" Wade said. "Just look."

I reached into the bottom of my stocking and pulled out a rectangular box haphazardly wrapped in star paper.

"Open it," the twins cried.

I peeled off the paper and popped the box open. Four snowflake charms sparkled at me, a gem in the center of each.

"They're our birthstones." Katy twirled. "For your bracelet."

"Peridot for me," Wade said. "Pink tourmaline for Katy and Daniel. And garnet—"

My vision blurred. "For Lily." I attached the charms to my bracelet, my hands trembling, and ran my finger over each one. I'd never take my one-of-a-kind snowflakes for granted again.

❄

Just after Wade got home with the cake and takeout, my in-laws' car pulled into our driveway. Would Leslie remember me? I opened our wreathed door and studied the clear sky. Snow would've made this day perfect. I shook off the thought. I had my family back—the day was already perfect.

Leslie hurried inside and I embraced her, breathing in her peppermint-scented lotion. She knew me. She really knew me. "I heard *Fox & the Magic Forest* just came out," I said.

Her eyes lit. "I can't wait to read it to Daniel and Katy later and show them how the illustrations turned out."

"What number are you up to now?" Wade said. "This has gotta be at least number seventy-seven."

"It's only my third children's book."

"Children's book, yeah, but what about all the novels, nonfiction books, articles, Popsicle stick jokes, peace treaties, astrophysics textbooks—"

I giggled and turned to Frank.

"How you doing?" he said, hugging me.

"Better than ever."

"Really?" He laughed, the contagious kind that comes from someone's soul and spreads to the rest of his body.

It always made me smile. Today, my smile must've been brighter than ever.

"Good to hear." He knelt and opened his arms to the twins. "Where are my favorite rug rats?"

Katy and Daniel squealed and raced to him.

I turned to Margaret, beautiful Margaret, who wouldn't have been. "Happy birthday," I said, those two words meaning more than ever before.

After dinner and cake topped with fresh strawberries—I ate two pieces—we gathered in the living room to give Margaret her presents.

Leslie saved hers for last. She handed it to Margaret with moist eyes. "When I found out you got the lead in *Swan Lake*—with the Joffrey Ballet, no less—I knew what I had to give you."

Margaret removed the paper to reveal a faded pink box with gold and midnight blue butterflies. When she opened it, a ballerina pirouetted to a melody from *Swan Lake*.

"Your father gave me that music box thirty-six years ago." Leslie glanced at Frank. "He knew I loved ballet and dreamed of starring in *Swan Lake* someday. When I gave that up for something more important, I never realized that one day I'd get to see you star as Odette. I'd like you to have it now."

Margaret kissed her on the cheek. "Thanks, Mom. I'll find a special place for it in my room." She ran a hand over the box. "Do you ever regret giving up dancing?"

"Sometimes I wonder what might have been," Leslie said. "But having you and Wade were the best decisions I ever made. And marrying your father, of course. I'd never trade the lifelong joy you've given me, not to mention Katy and Daniel, for a mere decade of dancing."

She locked eyes with her daughter and smiled. "Sometimes life doesn't turn out how we hoped. Sometimes it turns out better."

"And on that note." Frank rose and took an envelope out of his jacket's inner pocket.

Leslie narrowed her eyes. "I thought we weren't exchanging presents until Christmas Day."

"This one couldn't wait."

"We've been married thirty-five years and you're still full of surprises."

"That's right, baby," he said with a lopsided grin. He took her hand, and his face grew serious. "Remember the first night we kissed?"

"How could I forget?" Leslie smiled. "It was the spring dance our senior year of high school."

"Remember the theme?"

She closed her eyes. "Springtime in Paris."

Frank whipped out two plane tickets. "Ready or not, Paris here we come!"

Leslie gasped and jumped out of her seat.

Frank dipped her and planted a kiss on her lips. "We're going in March."

"The same month as the dance," she said.

"And while we're there, we'll see the Paris Opera Ballet perform *Giselle*. They better end it better this time though."

Leslie giggled. "We already did."

"It's snowing!" Daniel dashed to the window.

Snow continued to fall for hours but this time, instead of disappearing, the crystals clung to the ground, the windowsills, and the evergreen trees in our backyard.

Wade, Margaret, and the twins lay down in the powdery blanket and moved their arms up and down, their legs side to side.

Even Buster in his Santa snowsuit joined in the fun.

Leslie and I stood on the deck sipping peppermint hot chocolate. "Our snow angels," she said, her cheeks glowing.

When our noses got chilly, we headed inside.

"What's that?" Frank gestured toward the present Travis had left at our door.

"A Christmas present from one of Wade's students." I tore the paper off to reveal a portrait of the Cratchit family celebrating Christmas. Their faces bore a striking resemblance to our own.

Margaret stomped the ice off her boots and pointed at Mr. and Mrs. Cratchit. "It's you and Wade."

Daniel gawked at Peter and Martha. "And me and Katy."

Mrs. Cratchit was kissing the head of an almond-eyed infant.

"And our little one," I whispered, putting a hand on my stomach.

Leslie gasped. "You're pregnant?"

"Told you," Margaret said.

Just then, Wade came in carrying Katy on his shoulders, snowflakes on her nose and eyelashes. He laughed when he saw the portrait. "God bless us, every one!"

Epilogue

Shannon: April 2015

How's your husband?" Wade said, picking up a piece of calamari.

My chest tightened. My husband? Was I having another vision?

"I'm assuming things aren't going too well since you're out with me tonight," he said loudly enough for nearby diners to hear.

I grinned. "He's as smart, charming, and handsome as you." I dipped my squid into the marinara sauce.

Wade went for it at the same time, pushing my hand away.

"I take that back," I teased. I munched on the crispy calamari then washed it down with ice water. "Your mom suggested we write plays together when I'm not teaching."

Wade's mouth fell open. "Oh no," he groaned. "I already feel like a gorilla in the mist at her house. Now I'm going to feel that way at home too?"

I frowned. "A gorilla in the mist?"

"You know that Sigourney Weaver movie about the woman who studies primates?"

I nodded.

"Mom's always jotting down things I say to use as dialogue in her novels, like I'm some gorilla she's studying."

I giggled. "You have to admit, you are a very interesting subject."

"Ha-ha," he said in a mock-snooty voice. "The *most* interesting."

I mixed olive oil and Parmesan cheese together on a plate. "I love the idea of writing scripts together. It'll give me a chance to be creative and stay connected to drama while also being home with our daughter for her first years." I dipped a piece of bread into the oil and cheese. "Speaking of our daughter, she's due a month from today. Can you believe it?"

Wade's eyes widened. "Wait. We're having a baby?"

I smiled and rolled my eyes. "What do you want to name her?"

"I thought we'd decided on Princess Leia."

I laughed. "I don't think that's going to work." I chewed my bread, savoring the fresh-baked goodness and the tang of the cheese. "How about Amanda, your mom's middle name?"

"Amanda," Wade said, trying it out.

"It means 'worthy of love.'" My eyes filled. "Which is what she is."

"The baby or my mom?"

"The baby."

Wade laughed.

"Honey!" I glared at him. "You know what I meant. Both of them, of course."

Wade reached across the table and took my hand.

I caressed the soft strength of his.

"I love you," he said.

"I love you too," I said as if it were the last time. I wasn't taking any chances these days.

"Eggplant Parmesan." Our waiter set a plate in front of me. "And lasagna with meat sauce." He set another in front of Wade. "Can I get you anything else?"

"No, thank you," I said and took a bite of the breaded

eggplant smothered in provolone. When the waiter walked away, I brought up my other idea. Hopefully, Wade would go for it. "I was thinking Jean for her middle name."

Wade made a face.

"It means 'gift of God,'" I hurried to say. "And it's Peggy's middle name. If it wasn't for her," I said with a lump in my throat. "You might not be here." I put a hand on my belly. "Our daughter might not be here."

Wade nodded slowly. "Gift of God, worthy of love." He lifted his glass and clinked it with mine. "Perfect."

Just then something popped inside me and a gush of warm liquid soaked my pants. The faint smell of sweet sweat filled the air. I stared at the wet carpet. Did my water just break?

❄

I rested in the hospital bed and gazed into the perfect pink face of Amanda Jean Henry.

"Love me," her almond eyes seemed to say.

I nuzzled her head and breathed in her fresh scent. Heat radiated through my chest. Could I ever love her more?

She cooed and put her hand on my cheek.

Wade kissed her forehead and mine, his lips warm against my skin. He sat beside me and handed me a small box.

"What's this?"

"To complete your collection."

I opened it, and a diamond sparkled at me from the center of a snowflake charm. My eyes watered as Wade attached Amanda's birthstone to my bracelet. We gazed outside at the snow falling from the sky, each flake as unique as the next.

"The snow's a bit out of season for April, don't you think?" he said, putting his arm around me.

I smiled at him and then at our precious daughter. "Sometimes that's the best kind."

About the Author

Ever since winning a Butterball turkey in a short story contest in sixth grade, Christy has dreamed of penning novels, memoirs, and children's books. But first she met other adventures. She earned a degree in English and writing, moved to China to study Mandarin and teach at a university, and then returned to the States where she attended seminary, taught drama and music, and fell in love with a zany youth pastor. After Christy got married, a story grew in her heart, one she felt compelled to share. *Snow Out of Season* is her first novel. It won third place in the 2014 Jerry Jenkins Writers Guild Operation First Novel contest.

Discussion Questions

If your book club reads Snow Out of Season and is interested in talking with me via Skype or speakerphone, please contact me at christy@christybrunke.com, and I'll do my best to arrange something with you. Thanks for reading!

1. Snow is mentioned throughout this story and is even part of the title. Consider Wilson Bentley's quote in the book by Jacqueline Briggs Martin: "I found that snowflakes were masterpieces of design. No one design was ever repeated. When a snowflake melted, just that much beauty was gone, without leaving any record behind." How is snow used symbolically in this novel?

2. If you lost an infant and then discovered you (or your wife) were going to have another baby, what thoughts would be racing through your head?

3. Do you believe it's okay to terminate a pregnancy because your child has a disability? Is your decision a solid yes or no, or is it conditionally-based on the type or severity of the handicap?

4. With which character in the novel do you most identify? Why?

5. Before Leslie makes her decision, she retreats to her room in chapter 28: "Thunderstorms always made me want to stay curled up in bed with a novel, where the prince was always that—a prince. Where the enemy was as obvious as a witch or a dragon and relatively easy to slay. Where the right path was clear and the voices drowning out your own could be drowned out themselves." If you were in the novel, what would you recommend Leslie do? What characters in the book support your recommendation and which oppose it? Compare/contrast with Shannon's situation.

6. Put yourself in the shoes of the people in Leslie's life. How did her pregnancy impact them? What do you think motivated the advice they gave her?

7. What do the following quotes from Charles Dickens' *A Christmas Carol* mean, and how do they tie into the plot of the novel?

- When Scrooge asks the Ghost of Christmas Present what will happen to Tiny Tim, the spirit says, "If these shadows remain unaltered by the future, the child will die."

- After the Ghost of Christmas Future shows Scrooge what will become of him and Tiny Tim, Scrooge says, "Assure me I yet may change these shadows you have shown me, by an altered life. Oh, tell me I may sponge away the writing on this stone."

8. Near the end of the novel, Leslie says, "Sometimes life doesn't turn out how we hoped. Sometimes it turns out better." Can you give an example of when this was true in your life?

9. After reading this book, has the advice you would offer a pregnant woman contemplating an important decision about her unborn child changed in any way? If so, how?

10. What do you believe was the author's main intent in writing this novel? Do you have any ideas as to what inspired her to write the story?

Your eyes saw me when I was only a fetus.
Every day [of my life] was recorded in your book before one of them had taken place.
Psalm 139:16, GOD'S WORD translation

READY TO SHARE YOUR MESSAGE WITH THE WORLD?

Discover the secrets of powerful writing from Jerry B. Jenkins, author of the mega-bestselling *Left Behind* series, and learn to write a story with the potential to impact millions of lives.

If you'd like Jerry to be your virtual writing mentor starting today, just enter this link into your web browser:

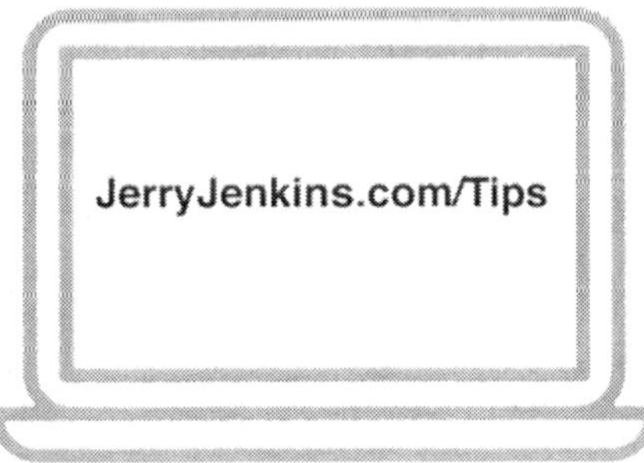

You'll instantly gain free access to Jerry's five things you *must* know if you want to write a book—as well as plenty more tips for aspiring authors.

Read the First Place winner of the Jerry Jenkins Writers Guild Operation First Novel contest

The Calling of Ella McFarland
By Linda Brooks Davis

Ella McFarland's dream is a teaching position at Worthington School for Girls. But scandal clouds her family name and may limit her to a life of grueling farm labor in the Indian Territory. Her fate lies in the hands of the Worthington board, and there happens to be one strikingly handsome man with a vote. Will they overlook the illegitimate son recently borne by her sister, Viola?

1905 brings hope of Oklahoma statehood and the woman's suffrage debate is raging, forcing Ella to make decisions about her faith, family, and aspirations. When she comes to the rescue of a young, abused sharecropper's daughter, her calling begins to take shape in ways she never imagined. Education is Ella's passion, but a new love is budding in her heart. Can she find God's will amidst the tumultuous storm that surrounds her?